Odds

Also by Patty Friedmann

Too Smart to Be Rich
The Exact Image of Mother
Eleanor Rushing

Odds

Odds

Patty Friedmann

COUNTERPOINT
WASHINGTON, D.C.

Chapter One appeared originally as a short story,
"Just So Much," *Louisiana Literature*, Spring 1994

Library of Congress Cataloging-in-Publication Data
Friedmann, Patty.
Odds / Patty Friedmann.
p.   cm.
ISBN 1-58243-087-X (alk. paper)
1. New Orleans (La.)—Fiction.   2. Mother and child—
Fiction.   3. Twins—Fiction.   4. Boys Fiction.   I. Title.
PS3556.R538 034   2000
813'.54—dc21   00-035887
First Printing

Jacket design by Wesley Tanner / Passim Editions
Design by Elizabeth Lahey

Counterpoint
P.O. Box 65793
Washington, D.C. 20035–5793

Counterpoint is a member of the Perseus Books Group

00 01 02 03 / 10 9 8 7 6 5 4 3 2 1

My mother knew this dedication was going to read,
"For my mother, Margie Friedmann,
who gave me everything."
Instead it must read, "To the memory of my mother,
who gave me everything but today."
I am sadder than she could ever have imagined.

Acknowledgments

With a title like *Odds*, and an exploration of matters of risk and probability, it is tempting to make a bad pun for every thank-you. But I feel too seriously grateful, so for once in my life I'll play it straight. (Oh, the English language: Is there no end to the groaners?)

Jack Shoemaker, Jane Vandenburgh, and Trish Hoard: I am so proud to know and love you. Heather McLeod, John Hughes, John McLeod, Carole McCurdy, and all the rest of the prodigious talent at Counterpoint: I know how lucky I am to work with you.

Muriel Nellis, my agent: I adore you.

David Hanson and Joe Brown: You gave this book its start, publishing "Just So Much" as a better short story than I originally wrote it, so it had to expand into a full-length work.

George Sterne, the Renaissance man who's a pediatrician by day: You gave me all the knowledge I needed to raise kids and write a book—then let me play fast and loose with both.

To friends (and my two best cousins) who gave answers and assurances as I wrote, I needed you more than you know: Marie-Rose Adler, Rosalind Bell, Connie Buchanan, Carole Gottsegen, Melissa Gray, Michael Hershfield, Susan Larson,

Acknowledgements

Bryan Moody, Caren Nowak, Axel Orlow, David Parker, Margot Stander, and Margaret Wade.

Lynda and Tommy: We claim each other and that makes me very happy.

Esme and Werner: You make me know I'm alive, even if it's only because you routinely override the Prozac.

And to my husband, Ed Muchmore, I say you've made only one lapse in judgment besides marrying me: You said it's impossible to have a happy ending with a fireman.

O N E

I wasn't an asthmatic or allergic or demanding child. I think maybe twice I told my mother that I *needed* a cat, but she felt my father had left her with enough as it was, and she wasn't going to go out and volunteer to take care of anything extra. I was three when my father blew out an aneurysm an hour before the topping-off ceremony of a building on Loyola Avenue. Maybe he wouldn't have survived either the fall or the insult to his brain, but even when I was older the subject never came up between my mother and me. I could step dreamily into the traffic on Canal Street, or press my hands and face up against the glass observation tower atop the Trade Mart, and she would become very pale and whisper, "No accidents, Anna, you better remember that; there are absolutely no accidents," and I would shrug and silently press forward, surviving.

She let me keep a cat when I was seventeen and she had decided I was almost ready to go. The cat showed up one morning, in the window next to the kitchen table that looked out onto the side gallery. He had no more than a three-inch ledge, but at the time he found me he was a rather lithe, busy cat, and he could balance there and wait patiently, not slip off, look longingly at my buttered muffins and café au lait, as if he would give up all the emerald lizards in the graveyard if he could just come in, please, and sit on the empty chair at the table and get ready to take my place.

I named him Ansel Adams. Ansel Adams did brilliant things with nothing more than black and white. The cat was, I realized much later, a type, a mostly black cat with white on his belly and splashes of white in arbitrary places, creating no symmetry, but making me look for balance through squinting eyes, an oriental screen sort of cat. After he came into the house and began to grow fat and lazy, I would lie on the floor and study him, curled up, trying to figure out where his patterns came from. "Do you think, Mama, that maybe in the womb there is just so much white to go around, and it spatters around from the walls, so if you could lay the kittens out in the right array, you'd see pictures, white on black?"

"If you are there imagining God with a paintbrush, lying with his back up against some cat's viscera, you're not as ready to leave as I think," she said. "Come here, Ansel Adams, you may be out of a job soon."

"You told me I should have imagination," I said, and she laughed.

Once I was finished with high school and my mother was letting me wait to begin my life, I spent my days at the library on St. Charles Avenue. The library was a mansion donated in memory of a son killed in World War II, and most weekday afternoons it was mine, the broad porches and stone steps, the separate garages the size of Mama's house, the man-made hillocks. I'd lie on a patch of grass, oak pollen forming a blanket under me, and read *The Castle* and *The Voyage of the HMS Beagle* and *A Brief History of Time* when I wasn't just watching. I stayed away from those dusty, jacketless books full of facts that were in the upstairs back stacks and avoided, too, the slick journals full of science that sat on the reading desk in the front room, the ones my mother went over to read page by page on Saturday mornings while I slept. My mother had never gotten past the fact that, by the time she was thirty-one, she was the widow of a construction worker, a woman who had no more schooling than it took to decapitate rats for three dollars an hour in the cytology lab at the medical school. I sensed it pleased her that my father's government check let me spend my days slipping out the side door of the library and into my dreams, happy to learn nothing more than that the idle rich have marvelous things to look at all day. She was planning on my becoming one of them.

I married George after a year, and Ansel Adams had his place secure in my mother's house. He grew a fine inguinal pouch that sported two fat, useless teats under his white belly, and lay around waiting for my mother to say something so he could ignore her. Because my mother said it was time, I became pregnant a respectable two months after my wedding, and George went downtown to work in a law firm in the same building where my father had plummeted to the ground fifteen years before. The corridors were narrow and needed paint, signs of respectability and dignity in New Orleans, and the sidewalk had been replaced at least twice since my father's death, but George didn't think about much more than going down to that building twelve hours a day so he could become a partner. I didn't know him particularly well, so his long days were fine: I could get by effortlessly, promising him nothing more than that I'd never tell anyone how my father had died. "It was no crime not to finish high school," I said to him once, and he said, "Well, in *my* family it *was*." Days, I sat around Mama's shotgun house and got as fat as Ansel Adams, and since I was not even nineteen years old, the doctor gave me vitamins and pushed his hand up inside me until I yelped in pain; it was not until my eighth month that he noticed I looked frightfully huge and pressed a stethoscope all over my belly for a few minutes and said distractedly, "No doubt about it, you're not big. *They're* big."

"'They're?'"

"Two of them," he said. "Are you ready for two of them?"

All George said was, "Don't have an ultrasound. I don't want weird pictures on the mantel."

Twins are supposed to come early, but the entire month passed without any sign that they were ready. I could have spent my days at my own house, two solid levels of stucco painted the color of crab fat, with a shell of a New Orleans raised basement and a queer L-shaped pool that wrapped around, side and back. It was a house that George had chosen because it was a half block off St. Charles Avenue. "It's unsightly," I had said, trying to sound as if I were joking, when I saw it the first time, marveling that anyone who had to put a fresh coat of paint on a house to sell it would choose such a color. "With the house in the way, you can't see anyone in the shallow end of the pool if you're in the deep end; what's the fun of that?"

"What counts is the address," George had said with the air of someone who's had seven more years of schooling and is entitled to a lot. "And you can put your mother in the basement." I'd shrugged, ashamed to be glad I was pregnant because soon I wouldn't have to let him touch me.

It was June, and I could have lain out by the pool; I could have floated and pivoted in the pool, weightless even with the water sac that held two babies inside me. I could have lain on a raft, navigating through the sharp right angle where the pool filled the back corner of our lot. But I spent the days instead at my mother's house, staring at Ansel Adams and half-listening to my mother saying good things about George. "Your father was intelligent, too, same as George," she said. "Probably you'll have two smart babies. They'll create monumental things; they just won't be dumb enough to go standing on top of them in the middle of June until the blood boils in their heads." My water broke on the anniversary of my father's death, June 21. I was in my mother's kitchen, and the last thing I saw when I left the house was Ansel Adams tiptoeing behind me, lapping up the liquid on the floor.

The first baby came, and the doctor said, "A boy, ten twenty-nine," and I lay still on the table, myopic and dazzled, feeling nothing except vague impulses from the waist down, and one minute later the nurse said, "Oh, Jesus, oh, Jesus, oh, Jesus," and the doctor said, "Get her the fuck out of here." A curtain went up over me, extended across the point at my middle where sensation ended, and the nurse who had not been thrown out said, "Honey, you go to sleep now, you're all right, okay?" The funny thing was, I was in a room full of strangers, with George in his office knowing nothing and my mother somewhere in the hospital pale and full of misgivings from what I could tell when I last saw her, and going to sleep seemed like an excellent option. "What happened?" I remember whispering through the sort of sleep that only breaks if I open my eyes. I wakened later to hear my mother telling George, "The doctor says he thinks it's called mosaic scrambling, maybe there's an error in the DNA, a translocation error." I heard myself saying, "But what *happened?*" and my mother went on about chromosomal changes not being hereditary, as if she'd never heard me, and I dozed again.

We named the first one George Junior. George Senior did not want to name the second one because he was positive the child was going to die. The boy had no arms or legs to speak of, just stumps of varying lengths, none reaching as far as a knee or elbow joint, tubes of flesh over bone with smooth, rounded tips. But I loved touching him, learning his bones, his skin as warm and alive as his brother's. I named him Gregor, after Samsa and Mendel; it was almost an anagram of George, an extra *r,* one less *e.* "Gregor, he's the one who'll have imagination," I said to George Senior, who had both eyes on the television set. "Not even thinking up a new name for a child doesn't give him a lot of options. Poor little George." My husband wasn't hearing me. "Poor little Gregor," I said for my own benefit, lying supine in that hospital bed in that private room with no flowers, tears streaming down into my ears. No one knew what to do, congratulate or condole, and so no one did anything, not even the secretarial pool on the third level of George's firm. People's silence helped George, made him feel once again that he was right and I was wrong.

I cried over Gregor until he was old enough to notice, by which time he had so much spirit in him that I didn't need to do so much crying. I could change George Junior's diaper and he'd kick at me so hard that it would hurt; he was the sort of boy who would rock back onto his neck when he was two so that when his heels hit my arm simultaneously he'd leave two perfect round bruises side by side; I'd want to smack his leg, angrily, reflexively, disliking him for a fraction of a moment, and he'd smile with pleasure. Gregor, on the other hand, had no time for mischief, and of course no power for it, either. He was too busy concentrating on figuring out new ways to do things, rolling over through pure will, scooting on the carpet on his stubs until they bled, so my mother began crocheting him tiny heelless red socks with elastic to hold them around his limbs, and after a morning of clumping around the house he would have rings of purple bruises on the stumps and a look of triumph on his face that George Junior never had unless he was stealing something. I would be sure to *tell* anyone that they were identical twins.

"I *told* you prostheses were unnecessary," George Senior would say. "He gets by with what God gave him."

"*I'm* the Presbyterian here," I'd say back, but George didn't laugh or acquiesce.

Gregor gave up trying to get around when they were both two and George Junior began to run so fast that his head bumped into low tables; George Junior would let out a shrill of pain, look back at Gregor, who was full of simple amazement, and then George Junior would keep running until his feet carried his head straight into another obstacle. Gregor perfected the skill of sitting up straight in a stroller, and his body became thick and wise while his brother ran about, knees covered with skin like that of old reptiles, stitches in three places on his face from three separate trips to the hospital.

George Junior had as little sympathy for Gregor as he did for Ansel Adams, the only difference being that he could torment the cat by chasing him. George Junior would not fetch anything for Gregor. Not that Gregor asked, even from the earliest times in his life, when he had no words, only grunts, sounds that George Junior didn't need to make because he could grab whatever he pleased. George Junior treated his brother as if he were a beggar at an intersection where his car was stopped; he moved slowly past, not letting his eye be caught, not having to give, not having to feel anything, either.

It was a few weeks after their sixth birthday. My mother had been living with us for some time, hiding in her basement rooms in the evenings when her son-in-law was home, otherwise roaming the house freely. Ansel Adams had no such scruples, no fear of being told to go away. George took a liking to him when he moved in. "He was probably a terrific litigator in a previous life," he said about Ansel Adams. "This is one no-bullshit cat."

"They're all like that," my mother said, missing the point.

George had not touched one wall or tool since he bought the house, but he went out one day and bought all the makings for a pet door, and in three Saturdays of skinned knuckles and cursing with tears in his eyes, he installed a vertical swinging door at the head of the basement stairs so that Ansel Adams could choose where he wanted to spend his time. When Ansel Adams came into the bedroom at night and slept on the backs of George's knees, George would come to breakfast complaining in a way that let my mother know he felt he had won her cat away from her. Ansel Adams still had his claws, and George respected him for that.

I was getting ready to go outside by the swimming pool with the two boys that afternoon after day camp. It was one of those summer days when a black cloud would stretch all the way from Texas to the Atlantic Ocean, leaving the Deep South awash in rot and sweat while everyone waited for the thunderstorms to break in a band moving west to east, cooling everything off for half an hour before the steam rose again a few hours before sunset. "It is going to absolutely storm," I said to George Junior.

"We have a lightening rod on the top of the house," George Junior said.

"Lightning, George, lightning," Gregor said. "Besides, lightning likes water better."

"You want to go out to the pool or not?" George Junior said.

"Well, not if I'm going to get killed," Gregor said, and my mother whispered to me, "You've done a good job." I gave her a blank look. "He doesn't want to get killed," she said.

"Oh, I am a terrific mother, all right," I said.

"You're kind of dead anyway," George Junior said. He looked like his father at that moment, and I tried to pretend he was Gregor so I wouldn't hate him.

"Mama!" Gregor said.

"Sorry," George Junior said, not meaning it. "But it's true," he whispered into my mother's ear loudly enough for me and

Gregor to hear him. He took the basement steps two at a time, almost tipping Gregor out of my arms, leaving my mother there, squinting into the semidarkness after him.

Gregor had his own special pool raft, cumbersome and safe, an inner tube balanced on three-foot pontoons and rigged inside with straps that kept him upright in the water. Gregor could actually navigate well, though of course there was nothing propellant about his limbs, no cupped hand or flattened foot that would push water behind him so that he could move quickly. I would race him with my fists outstretched in front of me, using only my legs for moving forward, and it was a fair race, though George Junior would thrash alongside us, face in the water, arms churning, passing, hitting the far end of the pool, taking a breath, coming back and making a circle around us, crashing past us again, often beating both of us on his second pass. "Well, Mama's the rotten egg," Gregor would say, and George Junior would say, "You're the rotten egg, Gregor," then clamber up onto the side of the pool and belly flop in next to his brother, rocking the raft and sending water up into Gregor's nose.

I watched the clouds over the river for streaks of lightning, but none came, and the clouds didn't move toward us, so I let George Junior into the deep water that ran alongside the house, rigged Gregor up, launched him in the shallow portion at the back of the property. The water was surprisingly cold for the dead of summer, shocking each little pocket of fat unpleasantly as I lowered myself into the pool. The sunlight was stronger because it had fought through the cloud cover; not thinking, I put my hand up to shade my face, then lowered it, preferring the warmth.

Elbows up on the edge of the corner of the pool where it turned at the back of the yard, chin thrust upward, feet pedaling gently, protected now from the sun by blooming bougainvillea that hung out over the water and left the pool full of lipstick-pink petals each morning, I didn't notice George Junior going into the house for a snack, didn't notice him until he came out. Gregor was floating past me. "Mama, you know Ansel Adams is out here," Gregor called to me after a while.

Ansel Adams stood next to the pool, blinking in disbelief at his good fortune. He had not been outdoors in years, except in a carrying case. George Junior went over to crouch next to him, laid his ice pop on the slate surface; it puddled in the heat. He put his finger to his lips, reached for the cat, lifted him up under the pits of his front legs, most of Ansel Adams's bulk bumping against his knees as George Junior carried him toward the deep arm of the pool. "No!" I said. George Junior kept walking, his back arching with the effort of carrying a cat fully one-third his size. He was moving toward the deepest end, where Gregor had drifted. "I mean it, George," I said. George Junior sat down on the edge of the pool, lowered his feet into the water. Ansel Adams wriggled a little, showing dissatisfaction but not particularly wanting to escape. And then, cat and all, George Junior jumped into the pool.

It was all too much for Ansel Adams, who perhaps could have managed being gently lowered into the water, for all I know. The cat went under with George Junior, and while the boy bobbed up fine the first time, the cat came up fighting as if someone had shot him full of amphetamines. He flew into the air, flailing at George Junior, coming down onto Gregor's raft, catching his claws in the taut rubber and puncturing it. I tore through the water as if it gave as little resistance as a vacuum, reached into the fray, pulled back instinctively when Ansel Adams raked me with his teeth, grabbed for him again, and then he sunk his claws into me so deep that I wanted to let him drown. Both boys and I were in eight feet of water, and now all I could see were the identical faces of my sons, one with his hair dry and soft and almost white in the sun, the other with his hair dark with water, one with a look of pure terror on his face, the other with a look of mild annoyance as if I'd come along and ruined his perfectly good idea for amusing himself. I caught the cat around the middle, and he slipped through my hands, landing on top of George Junior, covering his face and scratching at his eyes in panic to get a hold. "Mama!" Gregor said. He was now snared in the straps of a heavy, sinking, tipping vessel, a craft we trusted as long as everything went all right. I tore at the straps, made no headway, began pushing him toward the shallow end; I would have to move him a full twenty yards and around a bend to get him moored at the steps. I screamed for my mother, my voice echoing in the empty summer neighborhood.

I looked back toward George Junior, and I couldn't see him or Ansel Adams anymore. I pushed Gregor to the steps. It was all I could do.

T W O

I met George's mother at the funeral. Rather, I saw her at the funeral for the first time. Was told of her, was aware of her. It was a day of Valium and lavender and not much else; I had hoarded the ten-milligram pills, taken three that morning; with no sensation in my feet I was able to walk into Lake Lawn with the slow, steady gait of those who are forgiven everything by strangers, nothing by those who are close. George had said the night of the drowning, "I don't hate you, but I will never forgive you."

"What would you have done?" I had whispered.

"I'd have saved them both."

"Not true," I'd said softly.

He grabbed me by the shoulders, slammed me against the wall, leaving a crater in the plaster, no pain in my head; I felt nothing but the noise of the impact. "It wasn't physically possible," I said, though that wasn't what I'd meant at all. He slammed me again, and I deserved it. "What's that?" Gregor called from the next room. "Nothing," I said, too low to be heard. "Something," George called back, then he cried as if his heart was broken, as if he would never be able to stop. I had not cried yet. Nor had Gregor. He had screamed after the accident until a first responder from the fire department had taken us both upstairs, and neither of us had spoken above a whisper since.

George's mother didn't approach me, stood as if she couldn't move, but watched me from across the room, not seeming to accuse or reach conclusions, as if taking in every moment until she saved up enough for later judgments. She wore a black pantsuit, a lavender crepe blouse. So much lavender in the room, not in offensive patches but in touches, here, there; it was summer, and it was a little blond boy, and lavender was good on everyone else until I saw it on her. "Who *is* that woman?" the principal of the boys' school said to me. The principal always found reasons to talk to me, and I had noticed that she liked the freaks, the spina bifida boy, the slow girl whose brother went to Harvard; she was largely bored by the ones who stuck to predictable paths. Gregor was going to be getting a lot of her attention, now that he had grief of a sort on top of everything else.

"My husband's mother," I said. "I don't know her." I corrected myself: "She doesn't know me." The principal gave me a sympathetic smile, found a phantom in the crowd, moved on.

I could have fallen asleep standing up. I had no peripheral vision, was waiting for darkness to move all the way to center, and I took another Valium, drifted over to Gregor's wheelchair. Someone had left him next to the casket, too low to look in, high enough for everyone to walk past, take in, give a phony pat on the head, as if he were a model of what the boy in the box might look like if one didn't observe too closely. "You want me to move you?" I said into Gregor's ear.

"I think this's what I'm supposed to do," he said.

I squatted down beside him, with little sensation in my legs, content to stay there for as long as possible, to put my head between my knees, close my eyes. "Honey, a boy your age shouldn't even have to be here at all."

"That lady pushed me here," he said, gesturing with his chin toward George's mother, who was looking at us with a neutral expression.

"She talk to you?"

He hesitated. "Not a lot," he said. "He has a picture of her. I knew her."

"I don't know why she doesn't know us," I said, my words slow, groggy. It wasn't true, but I believed it right then.

"She doesn't look like she's better than Gammy," Gregor whispered.

"Oh," I said. "Oh."

I didn't want to stand, I didn't want to move. I wanted to be home. I didn't want to rise and see George Junior, in his blue blazer, clip-on dark red tie; what upset me most was that I'd sent over his black leather belt, which he had learned to close himself only recently. He'd pull it tight, make a sack of his pants, remind me he was six and loved knowing how to do such things. A flicker of impatience passed over Gregor's face, and I saw his brother. "What's the matter?" I said, wanting to do whatever he needed to make that expression go away. Gregor shrugged, his little arms popping up involuntarily. "Mama, they look like chicken wings," his brother had said the last time Gregor shrugged. They were four at the time, and George Junior had meant almost no malice, but Gregor hadn't made the motion since.

I wanted my mother to come. To be in the parlor, to know I needed her, to march over, in charge, move Gregor, cover me so I couldn't see. She was at the house, attended by Ella, who had a twenty-dollar bill stuffed in her uniform pocket in case my mother became willing to take a taxi. Ella cleaned for me once a week; Ella had baby-sat only once, when the boys were two. She had greeted George, my mother, and me at the door after our evening out. "They show that thalidomide child in

England on TV; least you can do is give that boy a arm." George had sworn he could not be held responsible if he ever laid eyes on Ella again, and my mother did our baby-sitting after that, content with her good reason not to have to go out with George. Since the accident my mother was taking Seconal at an alarming rate, sleeping for two hours as if she were dead, sitting in the kitchen nibbling on crackers and waiting for sleep the rest of the time. "A woman screaming sounds like little boys playing," she said whenever I remembered to check on her. "You know that."

My mother was my only friend, because somewhere along the line she had decided I was the only person good enough to be her friend. She was not going to let me go, even when I was fully formed, as if any fragment of my love for another was a small death for her. School had been easy, because girls were foolish in school, and when my mother talked about science and mathematics and logic, I learned to believe that dresses and shoes were not worth a phone call. "The odds are against finding a girl who thinks in school," she would say. The exception had been an underfed girl who wrote dark stories, a girl my mother approved of far too much for me to ask over. What about college? "College would ruin your ability to imagine." She let me have George, because she expected I'd marry for nothing more than comfort; she was relieved when I had twins, who could play with each other and protect me from sitting in parks with mothers who didn't think but loved one another forever, raising their babies together. In the parlor were women who had tried with me, and with whom I'd wanted to try back, but they came up and put their arms around me as if they didn't mean it, and I wanted my mother, who had owned me so deeply that now she should have been with me, been everything to me as she had planned.

Mama would have approached Mrs. Duffy, George's mother, taken her hand, sacrificed her dignity. *I think you should get to know Gregor*, she would say. *And Anna, you'll find Anna's quite good for George.* Her implication, of course, would be that she, Gregor's Gammy, Anna's most important person, was not so trashy herself. I scanned the room for Ella, who would have been easier to find in a white crowd, saw no graying black women. I hated the funerals George brought me to where old black women who had raised the rich white children sat with the widow and her now-grown sons and daughters, the black woman grieving for a man who had teased her each week over her pay envelope, a man she never knew by first name though she had cleaned up his most shameless messes. No Ella. No mother. I looked at Mrs. Duffy. She looked back at me, but didn't move, not toward me, not toward George, as if she did not want any of these strangers to learn who she was and judge her accordingly.

I was still squatting in front of Gregor when George tapped me on the shoulder. "Father McInvale wants to talk to you."

I shook my head no.

George gripped my shoulder. "We went through all this yesterday," he whispered.

"*You* went through all this yesterday," I said. Gregor gave me a pleading look, and I looked back at him as if to say, *You're about to see who's right, in case you have any doubts.* George had disappeared into our bedroom in the middle of the afternoon and arranged to have a Mass, just as he had arranged for me to go to RCIA when we married, no questions asked. ("John Calvin would probably say you were destined to become a Catholic," my mother had joked when I told her George had signed me up for conversion classes, and I'd laughed gratefully.) "Father McInvale will do it" was all George said when he emerged from the bedroom, red-faced, an hour later. I did not know Father

McInvale. I didn't know anyone with the Catholics, hadn't known anyone since George had refused to have an emergency baptism for Gregor in the hospital because, he said, he had no soul. Gregor had lived, of course, his soul more in evidence than most people's, it seemed to me. When George began planning a christening a few weeks later I told him to leave Gregor out of it. "We could swaddle both of them," he had said helpfully, and instead of walking out I'd said, "This child is going to be around awhile, you better get used to him." George Junior was as free of sin as any unreasoning Catholic, but I was not going to have a service in which I could remember that Gregor was once considered not worth saving.

"My mother's here," George said, his tone pleading. "She doesn't know anything."

I stood up, and in so doing saw George Junior, tips of profile. He had not had his First Communion yet, but he'd been getting ready for it, learning about good, hearing a need to set aside greed. He knew he was going to have a special dinner, receive holy gifts, but he had been told often enough that what mattered was the Eucharist, and on that subject he had been kind to Gregor. "Maybe I'll get, like, a rosary or something," I heard him say in the backseat of the car. "Probably that's not worth thinking you might drop Jesus."

I stood up, faced my husband. "Oh, I just can't be here for it," I said miserably.

"Just put your head down. You don't have to listen. You don't even have to take Communion, for Chrissakes, just keep your head down, everyone'll forgive you."

"I don't *need* to be forgiven," I said in a voice that told George if I had to repeat myself I was going to scream it.

"I meant people'll *understand*."

"What. Understand what." I was looking straight at him, my eyes full of tears; I was sure anyone watching us would see a different story. All I could see was how thin George's lips were; I wondered why I'd ever wanted to kiss his mouth.

"God, Anna, all I mean's that you don't have to take Communion, nobody's going to think it's an admission of anything; they're just going to think you're too damn distraught. Just act like you can't get up."

"I don't want to hear what he has to say, either," I said. "There's not a goddamn thing he can say that's not going to make me furious." I didn't mind using that sort of language; I hoped George *did* mind that he had.

"I told him what to say. We were on the phone for an hour."

I could imagine what George would try to tell a man who surely had a shelf of packaged speeches for children who died tragically young. George would have reminded him that there had been two, that I had chosen one; he'd have found a way to say it was the wrong one, that God didn't take a child at random, or even because he was special; rather, Anna had intervened and been more perverse than anyone had a right to be. I asked him what he'd said to Father. I wanted a fight. I wanted George to be terribly wrong.

"The boy is five, six? I said the boy is six. Not a lot to tell, Anna. Kindergarten, St. John's School; I *apologized* for Episcopal school, told him he went to St. John's because St. John's can handle his brother." I widened my eyes at him. "*Handle*, physically handle, for God's sake," he said.

"You should have told him Holy Name couldn't be bothered."

"Mama," Gregor whispered. The boys had just reached that age when, alone, they might eavesdrop with sensibility; they had been without each other so rarely that I hadn't learned to censor myself any more than I might have done with a two-year-old. "Honey, St. John's is a kind school; it's the only school where they teach you to be kind. That's why you go there."

"George was the meanest boy in the whole kindergarten," he said proudly.

I looked at his father, saw a flicker of pride on his face, too.

"You tell that to Father McInvale?" I said, and they both smiled. "Listen, it'll be okay," I said to George. "Nobody looks at the family. I mean, everybody looks at the family, but they can't admit it. I'll be outside, I'll take Gregor outside. People don't come here to find fault."

"My mother," George said.

Mrs. Duffy was stationed at the other end of the platform on which the casket rested. She wasn't eavesdropping, but rather seemed to be taking in George Junior, whom she'd never seen before, an odd farewell.

I said I could talk to her, and George shook his head no. "Gammy says that lady thinks she's better than us," Gregor said.

"No, son, she's just shy," George said. He never had called Gregor *son* before, but he hadn't called George Junior *son,* either.

"Then she'll understand," I said, and I wheeled Gregor out of the parlor, moving purposefully, my head held high. This was the way I'd always taken him and George Junior to the supermarket, not daring others to approach, but rather acting as if we were like them, no more worthy of comment than they were.

Lake Lawn sat at the edge of Metairie Cemetery, a few hundred yards from the interstate, the view largely unobstructed; all that kept passersby from staring was their own speed and the blind geometry of a mausoleum. "I want a three-story clock tower on my grave," my mother once had said when we passed the place on the way to the airport. "Give people something to think about."

"You'd need an electric outlet," I'd said back. "Or else a quartz battery. Or somebody to wind it. And I assume that'd be me. Until I died, of course."

"I told you it'd give people something to think about," my mother had said.

I wheeled Gregor along the paved roadway that led to the highway. Behind a statue of two sinuous, Modiglianiesque female figures, the hearse and two limousines were parked. This year's color was the palest bronze-gold; I had long had the impression that white funeral homes changed the color of their vehicles as soon as black mortuaries began to copy them.

"Why do they have those ladies there?" Gregor said, gesturing with his head toward the statues.

"They're angels," I said.

"I don't think so, Mama," he said.

I could push him toward the highway or I could push him toward the cemetery. Lake Lawn was so close to plots and tombs; I saw no reason for hearses and corteges when a processional on foot would have meant more. Particularly with a forty-three-pound boy in the simplest wooden casket. "I don't want to go that way," I said to Gregor, pointing toward the rows of aboveground tombs. "We could go looking for punch buggies," Gregor said. Punch buggies were old Volkswagen beetles; whoever saw one first could slug his competitor. George Junior had learned the game, brought it home; the rules in my car were that if they played at all they played for nickels, and Gregor won so much more frequently that I felt sorry for George Junior.

We were halfway down the drive to the service road when Gregor sang out, "That's Melvin!"

"Who's Melvin?"

"Ella's daddy, with the truck, he gots one with four doors, see, it opens backwards!"

Melvin was Ella's husband, who waited at our curb each Wednesday afternoon; I was always grateful that she had to leave on time, couldn't linger. I'd never told her of George's rage four years back, though if I thought about it George probably could not have picked her out of a lineup of black women in their sixties, even if they were of different heights and weights. I saw the heads of two passengers riding in the front seat, big heads of women, one in white, the other in black. "Oh, Lord," I said.

Melvin's windows were tinted within legal limits, the cheap film bubbling, and the images I could discern were no clearer than those of a security camera, blurs and gestures, black and white. I could tell, though, that someone had seen me, registered nothing, seen the wheelchair, begun to wonder, seen Gregor's pale hair, and then in a matter of seconds Melvin slammed on the brakes, rocking the two big heads around.

My mother shambled toward me, drunk with sadness. "We figured, why not give Melvin the money?" she said softly. Melvin already had the truck in reverse; using his rearview mirror, he was zigzagging backward in the direction of the service road. I couldn't remember how I had gotten there myself.

I looked at my watch. The service already had started. I had chosen the music, the boys' favorite, "I Believe I Can Fly"—"*I believe I can soar, I see me running through that open door . . .*" Last night Gregor and I had played the CD, and George had said, "That's hardly classical," but Gregor had said, "Me and George think it is." At nine o'clock at night George had found a violinist who could do an arrangement, and I had thrown my arms around him; he had stiffened at the touch. I didn't want to be inside, figured I was never going to be able to hear that song again.

"I'll take Gregor inside," my mother said. I searched Gregor's face, realized I hadn't thought about what he wanted or what was right for him. He was past the age when he would be an amnesiac about everything until it came back to him in senescence. "I want to hear the song," he said. I told him it wouldn't have words, the only warning I'd given him that day. "I could sing it?" he said, and I pictured him in front of everyone, singing for his brother in earnest high treble. I began to cry, cry so hard I bent over, the noise of me carrying out across the cemetery, out toward the highway, carrying everywhere except inside the tight mausoleum of the chapel.

"Oh, Jesus," I heard Ella say to my mother. "Miss Dorothy, you got to go get the smelling salts."

I lifted my eyes, saw my mother look around with the heavy-headedness of the overdrugged. I felt myself aim the loud sobs toward her, and Gregor began whimpering softly. "Oh, Lord," Ella said, feeling sorrier for herself than for any of the rest of us.

The glass door at the portico opened and one of the women in dark green suits who manned the reception desk came running toward us. She wore black pumps with low heels, and she jogged gingerly as if she knew she had three more funerals that day and no time to deal with scuffs. "Mrs. Duffy," she called, looking at me, knowing me by process of elimination and not because she had dealt with me. George had dealt with Lake Lawn. I had wanted Bultman, in our part of town, set where St. Charles Avenue went from one to two lanes. "She speeds when we get to the mansion," George Junior always said to his brother. "It's not a mansion, it's a funeral home, and don't call me she," I always said back.

"I'll bury you there, Mama," Gregor always promised, and George Junior usually chorused in, "Me, too."

"The guests are about to come out, Mr. Duffy wants you to come greet them, I'm supposed to say please," the woman said, breathless with her own drama.

I stood with George at the door, nodded, felt grateful after all that so many had come. Teachers who could say they were sorry they'd never get a chance to know George Junior, mothers who could say they regretted not knowing me before, but would remedy that, looking at Gregor with a promise I sensed they were afraid to deliver on. Men, so many men, in fine weekday suits, grieving for George because surely George had planned to hunt and fish with his boy. We were the last to leave for the burial, but George's mother had not come out. She was not at the grave, she was not at the funeral home when we returned. I didn't ask, and if Gregor thought about the woman at all, he kept it to himself.

THREE

I don't blame Ella for being empowered by the funeral. As a child I never again fully respected any schoolmate who threw up his lunch; as an adult I've refused to take seriously anyone I see screaming in public. Ella had seen me cry hard right out of doors, not in a pew where an usher lady in white could wave a bottle of ammonium carbonate under my nose until I forgot my troubles. On a Wednesday morning a few weeks after the funeral she timed her movements through my house to catch me. Ella never cleaned peripheries or high places; no one looked, and she had other interests. I figured she had something to say, and I stayed ahead of her, easing out of rooms that she'd have no excuse to abandon at a given moment. At lunchtime she chose to clean out the refrigerator, freezer and all, a task she could stretch out so long that the milk would spoil and the ice cubes all would stick together. Hunger got the best of me, and as I put room-temperature turkey, bread, and mayonnaise together and tried not to think about salmonella or rebuking the woman, she started in on me.

Ella fished a newspaper clipping from her uniform pocket. Mine was the only house where she worked, but she had a uniform, and she came on the streetcar in it, went off in Melvin's car in it, too. "I don't go saving the *Times-Picayune*, no," she said. "But this from last Christmas, I know one day you going to want to look at this."

I remembered the article. It was an annual item, always had been, coverage of the Doll and Toy Fund, a boring story now that they no longer separated blacks and whites on giveaway days. But last year was different. In a three-column photo, the mayor was handing a toy guitar to a boy in a wheelchair, a black boy, age eight the caption said. The boy had no arms. He and his daddy were looking skeptically at the camera, and the mayor was flashing his ceremonial grin. I'd shown it to George at the breakfast table, and he had said, "The firm donates," then had gone back to the Nasdaq. "My God, a *guitar*," I said, but he didn't answer.

"That boy in my neighborhood," Ella said. "I mean all over my neighborhood. That daddy you looking at, he the type move at midnight, you know, the rent due Saturday, they load a truck Friday night. But never go more than two blocks. You think, them sitting out there with that child, nairn arm and leg, landlords know where they at. Specially before they give them that chair. They carry that boy around in a milk box."

"Yes?" I said. All the cold food was on the counter, and I was doing a mental inventory of what I was going to have to discard when she left.

"Look, Miss Anna, they got a excuse. They going to be hauling that child around till they dead, or he dead, one or the other. But you got money. You got insurance?"

I nodded.

"I got to spell this out?" she said, as if she had raised me.

"We've been through this before."

Ella looked down, shook her head a bit, as if she were too shy to say what was coming next but she was going to say it anyway. "I say something *one* time, those children still babies, don't think I don't know I never sat for you since." Suddenly she brightened, as if she'd found a way to soften what she was thinking. "Back then you got *two*. You know the brother going to be around to take care of him. He not here no more."

I knew what she actually had been thinking, that Gregor had been an extra scrap of a child, that once I'd been able to get away with being indifferent toward him. Now he was all I had, and I needed to make him as whole as I could. My mother had told me that she heard one woman at the funeral say to another, "You know, with all the organ transplants, I wonder why no one thought . . . "

"You know as well as I do that George Junior was not particularly interested in taking care of his brother," I said to Ella.

"The boy *five*." I didn't correct her. "You show me one *man* besides my Melvin interested in taking care of anything, never mind a five-year-old. George Junior would of come around. Time you dead, anyway."

"My husband refuses," I said, and walked out of the kitchen.

This time she followed me. "What he's going to do, he come home, find a little bionic arm hanging on that child, he going to pull it off?"

I didn't know how to tell her that George had, in fact, promised to do exactly that. The night of the boys' first newborn checkup, George had grabbed me by both of my arms, squeezing slowly tighter so I never knew he was hurting me until the bruises appeared in the morning. "Don't talk to me about artificial anything. *You* need to figure out why *you* don't think he's good enough as he is," he said, and I believed him.

I told Ella I would think about it. I went into the bathroom, where the water was still blue in the toilet, and threw up my white lunch.

I was too hungry to eat dinner. My belly was full of poison air bubbles lined up in a constellation on the left side of my body and cramping me so badly I couldn't sit up straight. I told my mother before we sat down that I wanted her, please, if she would, to find a natural way to remove Gregor from the table as soon as he had eaten. Gregor had been eating slavishly since his brother died, not in any celebratory way but rather as if he would make us feel better by making the usual amount of food disappear. My mother and I always took turns feeding him, and he had perfected the art of signaling with his head when he wanted to pause, say something; it was nothing more than a polite thrust of the chin, a gesture he'd been refining since he'd begun taking solid foods as an infant. Most nights since the drowning, he had gone through the entire meal without a word. He had nothing to talk about, having stopped day camp after George Junior died. His father had wanted him to go to the Strive Center, which we passed every morning during the school year on the way to St. John's. "That's for retards," George Junior had told his father, but George had not been moved. The only reason I'd been able to put both boys in the same camp had been my argument that otherwise it would be too much driving. Gregor painted as well as his brother by gripping a brush in his teeth, and the sports coordinator had designated him as assistant coach; the only reason he was staying home right then was that I didn't have the energy for packing him up. Gregor waved aside a forkful of green beans with his chin. "I could have a dog?" he said. It was the first utterance of the meal from anyone. "I *need* a dog."

"That's what your mother always said," my mother said to him. "She *needed* a cat. I always told her nobody needs a cat."

"That's not what you said. You said you already had too much to take care of," I said.

"Well, nobody needs a cat," she said.

"But it's possible to need a dog," Gregor said. "I need one very badly."

"Dogs are for people who can't see and hear," George said. "You can see and hear."

"A dog could feed me. I think it could feed me."

I could not stand one more second of this conversation. "Hold it," I said. "When I told Gammy I needed a cat, I needed it as a friend. You don't have to pretend it's going to be useful." My mother interrupted me. "Much as I loved that cat, he was useless. Which is something altogether different from not being useful." I shot her a look that I hoped reminded her she was supposed to be getting Gregor out of the room for me, not prolonging the time before I'd be alone with George. "What I started to say was," I said to Gregor, "a dog's a good friend, but it won't take George's place."

"A *dog* would love me. That'd be even better than George," he said helpfully.

"Aw, Jesus," George said, slamming his napkin down on the table. "I never heard of a five-year-old boy, dies tragically, I mean *tragically*, and nobody has a good word to say about him."

"Six," Gregor whispered.

"Get him out of here," George said evenly to my mother, then pushed away his plate as a signal that he was leaving next; all he wanted was to have been able to put someone out, then find a different room to storm into.

"I need to talk to you," I said.

"Good God, Anna, we do a lot better when there's no talking at all."

"Honey, we don't do well at all," I said softly.

I had no idea where my words came from, and I wished I believed in angels and in George Junior's goodness because the intervention of a small, new spirit would have made more sense then than any other explanation. I hadn't called George by any name but his own since our first days together, when he chose to study for the bar exam on the library lawn. He had started out in the uptown corner of the library grounds, first creating a nodding acquaintance with me and then closing the distance by a few yards each day. When he crossed the front path, I began disappearing inside the library for comfortable stretches of time, leaving a challenging book face down to hold my place, then slipping into the children's section inside to watch and see whether George would find a way to check what I was reading. The first time he did so, I was in the middle of *Gödel, Escher, Bach*, and after that he quit pretending to ignore me. I would buy him strawberry sticks from the Roman Candy man, and he would talk to me and even kiss me out there on the lawn of the library, but we never went anywhere together until after the bar exam. I called him honey and baby and sweetie when he held me, out there beside the library, and I sensed he wanted to take care of this girl who showed up every day and read good books and gave him candy and called him honey and baby and sweetie. Something softened in George those days. I had no trouble convincing myself that he would be fine to marry, to tell myself I loved him.

My mother slipped Gregor out of the room noiselessly, as if what I'd said demanded reverent silence. But my intention had been to force the secrets out of George, to ask him why—why he wanted Gregor helpless, why his mother came and left, why he acted as if he didn't love me while I was still trying to figure out how to love him right. Maybe then I'd face the fact that I stayed because I didn't want to accept having married for comfort.

Instead I said, "I think you and I need to go away for a few days. Maybe not sort things out, but maybe feel better."

"We're not going to feel better," he said.

"One day we're not going to feel this terrible; all we can do is pile up some time." I had received a letter that morning from a woman whose son had committed suicide his freshman year at Loyola. "You think you want the passage of time, but it takes you farther and farther away from him, and you begin to forget him, and it's so difficult," she wrote, but I didn't believe her; all I wanted was for it to be a year from now.

"I'm not getting a thing done at work," George said. He wasn't looking at me. "That's not a reason to go away; that's a reason to stay, you know."

I said nothing. What George did at work had nothing to do with me. As far as George was concerned, the law and its practice never had come to my conscious mind. When he studied for the bar, I knew nothing about it until, years later, he said to someone at a party, "Oh, I was studying for the bar and Anna was learning for *pleasure* when we met." I hadn't seen the new office he'd been in for six months. I was no part of his legal corporation; I wasn't half-owner of our house, except statutorily by community property law, but he didn't know I knew that. "I sign the papers around here, and you're safe, I promise," he said from time to time. I stayed silent at those times, figuring that if he left me, my mother and I would take Gregor to live in a small house, and she would say accusingly, *We're worse off than we were before*.

"Maybe two days," George said. "Three days and two nights. Over a weekend, I could do that."

"What?" I'd expected a quite different response.

George shrugged. "I can't stand coming home. I go to work one morning, everything's ordinary and predictable, I get a phone call, you never call me, I come tearing home because I can't understand a word you're saying. Walking into this house makes me crazy. Eating at this table makes me crazy. Looking at the kid makes me crazy. Probably looking at you is the worst, but at least I know I'm not sane. I want to see you somewhere else."

"It wouldn't have to be far. Or special," I said, suddenly afraid.

"It's up to you," he said, and left the room.

F O U R

The Mississippi Gulf Coast was neither far nor special; possibly that was the reason George had chosen it for our wedding trip seven years before. He got the business of marrying out of the way the week between the end of his clerkship for Justice Perez and his first day as an associate. "I'll clerk, wait till I get a job; when I get a job, I'll take a week off" was the way he'd proposed. At the curb in front of my mother's house, reaching across me to open the door, motor running.

"A pragmatic man is a good man; he'll let you have time to stay inside your own head," my mother had said dreamily when I ran in to tell her, and at eighteen I was pleased to learn I had chosen well. Justice Perez did the ceremony in his office as a going-away gift to George; the only ones present were a secretary, two clerks who'd been there twelve years between them, and my mother, who had to take her lunch hour at ten o'clock for the occasion. I had a sore throat that day, and crossing the state line had worsened it, but George and I stayed in bed and made ferocious love for three days straight. We stopped once for George to go out for Chloraseptic because my throat was closing up; we went home to call a doctor when George felt feverish. In those three days the marriage was exactly right.

"The whole Gulf Coast's been *laminated*," George said when I told him where I'd chosen to go. Contempt was in his voice, not regret.

"We don't have to look." I'd seen the frantic ads for the casinos on television all the time, but I imagined them to be nothing more than luminous barnacles separated from one another by miles of good beach. We could go laugh at the casinos when we had nothing else to do. I couldn't picture us making love, gently or with ferocity. George's hands had not touched my bare skin in years. We would stay out of the room, talk on beaches and in restaurants, go into the casinos to mock the wheezing, hopeful people there, walk out quickly, liking each other. "This's your trip, suit yourself," George said.

I could not think of a thing to say in the car. I didn't quit crying until we were at the eastern limits of the city. My mother had carried Gregor down to the front lawn, held him as she waved good-bye, and all I had seen was his face, a face struggling for enthusiasm, but I thought he was covering up the fear of being dropped by a fifty-three-year-old woman who did little to stay agile. I rolled down the window to reassure him, and he called out, "There's waves in the Gulf of Mexico, Mama; they can go up twenty feet high in a hurricane." George had shifted into drive, pulled off before I could say a word, and I'd begun to cry with the same homesickness I'd had the first time I spent the night away from my mother; I'd been Gregor's age. "You just think I'm going to die," my mother had told me the next day when I came home and confessed that I'd spent a good part of the sleepover in the bathroom hiding the fact that my eyes were red. "Don't worry, I'm *never* going to die," she'd said, and I'd spent the night out happily a few more times before she decided I needed to be more discriminating in choosing my friends.

George was driving with his hands gripping the steering wheel at ten and two, like a boy in a lesson, even though we were on cruise control, even though we were on straight, empty interstate that wouldn't even veer until a bit before the Mississippi line. I had so many speeches planned, and I'd chosen places where they would work best. I'd thought the open highway would be good, with both of us facing forward, talking at the roadway, like patients in an analyst's office who stare at the ceiling and feel safe telling the doctor they are in love with him because they don't have to see his reaction. I was going to start with the Gregor business, but George was furious; I could see it in his hands. If I tried to speak, I'd cry, and the crying was what made him so angry.

"This isn't a very good beginning," he said evenly when we'd gotten as far as Pearlington without speaking.

"But I have a lot to say."

"I mean, you're miserable. This was your idea."

If I spoke, he would hear tears in my voice. I felt like a child whose father says, *Stop crying or I'll give you something to cry about.* I looked out the window, wanting to see anything that would be worth talking frivolously about. Mississippi highway in summer, with cars sealed tight from heat, looked and smelled like interstate anywhere, gentle grades, broccoli-head weed trees, filtered air. "We could be anyplace," I said.

"But you picked it," George said.

I fell silent, folded my arms across my chest, pressed back into my seat until my muscles ached. We were going east into the low morning sun, and it was difficult to face forward without being blinded by the glare. George was tall enough to be protected by the visor; I could not have driven. I closed my eyes, fell asleep, didn't notice when we slowed, cut south, stopped and started until we looped east, and George leaned on the horn. "You can tell you're in Mississippi," he said, swerving around a car going thirty in the left lane. I knew we were on Highway 90 only because a patch of gulf beach with a single stunted palm tree had appeared before a stretch of hotels and restaurants. "Oh, God, this is horrible," I said.

"This is what I was trying to tell you," George said, his voice surprisingly gentle.

Our wedding trip had been my first to the Gulf Coast since I had been a child, and that time I had grieved over the loss of the Beachwater Hotel. Every summer my mother had used up her week's vacation at the Beachwater, and I had gone into all the corners my mother knew nothing about. While she sat by the pool and worked on a tan that attracted no men, I monitored the romances of the bellhops and waitresses, watched the original *Man in the Iron Mask* in the side parlor, played checkers on the lobby chess tables with children much younger than myself. Our room always had a quill pen and green ink, and I wrote illegible postcards to girls who didn't know I existed. I read of the demolition in the *Times-Picayune*, a New Orleans story because everyone who struggled in New Orleans inevitably vacationed there, and I hurt as if it were my own house. When George and I reached the coast the afternoon of our wedding, I took one look at the shopping mall that stood on the site of the old hotel, and I said, "Aw, no."

George said, "It was just a building, you can't care about a building," and I believed him.

"The Beachwater was one thing, this is another," I said now, glad for it to be easy to be emphatic. "Why'd they have to build on the beach? Don't tell me anyone's in those buildings looking outside and admiring the view."

"They're boats," George said. "Everything you see out there is *floating.*"

"Oh, that's even worse." I imagined that the buildings were designed to rock and sway and ride out hurricanes, much like the new office towers in Japan could take quakes. For as long as I could remember, natural disaster had kept the beaches simple; my mother said anything garish would be washed away if we waited long enough.

George pulled over into the parking lot of a restaurant. An all-you-can-eat Chinese buffet. Biloxi was the place I'd first heard the word *smorgasbord*, and each year my mother would take me up the highway on our last night of vacation so she could heap her plate up with fishy little delicacies that didn't appeal to me no matter how bountiful the spread. The smorgasbord restaurant had linen napkins and reservations, and the tables never were full. Here it was eleven o'clock in the morning, and the parking lot had no empty spaces toward the front. Cars full of men in Air Force fatigues piled up behind us as George stopped to speak.

"You can't stop here," I said.

He drove to the back of the lot, found a place, pulled in. Before I could speak, he said, "I don't want to go in, either. I just wanted to stop."

"Okay."

"The I-110 to the interstate is only a couple of blocks back," he said. "We don't have to do this."

I shook my head no. I had too many speeches ready. I was never going to give my speeches if we turned around and headed back to New Orleans, where my mother was probably frightened that I would be alone with George just long enough to become shameless, forcing him out; give up the comfort and run. "The death of a child can destroy a marriage," she'd said before we left, and it didn't sound like a dispassionate warning. I took in a deep breath, enough to fuel a great spill of cheery words. "Tell you what," I said. "Let's wallow in it." I would go slumming with George, make him feel closer to me.

George, who didn't like dirt or deviancy or imagination, said, "What?"

Remembering all the hopeful people I'd planned to mock, I said, "You won't see anyone you know. We can be disgusting." I pointed at the restaurant. "For starts, we'll eat here."

"It's eleven in the morning."

"Pretty disgusting," I said, cocking my head to the side. We were in Mississippi, a better state, and I wanted to fall into playacting, see what would happen.

"Jesus, Anna, you're manic-depressive," he said. I didn't believe him, but I didn't chafe, either. He was going to be so confused that before he knew it he'd be talking to me.

We checked into the Oasis Casino Hotel before noon, full of barbecued pork and smelling of onions and green peppers. I felt no guilt over canceling our reservation at the Broad, where we'd spent our wedding night, me choking down teaspoonsful of cream of asparagus soup, George eating steak and potato, me more afraid of my throat closing up than of losing my virginity, George already thinking about the office with a window that waited for him when he returned.

There were yellow apples in a bowl at the registration desk, huge and free for the taking. While George did the signing-in, I ate an apple in great noisy mouthfuls that went down unimpeded. "You didn't want that apple," he said on the way to the elevator. I shrugged. "It *looked* good," I said.

The room had two double beds. "This what you asked for?" I said.

"I asked for a double, Anna."

We stood there, arms folded. After a while George put his hands in his pockets. I looked around the room. The drapes were closed. I walked over and opened them. George didn't move. We had a view of Highway 90, a double scallop—domed church to the east, construction to the west, the hotel garage in between. I couldn't make myself say, *Come look*, wish he would ease up behind me, peer out wistfully, and hold me.

"You're dying to call her, so go ahead," he said.

"I wasn't thinking about my mother."

"Hey, this is George you're talking to."

Now I *was* thinking about my mother. "Well, if something terrible happened, she wouldn't know where to reach us," I said.

"Nothing terrible's going to happen," he said.

"You're not trying to reassure me, you just don't believe there's anything terrible left."

"You come here to fight?"

"No," I said, but maybe it wasn't true. "Listen, I won't call her. Anything goes wrong, she can handle it. We're too far away to do her any good, and if Gregor dies it won't matter when I find out. When *we* find out."

"It was a star performance that woman put on when George was drowning."

"You *blame* her?"

"No," he said, in a way that meant, *I blame you*.

"I blame myself, too, you know," I said.

He paced the room, and I didn't watch him. George had skewed, chin-first posture, moving like a man with a migraine, and I could lose respect for him. "There's a bar downstairs," he said finally. Maybe we'd get along now, would have gotten along since the beginning, if I'd admitted I was wrong at every turn. I unzipped my bag, pulled out a light sweater that smelled faintly of cedar. "Don't come with me," he said.

"Oh," I said.

On his way out the door, he said, "I'll meet you here at five o'clock," and I thanked him. "For what?" he said. "I *always* come back." That was true. George had some traits I forgot about.

As soon as the door clicked, I needed to call my mother. Not to talk, especially not to say, *George is solid, rest easy.* All I wanted was for her to have the name of the hotel. She didn't need the phone number, didn't need the room number, just a lead for tracking us down in an emergency. But George would know if I called, the charge registering on the room bill or the phone bill or the credit card bill. He would look at the log of calls, see I had talked to my mother minutes after check-in, and whenever he found out, at check-out, at bill-paying, he would come to me and say, *We exchange maybe five words, you have to go tell her.*

I took one of the vouchers for a free roll of quarters that the hotel gave us to lure us into the casino and went down to the concierge to cash it in. I had to go upstairs in the casino to do so, she said, tired, as if every day some woman came up with the bright idea of taking home ten dollars' worth of quarters and feeling as if she'd gotten away with something.

I found a pay phone near the cashier's desk in the casino and all the noise around me was white, untelling. When my mother answered the phone, I said, "I've only got a second. We moved to the Oasis in Biloxi."

"Is he trying to hurt you?" she said. What? "You sound like you've got a gun to your head." I asked her if Gregor was all right. "How'll I tell if you're safe?" she said. I could hear Gregor in the background, his little-man voice asking for assurance, hearing only one side of the conversation; now I didn't have to ask how he was, and I was proud of myself. "Mama, you read too much garbage. Tell that child we're having a good time." When she moved away from the neighborhood near the library, she began getting her reading material from what was then the K&B drugstore and so she hadn't seen an uncommercial fact in years.

"So, *are* you having a good time?" she said.

"We just got here," I said, and got off the phone two minutes before an automatic operator could ask me to deposit more coins.

I had six dollars and seventy-five cents left from the ten. It was more than a fistful for me, but I resisted taking a plastic cup. I stuffed the quarters into my pockets, liked the weight of them. In fact, I liked the weight of them a lot, remembered the joy of having ten quarters when school lunch cost seventy-five cents. My mother would cluck, tell me that for one quarter she could get a ham po'boy when she was a girl; each time she told me the size of a nickel Hershey bar it got bigger. I went to the cashier, told her I wanted to trade in my quarters for nickels. Three two-dollar rolls and change; I broke a roll into my right pocket, patted it contentedly, strolled around the floor, looking for old people who also cared about coins. I wanted a story to tell George. At five o'clock, he would come back to the room, a bit numbed by drink, feeling he had punished me, leaving the girl who never had an idea of her own in a strange place, and I would have a story.

I had never been inside a casino before. Except for a half-empty poker room, all that filled the hall were slot machines. Dark alleys full of steady noise, backlit plastic so low in wattage that even the hot pinks of the women's clothing was muted. At first I walked around the edges, figuring that those who took the end machines expected to be watched. But I kept moving, pretending I was on my way, until I saw that no one took notice, and then I stepped into the rows. These were the dollar slots, and everyone knew what to do. No one pulled the levers; rather, each pushed buttons as fast as a touch typist repeating a syllable, the rhythm steady, unstopped even when coins rained out. Though few let the coins fall, I saw; instead they held the credit in the machine, not cashing in until they moved on to another, luckier machine.

"Don't forget, if you play when you're losing, you have a problem," my mother had instructed me the day before.

"That's not a great rule to live by," I'd said, feeling clever. She said she only meant when I gambled. "I'm not going to Mississippi for that," I'd said.

"Maybe I *don't* just mean when you gamble," she'd said.

In the second row of quarter slots, two women caught my eye. They were playing side by side, two very fat women, stuffed in between other players in a full row. All I could see were the backs of them. And their backs were identical. Broad backs, sheathed in the same vertical multicolored stripes, their shirts bulging where nice round pockets of fat spilled out over the tops of their bras. Each had a tight peppered gray perm, the curls so short and flat that their heads seemed freakishly small atop their shoulders. They were playing their machines with the same pattern, rhythm, right arm flapping. I had to know whether they were twins. But neither showed her face, and as I stood behind them and adjusted to the light I could see both had credits, the one on the left $128, the other $49. If they had any control over those machines at all, then they didn't have identical musculature, identical power. Unless they had come to machines with different figures left by the preceding players; where they started might affect where they ended up, though I'd heard randomness was built in.

Neither woman moved from her machine; neither had reason to do so; each seemed to be winning enough. I walked around to the next row, couldn't see through to their faces, went back quickly in case they decided to get up. I found myself wishing them to lose, thrilling as their credits dropped, sorry when they won. One losing would be enough; she would get up, and I could look at her, slip into her place, look at the other. I stood behind them for half an hour, gambling against them, losing on their wins, and a third woman came up the aisle. She, too, was wearing the vertically striped shirt; she, too, was carelessly fat. But her hair was dry strawberry blond, pulled back into a ponytail. "You two going to miss the buffet, rate you're going," she said good-naturedly to my identical women. Each held up her left hand and made a tight wait-a-second wave, each hit a single button at the left of the panel in front of her, both looked down as coins spilled into the tray, the one on the left taking twice as long to get her full payoff. I stood back, as if one of them were playing at my very luckiest machine and I would wait forever for it to be free. They turned, and I saw twenty years' difference in their faces. I wished I had bet against myself.

F I V E

I returned to the room having played only one nickel, which paid off two, though I didn't understand why, since I'd had nothing on my payoff line. It was midafternoon, and two hours alone in the room wouldn't be bad, with all the soap, shampoo, conditioners, and pay-per-view channels, none of which I planned to use, but I would like knowing they were there. I hadn't been away from Gregor overnight since he was born. George Junior had spent the night out, and I sensed that mothers who invited him thought they were quite brave, *not* inviting his brother. My arms had that peculiar lightness that comes after a long strain.

The room was dark, the drapes drawn effectively for day sleepers, but I sensed George's presence even before my eyes could adjust. It may have been the subtle sweet odor of alcohol recently drunk; it may have been that I knew he'd be there. "Come sit," he said from his bed, and I walked over slowly, protecting my shins from a room I didn't know well. I sat down, cross-legged, on my bed, which was the one farther from the door; wherever we slept, I always had the side farther from the door, even though George never got up in the night.

"I've never seen you drunk before," I said.

"I don't think I'm drunk," he said, his mouth not working at making his words. "I'm just so damn sad." My eyes had adjusted to the bit of light in the room, and I could see he was lying on his back, his face wet with tears. "Jesus, Anna, I never stopped to think."

I sat in silence, not knowing what he meant, not knowing, either, what to say to such a statement. "Now I think all the time, and I fucking can't stand it," he said. "You know, you get on this life plan, and you follow it because no one is going to be pissed with you, and then one fine day you figure out that you don't know what you're doing."

"You're not making sense, George," I whispered.

"I'm not trying to make sense. I don't need to make sense."

I asked him whether he'd mind a little light in the room. The dark was frustrating me terribly, though I could make out his expression, and it was one of contorted agony, which made him unattractively weak. I'd always been grateful that George had a strong, square face, so that from a distance I couldn't be disturbed by the thinness of his lips. His lips made him remind me of a hand puppet, a lesser primate, a nonpoisonous snake. "Please don't," he said. "I don't think I could take the glare."

"I saw these two women downstairs," I said.

"You want to talk to me or not?" I told him go ahead; I never heard of a drunk whose idea of conversation was to listen. "Know what I mean, I never stopped to think?" I shrugged. "Tell me the truth, you get the impression I did a lot of thinking about marrying you?"

It was almost a fact-gathering question, the way he said it, but it took the breath out of me. He'd married me because I was in the right place at the right time. "Look, I wasn't exactly going to call *you* down for acting on impulse. Or marrying for appearances."

"I take it the answer's no."

"If you're about to tell me all your regrets," I said, "then we might as well go home now."

George sat up on the bed, slid both pillows behind himself, squirmed around with little control until he looked terribly uncomfortable to me. "I'm trying to *tell* you something here. All I'm saying is, I got these ideas of what I was supposed to do, damned if I know where I got these ideas. You know, you're twenty-four, you get married. Go through all the sacraments and you can't miss. So I'm living for this child, that's what I'm living for, I guess, and he dies, and what am I supposed to do?" He waved his hand at me, his wrist barely under his control. "He was a *whole* kid, Anna, don't give me any bullshit."

"He could run," I said.

"Yes."

"You want to tell me that that was what was going to matter?" I began thinking of ways in which Gregor was better than George Junior. I'd been doing that since they were born. But I pictured in my mind George Junior running, his thin legs churning, perhaps competing against only himself. I couldn't bear the image, and I squeezed my eyes tight shut, wanting black in a dark room. "I'm sorrier for George Junior than you can imagine," I said.

"You made him mean, you know."

"You can't make somebody mean," I said. An old black man had lived three houses down from my mother, and he had bought a sorry-looking black-speckled dog that he named Joe Frazier. He fed that dog pepper and hollered at him, and told everyone that Joe Frazier was going to be mean, and Joe Frazier had been scared of a moving blade of grass.

"You made him *want* to be mean."

I wanted to say, *Hey, you're the one who broke into a moronic grin when Gregor told you at the funeral that George Junior was the meanest boy in kindergarten*. "Tell me," I said, "how I could have made him *want* to kick the hell out of me when I changed his diaper."

"You never took psychology, did you?"

I had no comeback. That was the way George ended any argument that could be played out with data. You never took psychology, did you? You never took economics, did you? You could have used a course in chemistry, he said when I took it upon myself to clean the pool and found the walls of it yellow with algae in a week. George retained nothing of what he had learned in college from what I could tell, probably had held onto nothing the day after the final exam. "Read him sophomore year," he said when I asked him what he thought of Flannery O'Connor's "Good Country People." I'd told the story afterward to my mother. She hadn't gotten it; she liked science too much, didn't know one postwar writer from another, but I figured she was happy for the whorls literature put into my thinking.

"I don't want to fight," I said to George.

"Then what'd we come here for?"

"For time to pass. I thought if time passed we'd feel better."

George flicked on the bedside lamp, and the sudden light hurt my head. "You don't feel bad. You don't have any right to feel bad. Really, he was *my* kid."

"God, I hate you," I said, and he reached over and slapped me hard across the face.

I didn't cry out, didn't cry at all. A blow like that doesn't hurt any more than a needle stick; it is swift and unexpected. It was the hand he still held raised that frightened me, because surely the next slap on the raw flesh would hurt badly. "Say you don't mean that," George said.

"I don't mean that," I said, believing myself, and he lowered his hand.

He was sobbing now, in the light, his face red and uncovered, his mouth open and wet; I could see how crowded his teeth were. "I'm drunk," he whispered, though even before George Junior died he was capable of bursting into tears cold sober, a peculiar trait. He slid to the edge of the bed, tried to stand up, rocked dizzily, proving his point. I helped him sit on the side of the bed. All I knew about drunkenness was coffee; that was what hostesses offered guests on television before they sent them out on the road. Surely it was the caffeine in coffee that worked as an antidote against the alcohol. I told George not to move, that I'd get him something, I'd be right back. There was a soft drink machine on our floor between our room and the elevator. I forgot my wallet, fished nickels out of my pocket, deposited seventy-five cents' worth. The Coke button was unlit. I pressed it anyway, but nothing came. Caffeine. All that was left with caffeine was Mountain Dew. Mountain Dew was a good idea; I'd get Mountain Dew. I popped the top before I ran back to the room, preferring to spill a little in the corridor than to shake it up so it threatened to explode.

"I can't drink that," George said.

"Come on," I said, thinking of all the nickels I'd used. He took a few sips, reeled a bit, took a few more sips at my urging. "You're still drunk," I said, and he upended the can, figuring he couldn't lose.

He made it to the bathroom before he vomited, but he didn't make it to the toilet. Once he had fouled the floor, he kept it up, choosing not to step in his own mess in order to reach the bowl. He didn't stop until he was empty, and I watched because I couldn't turn away, couldn't keep from gagging, either. When he finished, he faced me, and he was deathly white but relieved, smiling with relief. "Call housekeeping," he said.

"No one gets paid enough to do this," I said, and I cleaned it myself with bar soap and a bath towel that I wrung out in the bathtub. I breathed though my mouth, retched, pulled off clothes until I was cleaning in my underwear.

"It smells terrible in there," George said when I finished.

"I hope you're not complaining."

"Jesus, Anna, why do you always expect the worst from me?" he said.

I apologized, suddenly became aware that I smelled bad now, and I washed my hands, my arms, my knees, changed my underwear. I waited for George to brush his teeth, but he didn't.

Sleepiness is the only protection I know that can be summoned at will, with no harm. When the boys were babies, I liked the crazed feeling that came from wakening every two hours; it was an analgesic, an escape, a promise that I could go to darkness if I just had a moment. I began feeling slurry and sleepy, and George couldn't hurt me. He didn't want supper, and I didn't care. He had no interest in watching the weekend news on television, and I didn't, either. George lay on the bed, staring up, and I sat in a chair, able to doze as lightly as a psychotic cat. In the silence I played games with myself, betting I could gauge the passage of five minutes without looking, then ten, then half an hour. I offered myself prizes; if I guessed correctly I would slip out for a free apple downstairs. Or buy myself a Sprite. With a dollar bill, none of my nickels. No Mountain Dew, I would never again want to smell Mountain Dew. My back was to the window, and the shades were drawn, but I sensed differences outside, an ebb of traffic as people stopped and changed for dinner. All my guesses were wrong, and I didn't improve. Time passed more slowly than I thought it did. "You keep looking at your watch," George said.

"We could do something," I said.

"They gave us an envelope."

I knew the envelope; it was where I'd found the voucher for ten dollars in gambling money. The packet had seemed to me similar to the thick envelopes that came in the mail full of coupons, good bargains for address labels and automobile mufflers and porcelain figurines. I gave them attention because they seemed so full of possibilities, sometimes even slipped a few into a kitchen drawer. The voucher for the casino was the first coupon I could remember acting upon. "They've got free tickets to see all these impersonators," I said.

"Right," George said.

"Nobody's going to know us," I said. "And if they do, so what? It'd be like going to Ruth's Chris Steakhouse on Good Friday."

"I don't get it."

"It wasn't funny," I said.

We went down to the show because at some point both of us realized we'd booked our room for three days and two nights, and it was going to get so small we would be compressed together more and more tightly until one of us would have to stop breathing. George didn't walk alongside me, but shuffled a step behind, down the corridor, into the elevator, through the walkway to the nightclub. We had to pass through the outdoors, and though it was night the air was thick and hot and wet. I heard George say something behind me. "What?" I said; I could have heard him if he had been alongside me.

"For all the sneaky marketing tricks they put behind this place, you'd think they wouldn't piss people off like this."

"Twenty seconds in the open?" I said, liking the hint of a fishy scent in the air. The Beachwater always had smelled of gulf water and chlorine; either scent by itself was often enough to give me a sense of well-being. When I watched the boys by our pool, sometimes I closed my eyes, tried to see if

I could pretend that almost twenty years hadn't passed, that I knew nothing yet of that time, but my mind filled with newer people, groped hopelessly for girls who would have filled my thoughts if I were truly seven.

"I am strictly not in the mood to break out in a sweat," George said.

Elvis was good; so was Roy Orbison. I ordered a glass of white wine so George could feel as if he were with someone better than the old women from Florida who lined up Brandy Alexanders. "We never had a date before," I whispered into his ear. The wine was working fast on me, with the sullen southern baritone of the Elvis, and I placed my hand on top of George's. I saw him look down out of the corner of his eye, but he didn't pull away, let me hold on until the music broke to fast. Gladys Knight and the Pips. "Are they dead?" I said. George shrugged. "You can't imitate someone who's not dead," I said, "and I don't think they're dead."

"Why not?"

"Why not what?" I said, and someone hissed behind me to hush up. I turned around. She was a white woman, my mother's age. Everyone in the room was white. "Are they dead?" I said to her. She put her index finger to her lips.

"Let's go," George whispered, and he took my wrist, led me out before I could reach for my second glass of wine, finish off the last sips.

I was as empty as I'd have been if I, too, had thrown up, and the wine made me wobbly. George took my elbow, guided me. "You're a cheap drunk," he said, and I giggled.

"We didn't have to leave," I said, feeling free. Madonna was next, he told me. "Now *definitely* she's not dead," I said. "She had a baby, and you can't have a baby if you're dead." I giggled again, pleased with myself. I might have to try drinking more often.

Back in the room, I wanted him to make love to me. He was sorry, I knew he was sorry, and to me there was nothing more tender than a man who wants to make amends. "Cry-y-y-ying, over you, cry-y-y-ying over you," I sang in my sweetest falsetto and I ran my hand across George's chest. The worst thing George ever had told me was that his mother said he was shaped like a shmoo bag. I'd never seen a naked man before George; I would have believed all men were shaped like shmoo bags—puny arms, girlish shoulders, wide hips—if he hadn't told me. I closed my eyes, didn't let my hand wander far from the center of his chest, didn't want to think of how upside-down he was, how weak, as weak as his mouth, as colorless as his hair. I needed to be skin-to-skin with someone; I needed, too, to believe George meant more to me than my mother hoped he did. "This is a very bad idea," he said softly. I didn't pull away from him. My hands kept moving over his body, my fingertips a bit numbed with drink, the cloth of his shirt protecting me from feeling much. An erection began to stir in his pants, and I moved my body against it, wanting to arouse him so he would touch me back. He took me by the arms, gently pushed me away from himself until he could look at me. "You can't replace a child," he said.

I was frozen sober. I backed off. "I just wanted you," I said, and as I spoke I realized I didn't want him at all.

"Don't tell me it never crossed your mind. It crossed my mind the minute I heard George Junior was dead."

"No it didn't." All that could have been on anyone's mind was George Junior. I was there, I saw George Junior; George was downtown, at his desk, surely all he could picture was the boy, all he could think about was the boy, whether he had been afraid. The first thing I'd said when George came home was, "He was surprised, he was too surprised to know what was happening, honest." When I had to speak, I imagined the cat, the face of the cat, angry in the water.

"Know what the trouble with you is, Anna? You think you can read my mind. That's why you're always expecting me to read your mind. Well, you can't. If you think I'd admit thinking about another child if it weren't true, you've grossly underestimated me. Which doesn't surprise me in the least."

I apologized. I didn't reach for him, didn't want to touch him, but I said, "If it's what you want, one day we could."

In six years the subject never had come up, and I'd assumed that both of us thought two children were enough, replacements for ourselves. Though my mother had pointed out that she and my father had never had the opportunity to produce the two to which they were entitled, and therefore I could rightfully have a third. We'd had to draw a chart, a family pyramid, because my first reaction had been that I should have four children, two for my never-born brother. "But your never-born brother would have had a wife," my mother said, and we frittered away an afternoon imagining this brother, what his name would have been, where he would have gone to school, what his hobbies would have been. "No sister, definitely no sister," I said, and my mother agreed.

"What if you got another one like Gregor?" George said.

I remembered "mosaic scrambling" because it was such a queer phrase, remembered a sense of blamelessness when I heard "DNA accident" through the grogginess after giving birth. I should have said, *Another Gregor would be all right*; instead I said, "We wouldn't get another one like Gregor."

"True," he said without conviction. "Believe me, I researched the topic thoroughly. No matter how much I trusted the doctor."

"Yeah?" I said, wishing I could believe him.

"I'm an attorney, Anna."

"And?"

He hesitated. "And you don't have to be a personal-injury attorney looking for trouble to smell a lawsuit when a baby comes out like that."

"You thought there was money in it?"

"For the kid, Anna, for the goddamn kid. A hundred years ago, you'd have put him in a sideshow, and somebody'd have carted him around and fed him for the rest of his life. What's he going to do when you die?"

"If he had a limb or two, he could do anything."

"Aw, Jesus, I'm going to bed," George said, and he kicked off his shoes, turned off the light.

SIX

At three A.M. George was snoring loudly enough to mask all noise, block all chance of sleep for me, and I slipped out of the room unafraid. I took my nickels with me. I liked the feeling of having those nickels, though their heft and number had been diminished by my trip to the drink machine. I thought I might keep a few loose nickels in my pocket for a while when I got home. Even in the house.

George had said "true" when I said we wouldn't have another child like Gregor. I had to think. I hadn't thought about that before, but I had once thought about whether Gregor could have normal babies. Women were going to be obsessed with George Junior, I'd thought, because he was tantalizingly out of reach, but women were going to love Gregor, too, and he would marry, make love in ways I couldn't picture because he was my son and it was better not to. My mother had said that the DNA story was just something the doctor spat out because it was full of fancy language that would impress George and exculpate himself. George had been relieved to run with it, evidently, as my mother could have predicted. Advanced degrees affected George. I had to think. My mother said freakish bodily damage had happened when the boys were growing inside me, and I'd better never tell George because he already had enough things to blame on me. I had to think.

I shambled over to the casino, cracked my two rolls of nickels into a cup, sat down at a slot machine. Feed a nickel, pull a lever. That was how I'd won before. None of this pushing of buttons for me, except on a win. I could be mechanical, think of what I needed to think about, but hear the nickels fall when I won.

My mother had looked in the *Merck Manual*. She was still living near the public library at the time, and it was as good a reference as she could get. George maybe did a computer search in his law library, or probably did nothing now that I thought about it, but George was starting out with believing the doctor. If he went with mosaic scrambling, of course he would find chromosomes that were accidentally messed up; that's what scrambling meant—I didn't need a lot of schooling to know that. Because he believed the doctor, George couldn't blame him, but also he couldn't blame me. And as a Catholic he couldn't blame God. No wonder George was so furious.

Ten nickels down, I won five.

My mother said, "I looked all through that book, all those damaged-chromosome problems, every one of them, you get a severely retarded child. You can tell me anything you want, but Gregor is not retarded." The boys were ten months old at the time, and Gregor had a vocabulary of twenty words while George Junior never stopped running long enough to learn to speak. " The way I figure it, he's got what they call congenital amputation. Somewhere along the line, it was too crowded for him to grow arms and legs. Knowing George Junior, you can see how it happened." I had laughed, skimmed over the page she had photocopied, found the description of stumps, the "any or all limbs" part, the "lead normal lives" part. I'd found myself watching George Junior for days after I read that, daring him to push into Gregor's spaces.

I got a one-bar, two-bar, three-bar combination, and fifty nickels rained down.

I didn't want another child. I congratulated myself. I'd come to talk about Gregor's life, and even though I'd been sidetracked, I'd brought George back to it. We had more than a day left, and I would let George sleep late, in the dark, waken with a clear, cool mind.

I won nothing back from the fifty nickels, but it didn't matter because they weren't mine to begin with, and they'd bought me excellent ideas. My fingers were black from the nickels. I would bet against myself, see if I could make my two rolls last beyond daybreak.

I never came closer to broke than six nickels, and only hunger made me realize it was almost eight A.M. I counted the contents of my cup, my fingers so dirty now they left prints on the white plastic. Eight dollars and thirty-five cents. The cashier had a machine that would have done the job for me, one pour, a digital readout, bills and change, but the weight of the cup thrilled me, and I carried it out of the slots area. Now I understood why a basket of packets that looked like wrapped condoms was on the desk at the exit. Wet wipes, free, just as the drinks were free, though no one sat at the desk expecting a tip the way the cocktail waitresses did. I took a fistful, loving plenty, used up four and still saw clouds of black on my fingers, lines of black in my palms. I was sitting on the steps near the glass doors to the outside, the cup pressed tightly between my knees; I was close enough to an exit that someone could walk off with my nickels, and I had no proof they were mine. I had three little packets left, and I felt deprived, walked over and took seven more. I thought it might have something to do with living in New Orleans all my life, where each year at Carnival everyone grabs for useless trinkets, fights over them, even, and walks home happy and bent over with the weight of so much plastic. "Anal retentives, that's all we are," my mother would announce to me at parades, then scrabble hard on the ground for a broken string of beads, stuff it into her sack, and laugh at herself.

George was not in the room when I returned. I went directly into the bathroom: If he were going to pack up and leave me in anger, he would take his toothbrush, comb, deodorant, and razor. The razor was still plugged in, and I was relieved, not because I wasn't stranded, but because now I knew I hadn't done something too wrong. I lay down on George's unmade bed, surprised by how soft and embracing it felt now. Cool sheets. Pillows without years of the musky scent of the oil in George's hair. The air conditioning was on high, humming and cold, the only sound that of full water pipes somewhere above me. George had opened the drapes; all I could see from where I lay was the blue of the sky, crisp blue, autumn blue if I pretended. If I used the light to see what was around me, avoided imagining, picturing my boys, either, both, I could have laid there until it was time to go home. George came through the door so fast I let out a little squeal of unhappy surprise. "Don't give me that," George said.

He was still dressed in the clothes he was wearing when he fell asleep, and he was unshaven, but his hair was combed. "I wake up at five in the morning, your bed's not slept in, you're not in mine, and you're gone—what am I supposed to think?"

I shrugged. "Maybe you're supposed to think I've found something to do instead of turn on the TV." (On our wedding trip, I had awakened because my throat hurt so badly that I thought it was closing a millimeter at a time, and if I slept I would miss the moment when I could no longer breathe. I had turned on the TV, and George had sat right up in bed and said,

"Are you out of your mind? Haven't you ever shared a room with another person before?")

"Do you know what kind of lowlifes hang around a place like this? You go walking around in the middle of the night, next thing I know you're lying dead on the beach."

I hadn't seen anyone much under the age of sixty, the casino filling in the early morning hours with old people who'd done all their sleeping decades ago and now couldn't bear to lie alone in the dark. "The only person I saw in that place who had the muscle tone to drag me anywhere was a guy who barked when his machine paid off. And he was *blind*."

"Doesn't it count that I was worried about you?" George said.

"Sure." I ignored his worrying about me because I never sensed worry behind it. George had a whole array of behaviors on which he'd slap a caring label. He could miss me, he could want me, he could admire me, and all it meant was that he wanted me around to tend him, fill my end of the bargain. He was worried about me. If I were indeed dead on the beach, who would raise the boy and take the packages from the deliveryman and get the fresh cantaloupe? My mother might take the boy, but George would be left with a house where he didn't know the location of the circuit breakers and had fully intended to live out his life never knowing. My mother had the pragmatic son-in-law she'd wanted, but I was a practical tool for such a man, rather than the daydreamer my mother planned for me to be. "Anything happens to me, my mother'll take care of Gregor," I said.

"I'd hope so," he said. I gave him an unbelieving look. "I'm not playing that game, Anna," he said, and flopped down in the chair near the window. When George sat, he was ready to grapple for as long as it took. He wasn't a litigator; he manipulated best from a sitting position. I had learned long ago that all I could do was sit, too, or lie down, getting an advantage only if I was more comfortable than he was. I slumped in the other chair, and three nickels fell from my pocket. I didn't know I had those three nickels. I scooped them from the floor and George paid no attention.

I held the nickels tight in my clean palm. "I want to talk about prostheses," I said.

"God, what a funny word," he said. "Here we are, haven't had a bit of sleep, haven't eaten in days, and what do you come out with? Pros-*the*-ses." I looked at him crossly. "Come on, Anna, say the word. Pros-*the*-ses. You've got to admit it sounds ridiculous at this hour of the morning."

I pushed out a little laugh. My laugh wasn't sincere, but then I had thought about it, and most laughs were nothing more than polite sniffs that made other people feel good. The only time I believed in my own laughter was when I was alone.

"That's better," George said and smiled. Thin lips can't look sincere; they look too much as if something is being held back. "Come on, we're here to play, remember?"

I told him no, I didn't think so. This was not an earned vacation. Losing a child wasn't a reason to go off somewhere full of relief. Though the smallest part of me found ease in not having to expect all the time that George Junior would harm himself.

"You said yourself we were coming to make time pass."

"So I lied," I said.

"Look, we are *not* going to talk about the kid. I have my reasons, and he's not going to get all hooked up to computers and walk around looking like something out of a bad movie."

"A prosthetic arm. One. Under a sleeve." I pictured a soft flannel shirt, brown and green plaid. I pictured Gregor using his left arm. George Junior was right-handed, so I assumed Gregor was left-handed, though so far I'd had no reason to know. I wondered how the doctor would figure it out.

"Deaf people think cochlear implants are genocide," he said. "At least I'm no crazy idealist." I tried to suppress a little sniff of amusement.

"Tell you what," George said after a while. "You start paying the bills around here, you get a say-so."

"That's mean."

"*You're* mean. You think I've got no good reason for telling you no. I don't think you've ever had a very good opinion of me. Which is all right. But you could kind of keep it to yourself."

I had learned a long time ago that I couldn't let George think he'd made me cry. It was fine for him to fill the house with sobs that frightened the boys, repelled me, but something about my hurt enraged him, made him raise a hand until I went numb with forgetfulness. I rubbed the nickels together in my hand, made a little stack of them, fanned them out, tried to figure out if the top one was heads or tails; I guessed I felt the contours of Thomas Jefferson's profile; Monticello would have a line straight across the coin. I forgot about crying, forgot what we were talking about. "I think we should go home," I said. I was sure that followed whatever he had said last.

"That's just what she wants," George said.

The door opened, and I saw the housekeeper before I heard her. I lurched out of the chair as if she had caught me at something. George rose, too, slowly, as if we were in a restaurant and someone important had approached our table. "Oh, ma'am, I'm so sorry," the woman said to me.

"We won't need housekeeping while we're here," George said.

"Oh, you got to tell the front desk or I get fired," the woman said. Her face was round and Mayan, her accent Spanish, her eyes afraid of error. I wondered how she'd found her way to Mississippi.

"George, the room stinks," I whispered.

"Tell you what," he said to the woman. "We'll use the door hangers." He escorted her to the door, ceremoniously hung the "do not disturb" sign on the handle, turned to me with the look of a lawyer who'd once again twisted his way into getting what he wanted.

"We were talking about your mother," he said.

"Oh." I knew perfectly well who "she" was.

"We go back now, she'll offer to help me pack." He did a little jig, imitating my mother, who would never show her joy in such a way. Besides, he was wrong: She *wanted* to live with George. As long as he didn't actually kill me. I watched his antics. George was not a fit man, and his center of gravity was so low I was embarrassed for him. "If we have to sit in this room for two days and look at each other, so be it," he said. "But we're not going back early. She'd *love* to think we're having problems." I felt a little jolly jolt of adrenaline. George had pictured himself in an apartment, not me and my mother and Gregor in a cramped shotgun.

I didn't smile. "You know, we could order room service and get movies on the TV and stay in bed, just lying around, not doing anything, I mean *anything*," I said, not sounding too generous or sorry. I'd always imagined myself in a hotel room with a linen-covered rolling cart full of butterscotch sundaes; whipped cream and maraschino cherries were an important part of the picture, a matrix of white poufs, each topped by a lipstick-pink circle, perfectly centered. The Beachwater had had a mirrored display of giant plastic sundaes in the basement drugstore behind the soda fountain. When the hotel was torn down, I wondered if anyone had saved them. Probably not, or I'd have read about it in the *Times-Picayune*. Most reporters at the *Times-Picayune* were nostalgic as hell about their childhoods, and most had grown up in New Orleans.

"Anna, I'm not in the mood."

I rubbed the nickels together in my pocket. I could feel my fingers getting dirty. I liked the aloneness of being in the casino. No one spoke, no one made me struggle to think of what to say next. I could very well sit in front of a slot machine and not play. Time passed there the way it passed under anesthetic. It had no value. I had thought over the past days that George Junior only had needed another minute, maybe even less than a minute. Even if he'd died anyway, I could have used that minute to tell him something, something good in its finality. I wondered whether George Senior thought about time. I doubted it.

He was lying on his bed with his back to me when I left the room, and I was uneasy, as if I were leaving a child in a hotel room alone. I took my cup with me. I also took the second ten-dollar voucher from the envelope. We had one for each night we were there, as well as one pair of show tickets for each night. The remaining tickets were for a country-and-western show; I left them on the dresser where George could see them.

I didn't use the money to eat, managed to make it to three o'clock on two free apples. I could smell the buffet in the poker room, hot meat mixed with cigarette smoke. I was grumbly hungry, but I wouldn't borrow from my collection of nickels, which grew, not steadily, but smoothly enough for me to feel no need to change machines.

The tray was littered with nickels, but still I played only one at a time. Elbow to elbow with people on either side, the seats filled as soon as vacated, I knew everyone else used the "bet three credits" button. Their machines made different noises from mine, a repeating scale of twangs; they, too, were aware of the difference, but no one spoke. I played a nickel. One red seven, two red sevens, three red sevens; nothing happened. I sat staring at the machine, and all action on both sides of me stopped. "One nickel, you only win with bars," the woman to my left said, and then she resumed playing. I read the payoff chart. Three sevens would have paid a thousand nickels if I'd bet fifteen cents. The man on my right was still watching me, and I picked up my things, moved away.

Now I played three nickels at a time, preferring the risk to looking foolish among my new neighbors. But the wins were bigger and more frequent and soon the cup, the size of a thirty-two-ounce drink, was within an inch of the rim. I would count it in the room.

"Your mother called," George said when I walked into the room. He was still lying on the bed, and the television wasn't on, though the Gideon Bible lay open next to him, spine up.

I was half alarmed, because I had fears for just two people, and my mother was only one of them. She could make a phone call, she was all right. I could learn nothing from George's demeanor about Gregor; a neutral expression could very well mean the boy was dead. "Well?" I said after too much time had passed.

"Well," he said, "she's not smart enough to have found us on her own."

"What's wrong with Gregor?" I said. When George's mind moved deliberately into disturbing places, I often found my own mind jumping past logic and sequence, and erratically but surely, to the worst conclusions. I hated that he was a lawyer, assumed his tricks had been learned in school.

He was on his feet, bumbling like someone who'd spent too much time in a hospital bed or on a ship. George was seven inches taller than I was and outweighed me by seventy pounds and always told me not to worry, that he was a man who pulled his punches. "Why in God's name did you call her?" he said, and I knew nothing was wrong at home. George was an angry man, but he wasn't a cruel man.

"I shouldn't have," I said. "I'm sorry."

"You're not here to come to the phone, the woman thinks I've done something hideous to you. She says, 'How's Anna?' And I say, 'She's just fine, Dorothy.' And she hems and haws and talks about what she gave the kid for dinner last night and finally when I don't say anything she says, 'So, could you put her on?' I tell her you've gone out, I don't know when you're coming back, and she gets really quiet. I'm tempted to tell you not to call, see how long before the state police come break down the goddamn door."

"I said I was sorry."

"Sometimes *sorry* doesn't cut it, you know."

"I used the pay phone."

"Oh, Anna, Anna," he said, and I knew he was thinking that I had no money sense, that it was all about money.

I wanted to leave the room. I could break so much in that room. Television set, plate-glass window, three identical lamps with fake-crystal bases. George, I couldn't hurt George if I tried; he could grab my wrists with the saved-up strength of a lazy man and hold me off until I realized I was a fool. Pressed-wood furniture, as easily cracked as dry bread. So terribly many mirrors, and the onionskin pages of the Bible. I could throw something at George. I felt my fingers tighten around the cup of nickels. It was full, ungiving, so I had a good grip. I wasn't going to throw it, but I wanted to hold it as hard as I could, make myself know it was there for the using. The motion was imperceptible, all in the muscles of my hand, but George knew, and with one swift upward swing of his fist he sent the cup flying. The nickels scattered, so many nickels, impossible to follow the trajectory as I might have with one, or even two.

"I'll never find them," I said. "Aw, George, I'll never find them all."

We created night for the next two days. We let in no light, paid no attention to time, just lay in bed and dozed, slipped out on each other when we couldn't sleep. We didn't come out and agree to pass time in this way; rather, George announced in the late afternoon that he was going back to bed, and from then on, no matter the hour, each of us pretended it was the middle of the night. While George slept or lay still, I went downstairs to phone my mother, went to the casino for a cheeseburger I couldn't swallow, and crawled on the floor picking up nickels as I felt them in the dark. I don't know what he did when I slept. Certainly he left, and perhaps twice I awakened to hear him slide into bed, but I smelled nothing from him, not food, not liquor, just angry sweat.

We were close to the New Orleans city limits when I realized I'd bought no gift for Gregor. I told George we had to stop. His voice was tired, the way a voice can be when one has slept too much and begun to crave more sleep. "He doesn't expect anything," George said. That was true. We'd never gone away before. "And we don't want to set a precedent," I said with the certainty of someone who never again will have reason to leave. George laughed at my joke, and I felt the knots and rocks inside me begin to dissolve. "We'll get him candy," George said. "He won't care where it's from."

I could tell that my mother was popping with pleasure, content to wait for George to go back to work Monday morning. She had that expression that came when she had a fat new book to read or a fresh sack of ginger snaps. When I heard the sound of the garage door mechanism stop, I turned to her and said, "I hope you're not expecting anything. Nothing happened."

"Right," she said, not disappointed.

"We had a rough time, but I figured we would."

"Right."

Gregor was still at the breakfast table, waiting patiently for my mother to spoon scrambled eggs into his mouth. He had long ago given up on eating food at the temperature of his choosing. Surely inside of him was a boy who'd prefer to sneak into his bedroom and eat half the giant Hershey bar we'd brought him. His lips were parted, at the ready, in case my mother remembered what she was doing. "You want your candy bar?" I said to him. He looked at my mother, not believing.

"Eggs don't grow on trees," she said.

"I'll eat the eggs," I said, and I went to fetch the still un-opened candy bar, popped squares of it into Gregor's mouth as fast as he'd have done so himself. His lips began to smear with chocolate, and he threw his head back laughing. "Lick your lips," I told him, but he was laughing too hard, couldn't quite get the hang of it, laughed until he was pink. "Want me to lick them for you?" I said, coming at him, my own mouth full of cold eggs. "No-o-o-o," he squealed, and his little tongue darted out and around, hitting and missing. I tossed another chocolate square into his open mouth. "I'm going to spoil you rotten," I said, having made the decision right then and there. "George said I was a rotten egg," Gregor said, pleased with himself.

"So what really happened?" my mother asked me after Gregor was off to day camp. He was going because my mother said he should; for his own sake, she said.

"I told you, nothing."

"Anna, I've known that man just a few weeks less than you have, and he sounded downright homicidal to me on the phone."

"He always sounds homicidal," I said.

"Ah, the words of a worshipful, devoted wife." Relief was in her voice.

"I hardly need to explain my marriage to you," I said. My mother had a system of putting George in such a bad light that I had to defend him, and half the time I didn't know whether I liked him or not. It was her way of keeping us in that house.

"Hey, if I'd thought your marriage was based on anything personal, I'd never have let you marry him," she said. She cocked her head to the side, gave me what we called her John Belushi look, one eyebrow raised, begging for a smile after the room has been reduced to shambles.

"God, I have to love you," I said to her.

She kept the eyebrow raised.

"All right, we exchanged about five words, and one of them was no."

"No's not an answer to a why question."

I smiled. My mother had dedicated her life to ruining me for everyone else, and I didn't care. No one could come out with the aphorisms that she spouted without thinking, and certainly no one had the raw materials it took to have a million private jokes with me. Long ago I had figured that if anyone had to have complete access to my soul, it might as well be someone as clever as she was.

"Did he hurt you?" she said suddenly.

"No," I said quickly. She had told me once that if he ever touched me she would insist we leave him. We? I'd said, but she'd ignored me. I'd make it easy, she'd said gently. My mother had all the equity from her little house in the Whitney Bank at 2.5 percent interest, and it gave her an empowering fallback I would never take away.

"I see a handprint on your face," she said.

My left hand automatically went up to my cheek, but before she could catch me in knowing, I raised my right hand to my face, too. "I don't think so," I said.

She peered more closely, and I recoiled.

"Please don't push," I said. Her anger would trump mine, her plans to malign George would eclipse any intentions I had to allow him to be a good man. Even though her need for me to find a provider had long ago reduced him to something less than a person. My mother always would be twenty-eight years ahead of me, flaunting all the rights of the first to arrive. Most times I liked having more wisdom at my disposal than I had earned; all I had to do was be still. I assumed she had complicated reasons for having wanted to weaken George as soon as I'd ensnared him; I was waiting to find out.

"You're a grown woman," she said, and I couldn't tell from her tone whether she believed herself. "But that child can't make a decision in the world for himself. And don't think he doesn't know it."

I told her George said he had reasons; I told her George had done research. I wanted her to think the two were connected, that a book had said Gregor was better off without the ministrations of science. "Maybe it's painful," I said. "Or maybe it's bad for him, psychologically, I mean, to think he needs fixing."

"I'll tell you what research George did," my mother said, unceremoniously dumping the remains of her coffee cup into the sink without looking, her aim so good nothing splashed up. "George talked to his mother, mark my words."

She sounded so frighteningly right that all my blood flushed cold, made me shiver. She didn't know Mrs. Duffy had been at the funeral. The parlor, the corridor, the walkway, the gravesite: Each grandmother had had her turn, as if they had planned it that way. I tried to trust my memory, but knew better. For all I knew, Mrs. Duffy was a stranger, or perhaps an illusion; she may not have been there at all. Lavender and black, dream colors; purple was the favorite color of schizophrenics, and I very well may have been crazy that day. I could ask Gregor, but I knew I wouldn't. I couldn't even ask my mother whether she herself had been at the funeral. Though I could ask Ella on Wednesday what she remembered. Ella would be too grateful for a chance to tell a story to notice that I was peculiar.

"You don't know his mother."

"Sweetie, the woman doesn't come to your wedding—even if it is a lousy excuse for a wedding, she doesn't come, doesn't call, doesn't visit."

"She sent Jefferson cups." Four pewter cups, for which I'd written a two-page thank-you letter. I'd learned where she lived in Virginia. Chesapeake sounded historic and costly; Number Four Wright Place drew me a picture of an eighteenth-century colonial. I'd been satisfied with what I could do with the information, never had asked for more.

"Yes," my mother said, and she gave me the look she'd used when I struggled with common denominators and poetic meter as a girl. I said nothing. "You're not good enough for the Duffy family." I'd heard that many times before, and she spoke quickly before I could say so. "And Gregor is *definitely* not good enough for the Duffy family. The Duffys don't waste their time."

The answering machine on the kitchen counter picked up. The phone hadn't rung; sometimes my mother turned off the bell for no reason I'd ever been able to discern. I fumbled for the phone, sure the caller would hang up if I didn't break through the recorded message. "Hello, hello, hello, hello," I called over George's voice. "I'm not home, leave a message" was all he had recorded onto the machine, thinking he was funny.

A young male voice, recently changed, free of pollutants and polyps, was on the line. "Hi, this's Brian," he said.

"Yes?"

"At camp." I still wasn't registering. "I'm calling about . . ." He paused, searching for the name. "Gregory," he said. "I'm calling about Gregory."

"Gregor," I said. "Oh, Lord." I tried to remember whether the camp did dangerous things in the morning. It was only 10:30.

"You want to come get him?"

"You need to tell me what the problem is, son."

"I don't think he's hurt. Like, this ball hit him in the chest, but it was, you know, a soccer ball, and those kids are too little to throw hard or anything, but he won't stop crying."

I pictured Gregor at the sidelines, unable to dodge, still sitting there crying while the game went on out in the sun. In public George Junior never had ignored him completely; he'd have moved him to the shade because Gregor wasn't afraid to ask him to do so. Gregor asked nothing of strangers, and over the years I'd learned that strangers volunteer little, even when they're paid to do something. My mother maneuvered her face full of questions in front of me, and I mouthed "He's okay" so she'd get out of my way. I had my purse but searched for my keys as I listened for directions on where to find Gregor at the camp. My mother scuttled off to my bedroom, returned with the keys, pleased with herself.

"If you don't sneak him in to see an orthopedist," she called after me as I took the steep basement stairs two at a time, "I'll do it myself."

Gregor looked as if there were no water left in his body. His hair was plastered to his head with perspiration, his shirt was soaked, his face was covered with tears that continued to flow even after he saw me. I pushed him under the only live oak that hadn't been cleared for the athletic field. "Which one's Brian?" I said.

"I don't know," he wailed.

Two high-school-age boys came toward me at a brisk pace, defensive the way they would be when they grew up and went into business. One ruffled Gregor's hair, said, "Hey, man, how you doing?" and Gregor looked up at him with admiration. The other reached out to shake my hand; his hand was remarkably dry under the circumstances. "I'm Brian," he said. "Guess we're having a rough kind of day, huh, Gregor?" Gregor, good; Brian would do well in business. "We know the situation, Mrs. Duffy," he said, his voice low. Then his volume and pitch went up, but he was still directing his words to me. "We'd probably do better going home for a while today, don't you think?"

I looked at Gregor. "My chest hurts," he said indignantly. "Maybe we should call Buddy Homer."

The two counselors burst out laughing, and Gregor grinned, hiccuping with pleasure. Buddy Homer was the first personal-injury attorney in New Orleans to go haywire when lawyers began to advertise, and no child who'd ever sat in front of an afternoon television screen could fail to identify him. He was one of that peculiar breed of celebrity that flourished in the city—large-nosed, slung-jawed men with port accents who went on the airwaves to sell vinyl and sawdust furniture or Fords and Mercuries or frivolous lawsuits when what they wanted most of all was to be able to walk into a party and know that everyone was whispering with recognition.

"You want to stay?" I said. Gregor vigorously shook his head no, and water came off his hair the way it sprays off a boxer when he's been hit in a late round. "You want to come back to-morrow?" I said, and he looked at the two older boys, who both had a desire for success written on their faces. "Yes," Gregor said, and I saw the counselors exhale slowly with relief.

We passed a water fountain inside the building, but before I could speak Gregor said, "You have to pick me up for that. Don't pick me up for that. Please. There's kids in there." How about a cup? "No!" he said.

I couldn't leave him in the car when I stopped at the E-Z Serve to buy him a Coke. In the heat of the summer, for a three-minute run-in, I could always lock the running car, leave the boys in air-conditioning, have George Junior unlock the door when I returned. Sometimes he refused, played games with me as I stood in the open parking lot and vowed never again to trust him, but I would wave his candy or his chips at him through the glass, turn and pretend to go back into the store, and he would open the door, then say he was just joking. Gregor couldn't open the door, and he couldn't be left in the heat. I would have to get an extra key, one to leave in the ignition, the other to let myself in with. George Junior had had more responsibility than I'd noticed, and I ached with regret.

Gregor wanted a lotto ticket. In the cool of the store, he'd forgotten he was thirsty. "We got lots of them in our room," he said. Lottery tickets? "George finded them. Well, *I* finded them, but he got them. Even on the play yard. He got one that's mostly silver." Oh, I said, realizing I knew very little of what was stashed in the boys' room. With the death of a twin, there was no reason to give away things. "He said half of them're mine. See, I'm a good looker. I can see one under all the leaves, know that? That's a fair deal. But I never got one not scratched off."

I told him they cost a dollar, and that was an awful lot of money for a scrap of cardboard. I'd pick them up for him outside if he wanted; the parking lot of a convenience store was bound to have them strewn all about, though I'd never noticed before.

"You can win a million dollars, I think."

"Maybe a thousand."

Gregor thought it over. "I win a thousand dollars, I'll split it with you; you could buy yourself a car or something."

I was going to spoil him rotten. A Coke, a scratch-off ticket, a bag of Chee-tos. Before 11:00 in the morning. With only chocolate in his belly. It was good the impact of the soccer ball hadn't emptied out his stomach. There was no explaining dark chocolate to counselors who wanted to do things right.

"I think I'm a winning boy. I think I know how to win," Gregor said as we approached the cashier who would sell us the ticket. "I want the Pirate's Treasure," he said as I shifted him on my hip so I could put the Coke and Chee-tos on the counter. The clerk didn't blink; she was working close enough to Lee Circle that she was accustomed to misshapen people who knew what they wanted.

I scratched it off in the car as Gregor bounced on his narrow little behind. Five dollars. I looked at it, not knowing what to do. "They give you five dollars," he said. "You just go in, they give you five dollars. You don't get to keep it, though. The ticket, I mean."

"You *could* keep it," I said.

He gave me the expression men reserved for sentimental women. "You get your dollar back, I get four, it's fair," he said.

I couldn't help smiling.

"I *told* you I was a winning boy," he said.

My mother wouldn't play along with my distractions, and maybe that's how she figured out about George before I did. The nickels, then the quarters, then the silver dollars held no magic for her. "A sack of nickels has the same heft as a sack of silver dollars; you lose perspective," she said. What of the passing of time, the bets against time? I asked her. "Anna, you're doing the same boring thing over and over. What's it going to leave you to fantasize about?" I couldn't tell her that I wanted to have nothing to dream about, that if I'd been able I'd have meditated my way into no thought at all. Each morning, I dropped Gregor off at camp, went against the traffic to the Isle of Magic out near the airport, and played slots until twenty minutes before it was time to pick him up. I had an ATM card, and I took whatever I needed from my savings account, put whatever I won into a canvas bag I'd bought at Pier 1. I lost more than I won: if I played a hundred dollars I might only get back thirty, but I carried the thirty home in the sack, poured it into an empty five-gallon spring-water bottle in my closet. It was almost too heavy to move within weeks, though it was filled only inches high. I showed my mother. "Coins weigh more than water," she said. "That's why a nickel sinks when you throw it in the pool."

George was kind, and that's what tipped off my mother. It was a late August morning when she brought up the subject. Because private schools were going to open in two weeks, the day camp was already closed, but I still planned to leave Gregor with my mother and go out to the Isle of Magic until three o'clock. I had a favorite machine, and in daytime it always was mine; surely to some I'd become the tattered-haired blond woman in the black shirt who took the third Red, White, and Blue every weekday morning at 9:20, stayed until 2:40. If I didn't show, someone would surely think, *She must know something; here's my chance,* and I'd never have that machine again. "Don't walk out that door," my mother said.

She spoke as if she were trying to be authoritarian but knew she couldn't pull it off, and I hardly broke my stride. "I'll buy you a lotto ticket," I said to Gregor, figuring that would cover whatever objections my mother had. "Only the ones I pick'll win," he said. It was true, but I didn't know he'd figured that out.

"Your mother and I are going to have a talk," my mother said to Gregor.

I wheeled Gregor into his room, set him up with a video game I'd rigged up myself. With broad pads attached to the control buttons, Gregor could use the tip of his arm to play with as much agility as anyone else his age. I'd been proud of my inventiveness, and George had said, "Well, that proves that you can change his environment without having to change him."

"Okay," I said to my mother, and I sat on the edge of a kitchen chair, my purse and canvas bag on my lap as if I were a visitor who'd hoped to drop by when no one was home and had been caught.

"Notice anything about George?" she said.

I said no. Since Mississippi, I'd thought a great deal about saying something to George, but I'd actually said nothing of meaning. All my images of him were from Mississippi, the vomit and the mean hand. He could be in our bedroom, putting on a new summer suit, its clean chemical smell filling the room, and I wouldn't find the secrets behind his respectability erotic. Or interesting. He could eat soup too noisily for a wealthy man and I wouldn't be annoyed. Nothing he did after Mississippi mattered one way or the other, and I didn't think I'd pay attention to him until I figured out what to say. It seemed to me a single phrase would do it.

It might be an apology, or it might be an explanation of why I'd pushed him to this point. George was a polite boarder in my house and I didn't mind washing his underwear. He was up to a size 38 waist and I didn't care about that yet, either.

"George is being terribly nice," she said.

And?

My mother looked at me as if to say, *Think*. I couldn't think. I couldn't remember, right then, what George had said or done in the past few weeks, or days, or hours. I scanned the room for clues as to what he might have done that morning. Breakfast. He hadn't finished his cup of coffee and he'd left it on the table, but he hadn't complained. "He doesn't complain?" I guessed.

She shrugged. "It's a qualitative thing; maybe I should've written something down before I spoke."

"It's not like you're accusing him of anything," I said. If George was being kind, there was no harm in it—no importance, either. He could become slim and muscular, he could declare his love for Gregor, and I couldn't imagine myself wanting to touch him anymore.

"Anna, you watch him. Just watch."

I could hardly wait for him to come home; it was as if someone had promised me a movie that I would like but had no preview of. I came out ahead at the slots that day, playing mechanically, trying to break through the thick membrane that separated me from the concept of George behaving well. The silver dollars fell in obscenely great numbers, and it occurred to me that maybe I was on to something. I tried being distracted as I played, but it didn't work; I didn't win now.

It was in his face. The contours of his face were smoother, the color of his eyes a more translucent green. I would have guessed a drug, something like the cough syrup my mother gave me when I was a child: The world had become soupy and kind and I'd felt freer to speak than ever before or since. George seemed to notice very little, or perhaps he quit noticing more than he was supposed to. George generally came in looking for dust and errors; tonight he walked in as if he loved all of us but took for granted that love. He reminded me of the king of Carnival, riding and waving slowly through the streets of New Orleans as if everyone he passed had slow film and he wanted to be accommodating.

He let Gregor talk at the table. The boy would pour out a string of sentences, so pleased he didn't think of stopping, and suddenly he would get quiet for a moment, see if anyone would jump in, then keep on prattling. He had a video game in which he could kill Adolf Hitler over and over again, though the ever-threatened Adolf would growl, "Die, Allied *Schweinhund.*" "Die, Allied *Schweinhund*," Gregor said happily, again and again, practically expectorating on the German word. George Duffy, whose father surely was Irish but whose mother could have been a German national socialist or a German Jew for all I knew, remained silent. "*Auf Wiedersehen, Eva!*" Gregor sang out, and George seemed almost to smile.

"Well, he's *tolerant*," I whispered to my mother in the kitchen after dinner.

I was scraping the plates and she was loading the dishwasher. "Look at his plate," she said. I didn't need to look to know how George had eaten. With a the tip of his steak knife he'd managed to get every shred of meat off his pork chop bone; it was as clean as if he'd picked it up and worked at it with his teeth. "Tolerant," I said. George usually pushed aside plain meat.

"Bet you five dollars he says something pleasant to you before the night's out," my mother said.

Of course. Since I was a child, she'd had a spectrum of certainty: *Bet you a nickel* was as low as she'd go; *Bet you five dollars* meant she had no doubt. Naturally, she tended to cast away doubt when the circumstance was one she could change. "You'll say, 'Doesn't Anna look lovely tonight?' And he'll say, 'Yeh.' That's hardly a fair bet."

"Oh, poor Anna," she said.

Poor Anna what?

"You're not taking this seriously at all."

I gave her an of-course-not look.

"It's not my place to interfere," she said.

Interfere. If my mother could have crawled inside the frame of me, popped herself into every corner of me, filled my skin, maneuvered my every action, surely she would have. She tried to keep from smiling. She had had a magnet on her refrigerator once that had read, "If you love something, let it go. If it doesn't come back, hunt it down and annoy it."

"You think I have no limits, but I really do," she said. "If I say something, it can't do me any good."

"And me?"

"Oh, sweetie, just pay attention, that's all I'm asking."

I had no interest in paying attention, especially if I didn't know what I was looking for. When I was in school, I needed to be told in advance what was going to be on the test. Otherwise I wasn't going to write down and learn all the facts that wouldn't entertain me. And when I was finished with school, generally I read without trying to absorb or recall. There were too many signals out there, there was too much information, and if I couldn't play with it, I wouldn't work at it. Sometimes I surprised myself with what actually *had* stuck in my mind, that Lopakhin had bought the cherry orchard, that 1.96 and 2.58 were the values t approached as the degrees of freedom approached infinity.

As if she were reading my mind, my mother said, "I'm not asking you to notice anything except kindness. Trust me, it'll flag itself."

I put myself in rooms with George. It wasn't easy, because he sat still while I moved around, an odd reversal. I found myself wishing he wouldn't be good to me, and it was a familiar sensation. Perhaps I liked the fact of George's meanness; maybe it explained why I didn't work hard enough at loving him. I walked into the family room, and he was alone watching television and I could have interrupted him. George raged at anyone who spoke when he was watching television, even during commercials. Early in the marriage he had said, "Only *I* know when there's no dialogue to follow. Even if you're watching with me; only *I* know." At first I'd felt as if I were in the presence of royalty, never able to guess whether I would have to stand by for fifteen seconds or fifteen minutes. Eventually I'd made up my mind that when he was in front of the set I'd pretend he was out of the house. And that would hold in case of fire.

I edged around until I could see the television, though I could tell from the breathlessness of the audience and the commentator that George was watching tennis. "Footage of Wimbledon," he said quickly and put his index finger to his lips. He never had spoken when I walked in on him this way;

maybe this was what I was supposed to look for. "Who's play-ing?" I said, empowered. He tapped his raised finger on his lips, not yet impatient. I stood to the side, watched. I knew nothing of tennis, but it looked to me like a game one could follow with the sound turned off; someone hit, that was good for him, someone missed and that was not good.

For about five minutes I was transfixed, pleased by the *thock* of the racquet hitting the ball, lulled by the liquid mo-tions of the two players' bodies. Between serves, one would walk along the baseline, racquet swinging smoothly, never quite stopping, never frustrating me. But the sameness of the game, the deliberate unshakableness of the voice-over, began to bore me, and I remembered why I'd never had an interest in tennis. It seemed to me that sometime George had said that he, too, classified tennis right up there with the rest of spec-tator sports, its narrow definitions too foolish for a smart man. "He's playing too close to the net," George said to no one in particular.

I tried to see what he meant, but I couldn't tell which one he was complaining about and so had no rejoinder. "I thought you hated tennis," I said when the commercial came on. "Shhh," he said. It was a Buick commercial; George did not believe in buying American-made cars, said self-sacrifice could go just so far. My mother was going to owe me five dollars. I sat down on the chair next to the sofa, decided to wait.

"It's never too late to learn something new," he said during the same Buick commercial. I knew this wasn't an invitation to speak, so I said nothing. "Right?" he said.

"Sure, but good Lord, tennis?"

"I guess you didn't play as a kid," he said.

I would have expected him to say, *I guess learning tennis wasn't a top priority for a public-school kid.*

I shrugged, preparing myself for when he would go back to watching. I didn't want to be in midsentence when he cut me off.

"I'm joining the tennis club," he said.

A person didn't simply announce he was joining the tennis club as if he were taking out a library card. That much I knew. I always drove past there on my way to the Winn-Dixie, and I saw only the old families' unpretentious but perfectly maintained cars going in, occasionally the children of the old families walking up the avenue, heads uncovered, skin burning in the sun with the carelessness of the rich and the formerly rich. George was the first of the Duffys to live in New Orleans, and if he made a lot of money his grandchildren would be able to join whatever societies they wanted; that was the way it worked in this city. I'd never had the heart to tell him that bearing himself around town looking like a first family of Virginia meant nothing. Especially since he'd married a girl whose only claim to dignity was that she didn't speak with the all the terrible local diphthongs, didn't drop her final consonants.

"Not everybody gets in," I said gently.

He looked at me with what I only can describe as generous sympathy. "I don't go for something I'm not going to get," he said softly.

I was satisfied. I had a single piece of evidence, like a dead-on quote in a scholarly piece. Though I didn't know what to build around it, the inverted pyramid that would rise to a big idea. When I went to bed, I lay awake trying to figure out why his kindness mattered, but I came up with nothing. I was no better than a child who overheard adults sharing the simplest feelings of resentment or pride and couldn't understand why they raised the pitch of their voices.

"You're going to have to tell me," I said to my mother in the morning.

She knew what I was talking about; my mother didn't exist between our conversations, as far as I could tell. "If he's being nice, he's sorry for something," she said wearily. "And you know he's not sorry for anything he's done around here."

True. That was not his way.

"He's doing something out there."

I asked her, please, not to play guessing games. Inductive reasoning made me crazy, and she knew it. She'd raised me on a special version of it.

"I think George is having an affair."

I shook my head emphatically no. I couldn't even imagine George having sex with *me*, making the slow, seductive moves, revealing his body, breathing on me with unbrushed teeth. George worked downtown, where no woman had such small expectations.

"Oh, please," I said, now picturing George naked in an office, a woman's eyes traveling down from his hairy narrow shoulders and finding the hips of a woman, wondering what she'd see next if her eyes kept moving.

"George makes a lot of money," my mother said.

"He bought me, but I was young and foolish," I said, and my mother gave me a glad-you-admit-it smile.

"If you were a twenty-year-old secretary from Chalmette who gets hollered at for every grammar mistake, wouldn't you rather sleep with George?"

"He's joining the tennis club," I said. He didn't need to do that to snare a poor little girl who didn't know any better.

"Look, Anna, you know how primitive people probably were more in tune with the spirit world because they didn't have anything else to look at?" I nodded patiently; her analogies never took long. "I don't see the light of day. My instincts are so keen I sometimes surprise myself."

I wanted to say, *So why weren't you sitting in the house sensing that I was out by the pool with two little boys and someone was going to drown and I was screaming so loudly you could actually hear me but you had no idea of what was going on?* "Okay," I said.

"You watch him, just watch him," she said.

"Okay," I said, and I left for the casino.

In the middle of the night, when any wrong move can be passed off as the flailings of sleep, I reached for George. I don't know what my dream had been just beforehand, but it had enough touching and longing in it to make me want George. At that moment, perhaps I'd have wanted anyone, man, woman, child; the ache was that strong. We kept our bedroom dark—carpet to the doorjamb, opaque drapes—the cave darkness that makes it possible to open one's eyes and see nothing. George set the thermostat in summer at seventy, and because the thermostat was in the warmth of the hallway, our bedroom was winter-cold, purified as if by ice. George could have been anyone, though maybe I reached for him because he *was* George, and my dreaming mind knew it.

He snapped on the light. "What?"

"Turn off the light," I said softly, closing my eyes before I could see much.

He sat up in bed, his hair thin and skewed, his pajama top open two buttons down. I didn't want him anymore.

"I can't do it," he said.

If he'd said anything but that, I'd have talked myself into letting him fuck me. George never knew whether he excited me; he pushed when he was ready, and if I let out little cries of surprise, he seemed to think they were sounds of pleasure, and he drove at me harder, the condom he always wore sticking to my tissues, leaving me irritated for days. I didn't have to pretend with George, because he was thoroughly content with himself.

"Oh," I said dully.

"I'd like to explain, but I can't."

I told him it didn't matter. He sounded too self-important, as if he wanted me to coax out a story he was proud of. That he'd pulled a muscle saving lives but was too humble to mention it. That he was so raw and sensitive he'd had a relapse of grief and sneaked too much gin to lull him into sleep. That he'd screwed six beautiful women today and had nothing left. I wouldn't ask.

"I'm so sorry," he said, and he turned off the light, was back asleep before he knew it; the interlude had been so short he might not remember it in the morning.

I did a lot of exploring of possibilities when I played the slots, and I promised myself I would make sense of George before I went home, even if I had to call my mother and tell her I'd be late. I'd half convinced her that the machines soothed me, elevated me to where I could feel excellent by feeling nothing, thinking quite open-mindedly and objectively. But I played only two minutes that next day. I punched the keys on the ATM for $100; my account didn't have sufficient funds. I tried $50, no. Twenty, no. Ten I got. Ten dollars would last a while at the nickel slots, but I couldn't go back to nickel slots; I couldn't even go back to quarter slots. I couldn't bear the thought of a winning combination that didn't pay off, or paid off only ten times what I bet. The $10 was gone without even a small payoff. I hadn't even had time to tell myself to consider George. I had to calculate, and in the car I figured out it was time to go into the bottle in my closet. I wouldn't count it all; I would take out $100, play it until it was gone, take out another hundred when I had to. The progressive jackpot on the dollar slots was more than three million. I was going to win that, see if having my own money would soothe me into leaving George for my own big house.

No one was home, and no appliances were on. I could not re-call being in that house alone. The air conditioner kicked off, riding at seventy for a while, and every old house sound was magnified. It was a place open to ghosts and burglars, full as it was with niches and doors, and in broad daylight I felt a need to keep my back to the wall. Maybe George Junior's spirit would come back; I'd heard many stories since his death, of the sounds and smells that came to mothers and reassured them that their children were doing well on the other side. Toast and roses, whispers and motors, whatever was unmistakable. Hallucina-tions and wishes, I'd thought, and I knew I wasn't wishing at all to hear from my son. Not because I feared his only possible re-turn would be full of tricks and menace, but because I wanted to believe that dead was dead, that one day I would stop think-ing and be done with it. But not yet. I feared a stranger in the house, one who would hit me hard on the head if I caught him. We had an alarm system, and we lived in a city where no crim-inal was clever enough to get around electronics, but I checked the closets, under the beds, locked the door to the basement be-fore I sat down.

I had nothing to do.

I put my feet up on the kitchen table, but didn't feel I de-served to do so and put them down again. I took off my shirt and skirt, walked through the house in my underwear, cooling off. The casino always was cold, the house always was cold, but in between, a few paces in a garage, a few minutes in a car while the air-conditioning slowly cooled it, and it was easy to be soaked. The door to the basement was locked. No one could come in on me unannounced; if the doorbell rang, I'd have time to dress. I lay down on the sofa in the living room, damp skin on leather, sensed I was doing damage, got up. Checked the boys' room. I could straighten it up, shower off the dust. But it looked orderly, the way it never had looked when there were two of them, when George Junior could strew MicroMachines all over the floor and say Gregor had done it. All the other rooms looked good, too, inhabited as they were by three distracted adults and one immobile child. I had nothing to do, and I thought idly for a moment about suicide.

It would involve thinking and planning, and I wasn't in the mood.

I strolled through the house, still in my underwear, cooled off enough to be self-conscious, stayed away from the windows. If I won the jackpot, maybe I'd want to get a house, and what would I take with me? I scanned the rooms, decided I wanted nothing. George had chosen the furniture, the rugs, the drapes, all in a single trip to Units. As a child I'd passed the Units window when my mother took me to the Quarter, and I'd marveled even then that throwing animal skins around could pass for good taste and imagination. We never had guests, not even after the funeral, so George never had needed to announce where he'd shopped before anyone could judge him. Instead, he lived in a house where everything seemed outlined in black, like a girl child's crayon drawing. Maybe he would have guests if I moved out.

It took all my strength to pull out my money bottle. Once in the light, it transfixed me, its layers of coins like so much sediment, marking the eras, nickels deep and thin, quarters telling of two good winning weeks, silver dollars filling the rest. I wanted to use the nickels first, and I dumped the bottle on the bedroom floor. I didn't intend to count it, but the

coins fell into a spectacular mound, a Scrooge McDuck trove.
I'd seen the dealers and cashiers at the casino when they
counted, taking coins or chips inside an umbrella of fingers,
dropping a neat stack, cutting it and cutting it again, until
they could see identical piles of four. That wouldn't work on
carpet; I used the white pages of the phone book as my counting table, its surface small and smooth, good for tracking and
sweeping. I had $2,691. At a hundred a day, I was down by
half. My mother once had shown me that I could keep halv-
ing to infinity; I'd known negative powers of two long before
anyone else in my class. Of course, she hadn't been talking
about money. I could only halve down $2,961 twelve times
before I dropped below a dollar. Though twelve times two
months was two years. I was making no sense.

I didn't hear the garage door open. I didn't hear footsteps.
Not until my mother walked into my bedroom and cried out
my name did I notice she was back. I let out a scream of surprise. "How'd you get in here?" I said. She always came in
through the basement when George's car was out of the
garage.

"Oh, I don't think I'm the one to answer questions," she
said. She hustled out of the room, and now I could hear her
footsteps on the basement stairs. She was back up with Gregor
before I could find my clothes and put them back on. "Lucky
for us I had the front door key," she said, out of breath, or pretending to be.

I turned my back, finished buttoning up my shirt. "Where'd
you go?" I said.

"The zoo," my mother said before Gregor could speak. I
looked at Gregor. His clothes had no droop, his hair was thick
and dry. I sniffed at him. Little boys who've been outdoors
have a mud smell to them, even those who don't get dirty. I
could still smell soap on him.

"No, you didn't."

"What're you doing home this early?" she said.

"Gammy, tell her we didn't go to the zoo," Gregor said.

This was their third visit to an orthopedist. She had taken my insurance card, and it had been easy, she said. "You know, no one questions that I might be his mother," she said proudly, as if people looked at her and saw youth.

"You were forty-seven when he was born," I said angrily. "Try to imagine what they're thinking."

She winced, and I was instantly sorry I'd said that.

"Anna, if he doesn't get help soon, he'll have a hell of a time trying to adjust to it later," she said. "All I'm trying to do is, he'll get a prosthesis, I'll keep it downstairs, all he's got to do is wear it when he can, you know, get used to it. Someday he's not going to have to live by house rules."

Gregor was watching expectantly. I told him I thought he should go into another room, that this conversation didn't include him. He cocked his head to the side, and for the first time I realized he was an only child, in the way that only children get wise quickly. "You like what you're doing with Gammy?" I said.

"It hurts."

I looked at my mother. I hoped she knew I was seasoned enough to wait for more.

"Still, you know what?"

"What?"

"I can make things move. Already I made things move. It didn't fit or anything, but he showed me." His eyes were like those of a deaf child hearing his first sound. It seemed that whenever a deaf child heard his first sound, someone took a photograph or made a tape; I'd seen it often enough on television. My mother had taken something away from me.

"Okay," I whispered, "okay."

T E N

While my mother set Gregor up in another room, I prepared a lecture on sneakiness and what it meant to a child. But I should have known better. "I told him his daddy was just plain wrong," she said as soon as she came back into the kitchen. "*I* wasn't wrong, *he* wasn't wrong, his *daddy* was wrong. All right?"

I envied her ability to question George's judgment behind his back and think she was getting somewhere. "You know, I've never had the fear that George would hurt you," I said.

"Oh, I tell just *everyone* I have the ideal son-in-law."

I looked up at her from under my knitted eyebrows. Everyone?

"So?" she said. So what? "So, was I right?"

For once I couldn't bridge the lacuna in her thoughts.

"Was he kind?" she said, having no trouble knowing what I was thinking.

I couldn't remember. I knew he'd been *un*kind, turning away from me, as if he already had done better things. But it seemed to me that at some moment George had done something unexpected, and I'd thought, *Oh, perhaps this is kindness.* "He might have been," I said. "He didn't compliment me or anything, but I think he eased up a little. Not enough to make an impression, though."

"The impression he made on you hardly matters," she said. "When I worked with the rats at the med school . . ."

I stopped her. She had had to kill them for a living, and when I began to love mice I began to rage at her, eight years old and swearing I'd never eat meat again. The doomed rats marched through my dreams too many nights when I was a child; she was not going to make me so sensitive again, not even for a minute. "Just come out and say it," I said.

"You wouldn't recognize decency in that man if you saw it."

I picked up the phone, the way I used to pick up the phone and tell George Junior that I would call Santa Claus or the Easter Bunny or his daddy if he didn't stop right then and behave. He would invariably fling himself at me, struggling for the receiver and begging for mercy, even though he was close to figuring out both Santa and his father. My mother did neither, just folded her arms and leaned back. "Call him," she said.

I dialed his new office number, which I only knew by heart because it was mnemonically easy, the way the general line for a law firm has to be. I asked for George Duffy, got a young woman who announced, "Mr. Duffy's office." I wondered if he had a direct line, if calls that came through the switchboard were treated differently from calls by people who had a familiarity with him. The last time I'd phoned, it was the day of the drowning, and I'd gone through this same sequence, so enraged by the young woman's pleasant voice that I began to scream. The rage came back, but I could contain it now.

"Mr. Duffy, please."

"May I ask who's calling?"

"Mrs. Duffy."

"Oh, Lord," she said.

"Nothing's wrong," I said, tempted to let her be frightened.

She let out a sigh of relief that didn't sound particularly sincere and offered to have him paged on his beeper. I didn't know he had a beeper. He never wore it at home, never left it on his dresser at night. "Why's he have a beeper?" I said.

"I don't know," the woman said with the tone of someone under twenty who's lived her entire conscious life dependent on electronics.

My mother slapped her forehead with the heel of her hand and started to hiss something at me, but I was concentrating on what came into the ear at the phone, so I heard nothing of what she said. Though I didn't need to. I told the woman not to beep George: "A note'll be fine; there's no rush," I said. She said she'd give him the message, her tone full of peevish impatience, as if she were talking to a cranky old woman instead of someone her own age who cared nothing for business speed.

George phoned back in less than a minute, pretending to be out of breath and frantic.

"I told the girl it wasn't urgent," I said before he could speak.

"How'm I supposed to know that was true?" I could hear morning television in the background, a voice dopplering past.

"Because I said so," I said, and my mother's eyes opened wide in mock astonishment. I wanted her out of the room, not because of what she would hear, but because I would feel a need to make every utterance worthy of a clap on the back. Her presence was like a cloud of marijuana smoke, making everything I said sound goofy and truncated. I'd only tried marijuana once and had given up on it as a bad idea.

"I *expect* you to call only in an emergency," George said.

"Are you having an affair?" I said, tired of defending myself. He would say no, then he would light into me again, but at least I'd have sidestepped this issue about my phoning, which didn't interest me at all.

"I don't think that's the kind of thing we talk about on the phone."

"Answer me, George." I thought I was far away from this conversation, watching it, but my whole body was trembling.

"Meet me somewhere," he said.

"Answer me, goddammit."

"What makes you think I'm having an affair?"

I hung up the phone in his ear.

It rang in the time it takes to dial.

"Let the machine pick it up," my mother said. Instead, I lifted the receiver to my ear, said nothing.

"I know you're there," he said. Then he paused. "Dorothy, that better not be you." I said nothing. "Well, I'll just assume it's Dorothy. You tell Anna we've got a problem, and we've got to talk about it, and I don't want to talk on the phone, and I sure as hell don't want to do it in that house."

"Leave my mother alone," I said.

"Your mother's the fucking problem," he said, and I could tell he had his hand cupped around the mouthpiece, protecting himself from passersby or my mother, I didn't know which.

I looked at the clock. It was a little after two, and George was not at his office, and I had broken the routine I'd built since the drowning, and I couldn't figure out how we were going to meet. A strange mental lapse, the sort I'd noticed more frequently lately. "I'll meet you somewhere," I said.

"Name the time, name the place."

"I don't know where you are."

"I said name the time, name the place, and I'll be there," he said, and I burst into tears. "Jesus, Anna, what in God's name is wrong with you?"

I couldn't have told him; it was as if I'd tried out every possible emotion in a span of a minute and I'd created such an updraft that it had made me cry. "Are you downtown?" I said with enormous difficulty. If he was downtown, for some reason I'd feel better.

"It doesn't matter where I am. There's not a single place in this city I can't get to in fifteen minutes."

"Café Luna," I said. I loved Café Luna, though I'd never been inside. It was nestled in a rambling Victorian house with a wraparound porch and mauve weatherboards, and when I drove by I saw many tables occupied by one person each and thought it was a place of much confidence.

"How about someplace *real*?"

"So what's not real about Café Luna?" I said.

"I don't know a damn thing about Café Luna. From the name I just assume they've got oils and crystals all over the place."

I told him I couldn't do this. I had about two more sentences left in me, and those would have had to require no thought. With George, talking was like a chess game, a process of charting out all possible responses—and one's own responses to those, and his next responses—before uttering a word. We disagreed on a place where neither of us ever had been.

"You want Café Luna, it's fine with me," he said as if I'd driven a hard bargain.

It was seven minutes from our house to the coffee shop, but he already was waiting on the porch when I arrived. Coffee shop etiquette dictated that whoever showed up first went in and settled in over a cup of coffee and waited; this much I knew. No one ever stood outside unless the place was closed. Café Luna was closed on Mondays, in spite of or because of its name, and from time to time on a Monday I'd see a woman or two waiting on the steps for someone who was coming, not knowing it was closed either.

The place smelled of dark coffees and I wanted to try something fancy, but I was too dry and cold on the inside, though it was pushing a hundred on heat and humidity outside, and I ordered herbal tea. Strawberry-kiwi was the herbal tea of the day, and it sounded like a happy flavor; it was red in the cup, gentle and medicinal. George looked around as if the place were not sanitary. I followed his gaze, noticed when he did that he was far from the only man there in a business suit. He shrugged, asked the boy behind the counter whether they served alcohol. The entire menu of coffees and teas was printed in pastel chalks on two small blackboards over the boy's head; all the foods in the display case were full of sugar and butter. The boy laughed, expecting George to be like the other joshing sorts who made lame jokes and threw only nickels and pennies into the tip jar. He's not kidding, I said to the boy. "Oh, no, sir," he said to George. George ordered two Prussians and black iced coffee into which he poured heavy cream, dumped three spoonfuls of white sugar. No daring, so much fat; maybe he wasn't having an affair.

I poured three packets of raw sugar into my teacup, and George said, "I'm in love with someone else."

I felt far less than nothing. All my senses went quiescent, so sound was muffled, light was suffused and dark yellow. I needed to take a sip of tea, to make a motion; instead I took a large mouthful, and I knew nothing of the burning until my tongue went numb. I didn't think I was upset, because for me being upset had more to do with anticipation, unless the news was a keen and unbearable loss, like the loss of George Junior. If this was a bad moment, it was because a huge effort was now expected of me. I said nothing.

"I figured you wouldn't give a shit," he said.

I couldn't think of what to say.

"I've tried my level best with you," George said. "I've never cheated on you, and Lord knows I had reason to. If I hadn't met Kathryn, this never would've happened."

"I don't want to know her name."

"That's all you can say?"

George was seated on an old church pew that ran the width of the coffee shop; behind it was a ceiling-to-wainscoting mirror. I glanced at myself in the mirror, my reflection next to that of the back of George's balding head. The silvering of the mirror was tarnished and flecked, and I looked far more tragic than I felt.

"For once, I don't think I'm the one doing wrong here," I said.

"Aw, Jesus, Anna, the woman's got you convinced I'm the bad guy, always the bad guy."

"I have judgment, you know."

He put his coffee glass down slowly, patiently, as if I were dangerous. "There's so little difference between you and your mother that I can't even blame you for thinking you have a mind of your own."

"You married me because somehow I had a mind of my own that didn't scare you; I practically *auditioned* for you, don't think I don't know it. And why am I sitting here defending myself?" I was getting shrill.

"I'm sure I don't know."

I wanted to throw hot tea in his face. Instead I took a sip, this time controlling the cup, but tasting nothing, feeling the presence of the liquid in my mouth only along the unburned edges. "So you're moving out," I said.

"That's what I figured you'd say. I can almost hear her hollering after you when you left the house." His voice went deep with a squeak. "'Now, Anna, if you find out he's fooling around, you call me and I'll change the locks, you hear?'"

I stood up to walk out, not because I was a no-nonsense type who was unafraid of doing so but because I had to get away. Run, if possible, run so fast I'd hear nothing, no one calling me to come back, no car screeching to avoid me. George reached for my arm. "I'm sorry," he said softly, gently pressing me to sit down again. "I love you both, and I don't know what to do."

I wanted to say, *It takes your loving someone else for me to hear for the first time that you love me.* "She know about me?" I said.

"What about you?"

"That I *exist*."

He nodded. "But she's not that sort of person."

I looked him in the eye. "The only women who involve themselves with married men are competitive bitches."

"I don't have to sit and listen to this," he said.

I shrugged.

"Well, I don't. It's hard to hear her talked about like that."

She was no longer just a possibility, the way my boys' wives were, hypothetical women who would affect me without my say-so. One idle day I had joked with my mother over what women would be most likely to seduce George. We'd built entire worlds around such women, the sorry texture of their hair, the illegitimate babies, bad spelling. Photographs of my father showed upper-body strength even under clothes; my mother knew before I did that George was not shaped the way a man was supposed to be. A woman would have to meet George in context, know that his name was on the letterhead, think of the softness money could buy. Some woman had done this and, oddly, all I could wonder about was the color of her hair. A blonde would be a fresh me, a woman with dark hair would be a slap. I asked George what she looked like.

"She's very pretty," he said, as if he knew I assumed otherwise.

"Thanks a lot."

"You *asked*," he said, then softened. "You're very pretty, too."
I didn't want to hear that from him. "You're just different,
that's all. You're fair, she's dark. You're large, she's very small."
I wondered what small meant, if I was large: I was five-six and
weighed 127, and every table I'd ever read put me smack on
the median. I pictured a ratty little thing, a stick with unruly
thick hair. I gave her olive skin, because olive skin blemishes
easily. "She's a doctor," he said.

Up to that second, I was willing to give George up, sacri-
fice my mother's comfort, let him go off with a scrap of a
woman who would bore him quickly, make him sorry when it
was far too late. Now I had to keep him, not because I was up
against fine competition, but because I figured I'd failed to notice something. I gave it one last chance. "Medical doctor?" A
Ph.D. in almost anything would mean total lack of judgment,
and I could let him go. Women who finished medical school
generally had no time to waste on foolishness.

"Medical doctor," he said.

"Oh, Jesus, just don't tell me she's a fucking orthopedist."

"What difference would that make?"

"A hell of a difference," I said, though for the life of me I
couldn't have spelled out why.

"She's a dermatologist," he said, and I smiled, thinking of
my efforts to pock her face in my mind. George looked
wounded; probably he thought that in the world of physicians,
dermatologists were about as good as personal-injury attorneys were in his field: They did whatever was necessary to get
the degree, then remembered one sickening process that paid
well. "*What* she does means nothing."

"So why'd you tell me?" I said.

"Look, Anna, I don't need to sit here and take this shit."
He pushed away his coffee glass, but the gesture wasn't par-

ticularly effective because he'd drunk it down to the sweet ice. "She's different from you, okay? I didn't say better, I said different. And mostly she's different because she's interested in me."

I couldn't answer that. I'd thought often of what I needed to do to make us one of those couples who look forward to the passage of many decades, to days alone when they stroll and talk; usually I pictured them somewhere in rural New England. I couldn't imagine a conversation between two older people in the Deep South. Everyone was too irritable and show-offy, and besides, men didn't last long in the Deep South. They ate too much salt; their wives saw to it.

"I am interested in you."

"Well, you have a hell of a way of showing it."

At that moment I finally understood why people went to counselors. To talk to him without someone else at the table was an exhausting prospect. Was it my idea to meet him in a public place? I couldn't shake him until his brain bruised into sensibility, and that was what I wanted to do. Though I wouldn't do it in private, either. "Really, you're just about all I have," I said instead.

"Maybe that'll be true when your mother dies," he said. "But by my calculations she'll probably outlive me. And I'm sure that's her whole reason for existing."

He was right, of course: More than once my mother had talked dreamily of the day when the boys were grown and George was dead and she and I would buy thin cotton shirts and roll them up in a duffel and go to China. "You know, you can't just attack my mother every time you can't think of anything else to say."

He grinned his lawyer grin at me, and I wondered again how a man who came from such a good background could have such crowded teeth. "Yes, I can," he said.

I stood up without speaking, walked out of Café Luna, across the porch, down the steps, the path, the sidewalk, no break in my gait, no looking back. Before I was out of earshot, George called after me, but I didn't pause, didn't turn. "It's my house," he shouted.

ELEVEN

The house looked different to me when I drove up. It had been a long time since I'd been put off by the crab-fat yellow color, the barn lines, the dullness of stucco. The house had become like a lover whose face is misshapen: He is good-hearted, so eventually the asymmetry, the funny jowls become beautiful, and film stars begin to look freakish. Now I needed to grow to hate the house, imagining myself driving past it when I lived elsewhere, perhaps coming by occasionally to pick up Gregor after a visit, remembering it concealed a swimming pool no one would ever use again unless it were sold. But George would not want visitation rights, surely. He also would not want to look bad to God and Father McInvale: He would have to figure out a way to get back with me, so he could live in the house with his own child. The flicker of disgust for the house didn't go away, and I decided to hold onto it, just in case.

My mother was standing in the kitchen with her arms folded across her chest, as if she'd waited in that pose for hours, sure it would be appropriate. She raised her right eyebrow—this was a hereditary skill I had not acquired—and waited for me to speak. I was in the mood to satisfy her immediately. But I surprised myself by the way I put it. "He says he's in love with someone else." An adrenal rush made me nauseated, not enough to vomit, but enough to be afraid.

"Perfect!" she said.

"This is not nineteen-fifty, Mama," I said.

"I'm not the one you should be angry at."

"Her name's Kathryn."

"You tell me that like you're proud of it," she said.

I asked her, please, to get out of the kitchen. She was too clearly delighted. "I'm here for you if you need me," she said, and she still sounded delighted.

I didn't know whether George was coming home. Now that I was inside, the next hour was all that mattered. I would plan for the next hour. I couldn't plan. I watched the wall clock, watched the second hand turn. It had been in my mother's kitchen, a starburst-face clock, and the second hand never had moved fast when I was a child. I could hear cars that passed on the block; we lived on a one-way street, and cars seldom had reason to use that route. Each one that came by sped my pulse up a little, and it didn't drop back, just went faster each time until I sensed no space between beats. I was shaking, the way I had shaken when I sat in the school auditorium ten years earlier and listened to the principal read off the names of the honor society members. I must have known I wasn't getting in, though I lost out only on the vote of the teachers, a setback I couldn't have predicted. I'd decided then that I only became upset when I wasn't certain, even if the knowledge that made me uncertain was buried too deep.

I heard no sounds in the rest of the house. George wasn't coming home. Right then. He would come home after work. He had to go back to work. Now he was in his office, thinking about what we'd said, though I'd read that men didn't recite conversations to themselves. I didn't know why I'd considered giving him the full hour; since he hadn't followed me directly, he wasn't coming now. I wanted my mother to walk back into the room so I could explain to her. I listened for her, heard nothing. She'd been out of the room seventeen minutes; she should have known to come back. I'd give her five more minutes. I was getting annoyed with her. She walked back in before the hand had swept a full three minutes. "He's not coming back," she said.

"I figured that out. He works for a living."

"At all, Anna." What? "He's not coming back at all."

"It's his house," I said, feeling triumphant for some reason.

"You know what I'm talking about," she said gently.

At that moment I realized I was alone. I couldn't put a shape to what was going on, I didn't know where my allegiances lay, I had no one wise to tell me what to think. This was how I'd felt at the funeral, in a room full of women who wished better for me but knew not to approach. Outside my house, maybe up the block, perhaps a few streets over, probably out along the highway, those same women were close to telephones. They could call one another, at this time of day or in the middle of the night, and expect answers, informed answers based on a lot of shared facts. I wanted them to know me. *Yes,* one would say, *I've sensed all along that George was a rotter.* Or *You know, Anna,* another might say, *your mother doesn't exactly wish you well; she's the one who made you marry for money.* Or *I'll be right over*—that's what the third one, who always fussed but never analyzed, would say, and in the short run I'd be the most grateful to her. "Oh, God," I said to my mother and burst into tears.

She reached out to put her arms around me, and I pulled back.

"Okay, okay," she said as if she thoroughly understood.

I walked out on her. She stood in the middle of the kitchen, not moving, filling the room from there, all points equidistant from her. My mother never seemed alone in a room. To me that meant she didn't mind if someone left her, because there was so little space for another anyway. I didn't feel sorry for her, and I was surprised: I could have left her alone in rooms long ago.

I needed to kneel in front of Gregor. I always sensed that he was straining from the inside to embrace me, sending impulses to the ends of his limbs the way amputees did, remembering an action, transmitting electric messages to nerve endings that weren't there. "Hey, sweetie," I said when I walked into his room. The screen on his television was dark.

"I think Daddy's not coming home," he said.

"Why?"

"Gammy told you that. I heard her tell you that."

I knelt in front of him. "God, I love you," I said. I looked at his wise little face and began to cry. Right then I pulled him into my childhood daydream of a ten-foot boat. I always wanted a ten-foot boat where everything doubled as something else; I could lie under the bow and stretch out my foot to touch all I owned. Sometimes I would love someone from afar, the man who taught me in fifth grade, a pretty girl in my class, and I'd put that person in the daydream, so close we were always touching. Gregor and me on a ten-foot boat. The boat wouldn't have to leave the dock.

"I want him to come back," he wailed, and I believed him, though he sounded as if he were mimicking something from Ella's soaps or a Beverly Cleary book.

"Baby, I saw Daddy half an hour ago. He's probably at his office."

He raised that right eyebrow he got from my mother, and I had to smile. "This is his house. He's going to tell you to get out."

"You think I ought to go?" I heard myself say.

"I think Daddy and Gammy would fight. A lot."

I could track his thinking as well as my mother could track mine, though I hoped he'd elude me by the time he was grown. "Gregor, if I go, Gammy goes."

At that he let out a shriek that brought my mother running. "What are you telling that child?" she said.

"Daddy won't take care of me," Gregor shrilled at my mother. "He'll put me in front of the TV set until I die."

"Out, Anna," she said. I didn't move. "For Gregor," she said, and I took a step backward.

"Where're you going?" Gregor screamed after me.

"The kitchen, just the kitchen," my mother said, her voice so soothing that it quieted Gregor and made me quit breathing.

I phoned George's office before I could think. When the general operator answered, I said, "This is Anna Duffy, I'd like to speak to my husband, please," and she bypassed his secretary; the next voice I heard was George's. "Are you coming home?" I said.

"It's the middle of the afternoon," he said, and I knew someone else was in the office. But not his doctor woman. She would have a waiting room full of acne and basal cell carcinomas at this hour of the day. "I'll be home for dinner." He hung up.

I dialed right back, told the operator we were accidentally disconnected. "You will not," I said when George picked up in the middle of the first ring.

"Beg your pardon?"

I spoke loud enough for the pitch of my voice, if not my actual words, to leak out into the room and surprise whatever client was paying $250 an hour to hear George be quick and rude with me. "You cannot come sashaying back into this house just like that after what you told me," I said.

"I think I can," he said and hung up.

"Okay," I said to the air.

I had almost four hours, a wealth of time, with a guarantee. For four hours I would still be married, I would still have a chance to understand why George was always right. Life with George was simple; all he required was an apology. A pure apology, with nothing attached. I had all afternoon to practice the perfect apology. I remembered a film my mother had rented once. It was black and white, and the man didn't take the job his girlfriend wanted him to take, and when he got home he told her he'd stood on a corner saying he was sorry to everyone who passed, and almost all of them forgave him. George loved the winning that came with an apology, and when we were first married I would get a dull ache in my belly afterward. Eventually I began believing that I was wrong each time and he deserved my remorse; the bellyaches went away, replaced by a confusion at such a low level I hardly even knew it existed.

My mother and Gregor didn't come out of his room until snack time. His eyes were dry and big, as if he were being brave about something he didn't quite believe. She set him up at the kitchen table without looking at me, went at Gregor for every detail of his snack. Peanut butter? Jam? Strawberry or grape? Oat bread or whole wheat? Toasted, crusts off, cut on the diagonal? Gregor always chose the same: grape jelly, whole wheat, untoasted, keep the crusts, cut both diagonals. Last year he had switched from strawberry jam to grape jelly, but he had announced the change; I never asked. George Junior had been the one to change each time, asking for what we didn't have. "I could've told you," I said to my mother. "He likes to be asked," she said back.

"Gammy's taking you to a movie tonight," I said when Gregor just had taken a big bite of sandwich and was chewing absentmindedly. He sent up a piteous howl, his mouth open, the unchewed food lump flopping around, threatening to choke him.

"Nice move, Anna," my mother said.

I ignored her, spoke over Gregor's cries. "Daddy and I had a fight, okay? We've got to finish the fight and make up, okay? So you and Gammy go out to a good movie; when you come back we'll be all right, *okay*?"

"I could see something rated PG?" he said, snuffling, his food still unchewed. I nodded. He could have driven a harder bargain and gotten away with it.

"You can have popcorn, too," my mother said triumphantly. Feeding Gregor popcorn at the clip at which everyone likes to eat popcorn was quite a task; George Senior always insisted on hard candies, even when the boys were little and prone to choking. Gregor had been right: If he were left to live with his father, he'd wither away in no time. All they would find would be a chair heaped with tiny dry bones, set so close to the television set that the irradiation alone would have reduced him to glowing ashes.

The film Gregor chose was playing at 6:10, and my mother fed Gregor his supper before they left rather than go out early enough for me to gather my wits. I took a cool shower, pushed the thermostat down, perspired anyway. "What are you trying to do?" my mother said when she walked in on me. I was standing in front of my dresser, wearing a pink silk slip and panty hose and putting on makeup slowly. "I don't know," I said peevishly, though I did know. I was going to find George attractive, and he was going to have to find me attractive, or this evening was not going to work out; I was not going to have any power over him. If I told her that, she would try to remind me that this was my opportunity—to have George's money, to punish him for having been thoughtless for so long, to live without the gloom of him.

"Look," she said, and I automatically checked the clock. "I don't claim to know what's best for you." I shrugged. "No," she said, "I mean it. If you want George back, that may very well be the right thing to do. Especially for Gregor."

I was relieved, not by what she said, because of course I didn't believe her, but by her struggle to shut herself up. "Please take him out afterward for ice cream or something," I said. "PG movies never last nearly long enough."

"Unless you're sitting through them," she said, rolling her eyes back and smiling good-naturedly.

"Thanks for not making me crazy," I said.

George did not get home until 6:30. I was ticking off my mother's minutes, travel time, concession stand, coming attractions, opening credits. If he was coming at all, he was using up my time. If he was not coming at all, he was meaner than I thought possible. Either way, my clothes were soaked, my makeup patchy, my bile gurgling up into my esophagus by the time he walked in. I didn't look at him. If I was still going to find him attractive, he had to say something before I looked at him. "Hey, where's everybody?" he said.

I still didn't look at him. The four hours I'd had earlier were now reduced to seconds. "I thought it'd be better if we had the house to ourselves," I said, not seductively, but not neutrally, either.

"I can't imagine what it is you want me to say." Out of the corner of my eye I could see him removing his suitcoat, loosening his tie.

"You need to say something quick."

"I've told you everything," he said, and I decided I might as well look at him.

George had green eyes. If I looked only at his green eyes, I couldn't be sickened by him. His lashes weren't long, but his irises were translucent no matter what color he wore, and I always pretended I saw accessibility there. My eyes are that cornflower blue that is so rare in this country because of the mood of hybridization; my mother would say, "Now, I'm no Aryan supremacist, but there's a purity in our eyes that means something, I don't know what." She'd watched the boys' eyes in their first year, holding them to the light, checking for a tinge of yellow pigment. When they stayed blue into their second year, she was relieved. But the blue was opaque, and I didn't like it as much.

"I don't want you to leave," I said, looking him in the eye.

"I'm not going anywhere."

"So you'll give her up?"

He said nothing, walked over to the refrigerator, pulled out a casserole dish half full of pasta with red peppers and sausage, began forking out mouthfuls straight from the dish. "When you give up your mother, I'll give up Kathryn," he said. I asked him if that was a rhetorical statement or an offer. George guffawed, his mouth full of a lumpy paste of half-chewed food. "Sometimes I really enjoy you," he said.

"A person doesn't give up her mother."

"I did."

All the other issues dropped away right then: I was panning for gold, and I was willing to wash away all the dull sand-grainsized bits when I found a glistening nugget. I stopped breathing the way I had done the first time George kissed me. "Oh?" I whispered, so he wouldn't know I was interested.

"Don't sidetrack me, Anna."

"The woman doesn't come to our wedding, I've never spoken to her, she shows up at the funeral, unless I'm hallucinating, doesn't say a word to anyone, like she's Mrs. God, disappears like she's got something a lot more important to do than go to her own grandson's grave; *you* gave *her* up?"

"Yes," he said. "It's not what you think."

He spoke so softly that I felt sorry for him. "So tell me," I said.

He shook his head no. "Some things I can't tell you."

The way he said it, I couldn't be angry at him. I almost couldn't be angry at him for saying he loved another woman. George could make me forget he was mean; his tears and his secrets and his funny sack of a body didn't make me sorry for him, exactly, but they did make me wish he were stronger, for his own sake.

"I thought your mother cut you off because of me," I said softly.

"I know you thought that."

"But you cut *her* off because of me."

"Anna, I'm not playing fucking Twenty Questions," he said.

"Get out," I said. He didn't move, waiting, I assumed, for me to remember that the house was in his name. "I mean, *get out*," I said again, this time with all the nuances of Louisiana civil law and common decency behind me.

When my mother was due home with Gregor, George was still packing. He was a strange sort of meticulous packer: He would fold his undershirts, not the way they came from the store, with the neckline framed nicely, but along the central line of symmetry, sleeve upon sleeve. He took his dress shirts off the hangers, folded them the same way he did his undershirts. If he hadn't always taken a long time to fill a suitcase, I'd have thought he was delaying deliberately. I'd imagined my own departure, should it have been necessary, and I'd figured I could get what Gregor and I both needed out of the house in twenty minutes. "They'll be back any time now," I said, standing in the doorway of our bedroom, watching George and wanting to refold. Or toss it all into a plastic garbage bag, as I'd have done with my own things.

"You're the one putting me out. Let him see you putting me out," George said.

"I'm not putting you out."

"You said 'get out'; you want to tell me what else that could mean?"

"You know damn well that's an invitation to negotiate."

He threw down the shirt he was trying to fold and couldn't manage to button up straight. "I don't let anyone go to the brink like that; if you'd listened you'd've known that." It was true: I'd heard fragments about companies trying to get his clients to violate federal tax law in the name of saving money, threatening to go elsewhere if he didn't play along. George would sit at the dinner table and boast about telling multimillionaires to fuck off, and the boys would stop chewing and I would make myself think about something else.

"I'm not good at these things," I said.

"Like fun, Anna. You play the stupid card more craftily than anyone I ever met."

"I don't want you to go." If he'd asked why, I couldn't have told him, but it was true.

He faced me, hands on hips, and what I noticed was that at the end of the day his shirt still had the creases starched into it. He would not look like this without me and Ella. "Look, you're just as confused as I am," he said gently. "Let me get away for a few days, sort things out." I asked him where he was going. "Not to her house," he said wearily.

"Where, then?"

"Right now I'm going down to my office."

His new office was on the fourteenth floor, his building reachable from the garage by an elevated walkway; I'd seen it from the street. If he trudged in carrying his largest suitcase, everyone in his firm would know his story by the beginning of business hours tomorrow morning. I would have dozens of witnesses that he had abandoned his family; he would have more attention than he could stand. "With all your stuff?" I said.

"That's not your problem," he said.

I heard the front door open, then close, heard my mother's heavy tread as she carried Gregor through the house. I gave George a now-what? look.

"He's not coming in here unless you carry him in, you know," George said.

"The kid's got object permanency," I said.

"I don't know what all that psychological bullshit means."

"It means he knows his daddy's threatening to move out and he'll *ask* where you are."

The door to the hallway banged against the wall, the way it did when my mother came through with a heavy load and kicked it. I heard Gregor's tremulous high voice calling both of us, one after the other. George picked up his suitcase and lumbered toward the kitchen. I grabbed his arm. "You could stay, you know," I said, but he kept moving, the case bumping the door frames and low shelves as he worked his way toward the kitchen.

Gregor took one look at the suitcase and let out the exact same scream he'd let out the afternoon of the drowning. George tried to speak to him, but I couldn't hear a word he was saying. He began to shout, and Gregor screamed louder. "Goddammit, stop it!" I finally heard him say, and Gregor shut up in midscreech, pulled a lungful of air through his nose, let out a few quavery breaths. "That's better," George said. "I'll see you tomorrow, Gregor. We'll have ice cream."

"You're not coming back," Gregor said.

George set the suitcase down on the floor with the attitude of a man who is about to miss his train for the benefit of someone he doesn't particularly care about. "I'm giving you my word, Son. You've got to take my word for it."

"I saw it in a book," Gregor said hotly.

George looked accusingly at my mother, who knew better than to speak, and Gregor said, "Mrs. Dunn read it to us in class," but George kept glaring at my mother.

We stood in silence, my mother straining under Gregor's weight. Finally Gregor said, "What time?"

George clearly didn't know what the child was talking about. "Daddy goes to work. After work," I said.

"After work," George said, reminding himself, it seemed to me, and then he walked out.

"I could have a dog?" Gregor said.

TWELVE

I went to bed with the greatest hunger for sleep I'd known since my baby boys had taken turns screaming in the night. I remembered the story about the American soldier, damaged by war, who says, *You take a really sleepy man, and he always stands a chance of again becoming a man with all his faculties intact.* I lay supine in the bed, on my side of the bed, and a heavy blackness weighted my head down, stifled my breath, but didn't put me to sleep. I tried to imagine George in his office, but I'd never seen this new office, knew the building only from the outside, pleats of glass that looked from some angles like stacks of mirrored box kites. Men like George had small spaces, compensated for by excellent views of the geometry of the city, but I couldn't picture him peering out the one-way glass and being glad he was there, curling up on the floor and smiling as he dozed off, the lights on the bridge over the Mississippi such a pleasing sight.

George could not sleep sitting up. If he had one of those headaches that worsened when he lay down and blood filled his head, he would stay awake until it passed. He wasn't in his office. He was at the doctor woman's house. I had enough facts—her name, her specialty: with first the yellow pages and then the white, I could find her phone number and her address. PHYSICIANS & SURGEONS——MD——DERMA-TOLOGY (SKIN); I wondered whether the directory copy-writers in more sophisticated places mentioned skin. Two pages, one of display ads. Skin, hair, nails—I thought feath-ers, scales, claws. Port wine stains, hemangiomas, warts, tattoos—I thought perhaps this Kathryn did not have such a clean life. Only one Kathryn on the page. Kathryn Gold, practice limited to aesthetic dermatology. I scanned the rest of the page. No one else made such a claim. What a spoiled woman. Her patients were so smooth and neat she didn't need to wear latex gloves. She would give George no dis-eases, but she probably would not give him much pleasure, either.

I found her in the white pages, State Street. No part of State Street was more than three minutes from Café Luna. No part of State Street was more than three minutes from our house, either. Though in New Orleans that wasn't a big, exciting co-incidence. The city wasn't the way I pictured large cities, squeezed thick and high, but it was moated by water, so dis-tances were short, with no traffic jams except among the whites who fled across bridges. Eighteen-hundred block. Houses that sold for three quarters of a million; surely she had a husband with a different last name. He would be a doctor. All I had to do was go through every doctor in the phone book, cross-check to find one in the 1800 block of State Street. Or I could drive past her house, look for George's car. If it was there, she had no husband, and I had no ally. I didn't even have the shared indignation of other women. It was two against one. Unless she had a husband.

I let myself into my mother's room slowly so I wouldn't startle her. The room was filled with that faint garbage smell of mouth-breathing and farting in privacy. "Mama?"

She sat bolt upright, turned on the bedside lamp. "You scared me to death."

"No, I didn't."

She tugged at the neck of the housecoat she slept in, ready for fires. The skin on her chest was smooth, undamaged by the sun, and I realized for the first time that she wasn't particularly old, that women her age often knew passion. "It's the middle of the night," she said.

"I'm going looking for George."

"It's the middle of the night," she said again.

"The woman lives in a good neighborhood," I told her.

Now she kicked off the sheet under which she'd been sleeping. We'd put a heat pump into the basement when she moved in, not knowing how costly it was to run, and George had been sure to tell her after the first utility bill came that she'd better watch her thermostat, that cooling her room cost as much as cooling all the rest of the house. Since then it usually was unbearably warm and damp in there, and Clorox never quite killed or masked the mildew. "You didn't want him when you had him," she said, more for her benefit than for mine.

"But there's something about competition," I said, shrugging with the knowledge that she had no comeback for that.

Her face settled into its cast of a woman whose life was as good as over. "As long as you're here when Gregor wakes up."

"I'll try," I said. I also needed to go to the casino. A win would solve all my problems. I'd ask for the jackpot money in coins, pay everything with coins, never tell George why I was doing so well, let him think I always had had money and had married him because I loved him.

"I mean it, Anna."

"For Gregor," I said.

I was back in twenty minutes. No cars were parked in the 1800 block of State Street. Most houses had gated drives, even though the drives were no more than a city lot's depth long. No cars were visible in the doctor's driveway. Not hers, not his; it meant nothing. I studied the house, smooth colorless plaster two-story, nothing breaking out of the rectangular solid. Quite a number of those houses had popped up in the sixties, my mother had told me: Parents with no imagination bought the last lots uptown and raised their children to scream about wars and rights. People who bought such houses twenty and thirty years later had even less imagination and less excuse.

I turned off the motor in my garage, suddenly awash in pity for this Kathryn Gold. Here she was, small and dark, Jewish by her name and not happy about being small and dark if I could go by the girls I once knew. George was thirty-one, so she couldn't be much older, though George was letting himself be old even more carelessly and effectively than my mother was. Poor Kathryn Gold, so afraid of doing the wrong thing that she'd gone to medical school and made her parents relieved that she could support herself. She'd bought a house with an address no one could fault, a design that dared nothing. She was too well behaved to fool around on a husband; perhaps she had none, perhaps she once had married a simple man who became befuddled by the powers of doctors. George wouldn't have to say the right things to her, and George certainly didn't know the right things to say to a woman. He must have played out the *apprivoisement* that he played out with me years ago on the lawn of the library, taking tiny steps closer each day when he thought I wasn't paying attention. George did have flawless skin: He probably made appointments over and over again until she finally asked why he came in at all, and he said, "Well, I like coming here." Soon she'd asked him what a man of his age and status was doing, being interested in her; surely he had a family. Oh, I could hear it, right down to the catch he put in his voice: "Our marriage didn't survive the tragic death of our child." Kathryn had clutched him to her insecure A-cup breast, and he'd smelled the costly antiseptic scent of her office and decided he finally had what was rightfully his.

I had wanted to walk up, ring the doorbell, and warn her that eventually he would hit her, soon he would home in on her fears about herself and call them by name. I could imagine reporting that to my mother, telling her that George was probably upstairs in the doctor's bedroom while I was breathlessly screaming the truth about him. *Hah*, my mother would say, *now you know how I always feel*.

My mother was waiting in the kitchen when I came upstairs. She was always waiting in the kitchen, ready to be right. She had a cup of coffee steaming in front of her; her body no longer expected to be cooled off in summer. "Well?"

I shrugged, half hoping she'd go back to bed. "There's not a lot you can find out in the 1800 block of State Street."

"*That's* where she lives?"

"Mama, I feel sorry for her," I said, picturing this Kathryn, whose face and furnishings already were making themselves up clearly in my mind. At night, she had no emergencies; probably she had chosen her specialization thinking she would have children to come home to at night. She drifted around that terribly clean house and thought about the possibilities of George. She was a medical doctor; I wondered how she made herself feel proud to be able to touch his body.

"Doesn't it occur to you that she's getting exactly what she deserves?"

"George lied to her," I said.

"Look, I'm the last person on earth who'd have a good word for George Duffy, but I've got to tell you, the man's no liar. Liars have imagination."

I thought about it. I could have argued with her, because some liars were crazy and simply didn't know the truth, others could say yes for no without having to make anything up. But George wasn't a liar, because he didn't have the patience for lying, which I supposed was the same as having no imagination. "Maybe he *is* at his office," I said, more to myself than to her.

"I'd put money on it."

"How much?" I said, surprising myself.

She said five dollars, and I took her up on it. If he was there, I'd feel good. If he wasn't there, I'd have five dollars, and I needed five dollars. But I had no way of knowing, short of driving down and corkscrewing through the parking garage until I found his car. I told my mother I didn't know his direct line, that the operator wouldn't be on duty at three in the morning. "Trust me," she said, "they've got a system in place. They don't risk losing business."

A recording instructed me to press my party's extension. "I don't know his extension," I whispered. "Just wait," she said aloud. The recording went on to say that if I didn't know my party's extension, I could punch in the first five letters of my party's last name. What if it had a Q or an X? I pressed 3–8–3–3–9, slow going. I never enjoyed the mnemonic tricks some companies used, selecting phone numbers that could translate into words. Though translating letters into numerals might prove interesting if I needed to bet on them.

I heard ringing, then George's voice. "What."

"Are you expecting someone?" I said.

"Obviously not. Is something the matter?"

"No, George, nothing's the matter," I said. "I'm just sort of up in the middle of the night because my husband kind of moved out and I don't know where he is."

"I told you I was coming to my office."

"Why should I believe you?" Gregor had the right idea. Spout the scripts from simple books; someone must have once used them effectively. I had no sense of whether or not I trusted George.

"Because I don't lie to you." I covered the receiver, whispered to my mother, "He says he doesn't lie to me." She was watching my side of the conversation as if it were the most natural thing in the world, and now she gave me an I-told-you nod. I turned so I couldn't see her, though she could still see me.

"Oh, Christ," George said. "Your fucking mother's in the room."

I denied it. "It's three o'clock in the morning; even my mother rests." She moved into my line of vision, giggled with her hand over her mouth, and I didn't feel like conspiring with her.

George hadn't heard her. "Look, Anna, I don't know what the hell I'm doing," he said. I had no urge to say, *You sure as hell don't.* "I'm not going to Kathryn's; give me a little credit. I've got thinking to do. I didn't know I'd have to think about all this."

"Oh?"

"Hey, some things can go on forever, you know."

"Only if you don't want to get caught."

I could imagine his expression, a narrowing of eyes and lips and nostrils and brows into angry parallel lines. "I hate it when you spout all that psychological babble," he said.

For the first time it occurred to me that sometimes I was right. "I'm right, aren't I?"

"Am I not." What? "Aren't I, are I not, I are not—your grammar's wrong."

My mother angled around me until she caught my eye again. I mouthed to her, "He's correcting my grammar." She furrowed her brow, shrugged, whispered, "What?" I grabbed a pencil, a furniture ad on the back of yesterday's Metro section of the paper, wrote, "He's correcting my grammar." "Hang up on him," she whispered, and I batted at the air in front of her face, hoping she'd go away. Instead, she poised her index finger over the hang-up button on the phone. I grabbed her hand. "George, no lawyer worth his license stoops that low," I said, and my mother pulled back, satisfied. I had a cramp in my belly, not a great, hurtful one, but a small, insistent ache that seemed to mean poison had begun to leak into some organ and would never stop.

"I'll take the kid for ice cream, okay?" George said.

"Were you asleep?" I said.

"No," he said and hung up.

THIRTEEN

All I had to do was tell Gregor his daddy was coming to take him for ice cream after work, and he eased off to play alone in his room as if his whole world had been quite fine lately. "In *his* car?" he had said, and I had said, "Sure," though Gregor never had ridden in the Infiniti. To put it fairly, George Junior never had ridden in that car, either. It wasn't that George feared sticky candy wrappers and muddy shoe scrapings, because Gregor, after all, threatened neither. It was that George never had had an occasion to go anywhere with the boys alone. He would not have known what to say to them. I expected Gregor would do all the talking, and George would come close to throwing the child's ice cream cone away after he learned what patience it took to let the meltings drip down his hand while Gregor jabbered and licked.

I was loading coins into my money sack when my mother walked into the room. "Don't judge me," I ordered her.

"If I were going to judge you, I'd have started a long time ago."

I dumped the contents of the sack onto the carpet. I'd planned on filling it with fistful of whatever came out of the bottle, nickels, quarters, silver dollars, playing whatever I had, keeping the winnings separate until I had a hundred dollars or ran out of coins. The Quartermania slot's progressive jackpot was more than three-quarters of a million dollars last time I was there, and that was a good sum. Not enough to prove something to George and never look back, because even invested with a 10 percent return it wouldn't make the best life for Gregor. But something about my mother's tone made me fish out only the silver dollars. I loved the silver dollars; the only other place I'd ever gotten one was at the stamp machines in the post office. They weren't for spending, because people mistook them for quarters, and the exchange of money is supposed to require no explanations. Money is a language learned in childhood. Some casinos sold tokens for the dollar slots, the woman with the change cart told me at the Isle of Magic. I said I wouldn't go there, and she said, "I hear you." Pushing the change cart seemed like an excellent job. Like working in a bakery, without the olfactory assaults that would make honesty more difficult.

"You've won a lot," my mother said in a voice that almost sounded sincerely encouraging. It was the voice that had beckoned me through school; I'd imitated it with my boys.

I told her thank you. I wasn't in the least tempted to confess that on balance I had won nothing at all.

"So," she said.

"So, will you feed Gregor?"

She took in enough breath to last her a full minute, and as she let it out I could hear a reluctant quaver. "Walking away from *this* disaster isn't going to make it better," she finally said.

"What's that supposed to mean?"

"After George Junior, you could go sit out in that horrid place, and time passed, and that helped *something.*"

"Mama, I do think out there." I wasn't going to tell her that all I was thinking was that I could win enough to tell myself I didn't need George, not for shared funds, not for child support. I'd be able to pretend I married him for love. She could argue against that, using figures and laws.

"Oh, please," she said.

"Hey," I said, cocking my head to the side. "This is the girl who had to have the TV on when she did her homework, remember? And the noise out there is constant."

My mother folded her arms across her chest, her signal that absolute truth was coming. "I was behind this woman at the butcher counter at Langenstein's—I don't know what someone like that was doing in Langenstein's—anyway, she says, 'I went to the casino one time; between the lights and the noise, I'm surprised no one has an epileptic fit.'"

I'd actually thought that the casino was an excellent place for Old Testament prophecies and apocalyptic visions, all of which I believed were products of brain lesions and ambient light. Lately I'd been surprised by how comfortable I was in the casino, my mood elevated by the lilting tunes of the machines that encouraged the winners to keep on, by the dances of neon lights that vied for my attention. I was supposed to be pleased all the time there; the designers had done studies. They made certain I was full of hope. "Mama, I'm happy out there."

"Fine," she said. "Just fine." I thought I heard in her voice a wish to make me sorry.

Ordinarily I parked in the lot, rode the shuttle over the levee to the landing where the paddle wheeler stayed docked in spite of all the fussing the state legislature did. The wait for the twenty-seater was never long; I could sit on the bench under a canvas shelter and still be cool from the car's air conditioning when I was picked up, even in the midmorning heat. That day the sky was dark, threatening a heavy, cooling rain earlier than usual. With an unobstructed view of the lake, it was possible to predict when the storm would come in: A gray column would move in from the northwest, taking an hour to arrive from the horizon. In the meantime, it was possible to walk across the unshaded parking lot and not be burned by sun and asphalt. I thought I would cross over to the park next to the landing, sit down on one of the piers, count the money I had with me.

No one was on foot. A park made no sense next to a casino; people who came here had no interest in being outdoors for any more time than it took to go from one tightly sealed cool space to another. Most carried sweaters or jackets, limp and soiled, to be worn when the cold air of the casino chilled old, thin skin, penetrated to unused muscles. I moved toward the seawall, somewhat reassured by the open spaces where no one could hide, somewhat spooked by the silence. The breeze coming off the lake was strong, but I could pour out my silver dollars and know that the wind wouldn't move them. I emptied the sack on the top concrete ledge, and two coins fell wrong, stood on edge, rolled down erratically, one step at a time, toward the lake. I chased them—each possibly the one that would win the jackpot—and caught them a step above the water. I stuffed them into my pocket, planned to save them for last, looked out at the lake. The water was choppy, ushering in the storm. I had no idea how deep the lake was, and couldn't see bottom through the silt and blue-green algal bloom. I moved gingerly, afraid of falling in, the way I always had been afraid of falling into the river. My mother had convinced me that a person who fell into the Mississippi would die from the toxins, and I imagined myself pulled out—skeletal remains, flesh burned away. The lake was full of algae and garbage, unloosed a few months past when the river crested and the spillway routed all its poisons into the lake. I could be out there alone, and if I slipped in, I probably could struggle out, but I would emerge already in the process of dying from a thoroughly compromised hepatic system.

The voice sounded so real I looked around to see where the child was. "Mommy." I heard it clearly, saw no one anywhere near me. "I don't mind," it said. Children's voices all sounded alike when they said "Mommy"; I could be in room full of solipsistic children, hear one call for his mother, chorus "yes" along with half a dozen other women. But "I don't mind"; that was George Junior. No one else's child, not even Gregor. That was George Junior. Maybe an auditory hallucination, maybe a strong wish, but no other child. I looked around for something to see to go along with it, saw nothing. Just water—pretty, lethal turquoise water. "You don't mind, baby?" I said, tears in my eyes, reasoning that I had to speak aloud because he had done so. I heard nothing more, felt foolish, realized I had no idea what he was forgiving.

I phoned my mother from the ladies' room pay phone as soon as I was inside the casino. She would have a scientific explanation. My mother put extrasensory experience into unexplored dimensions and sloughed it off. "I'd like to be cryogenically preserved just so I can live with people who already know the future," she'd once said. "I'd rather die," I'd said, and we'd both found that unbearably funny.

No one answered the phone at the house, and I began to feel all spiritual. I wasn't exactly filled up with *belief* or even faith; the sensation was more physical, the way I felt if I heard "Amazing Grace" played on bagpipes. I phoned George at his office. George was the sort who was unwilling to deny the existence of angels because he'd been told about angels. "What, Anna."

"George Junior spoke to me," I said, and I was surprised by the excitement in my own voice.

"Beg pardon?"

"He said, 'I don't mind.'"

He was silent for a while. "The boy is dead, goddammit," he whispered.

"I heard his voice, I know I heard his voice."

George took on the superior tone that had almost nothing to do with education. "You heard the other one. I defy you to tell me you could ever tell their voices apart."

"*I* could tell their voices apart," I said. "Besides, Gregor's not with me." No one else was in the ladies' room, and I hoped no one would come in. George didn't need to know where I was, though maybe he'd have believed me if he knew George Junior came to me at the edge of deadly water.

"Please don't call me every five minutes."

"He said, 'I don't mind,' George. That means something. Even if all it means is that I'm making it up. He doesn't mind. If I'd *dreamed* it, that'd be enough. But I swear I heard him."

"Christ, you've gone psychotic," George said.

For a moment I believed him. I looked around. Everything I saw and heard could have been a delusion. No one would make up such a place on purpose. The carpet had a wide rippling pattern of red and gold and black, even in the ladies' room. I swept my eyes across it and felt a wave of vertigo. The door opened and a woman in her seventies came in. She was tugging an oxygen tank and smoking a cigarette. I could not have made her up. "I'm not psychotic," I said into the phone, and the woman scowled at me. I put my finger to my lips, but she probably didn't have the breath to make herself heard. If she flushed the toilet, I could explain that.

"Stay right there, I'm calling a doctor," George said.

"You don't know where I am."

"I'll be right there."

"I'm not at home, George."

He was silent for a moment; he would have to start logging this conversation on his time sheet. George was worth $250 an hour. "What do you want from me?" he said.

"I thought this meant something," I said.

"Listen, I told you I can't think."

"No, you said you *needed* to think."

"Don't call me up and play semantic games with me, Anna."

I felt like crying. I had George Junior's forgiveness, and I figured that fixed something.

"You there?" he said. I nodded. "Anna?"

"I'm here."

"Go take a nap. You need a nap," he said, and hung up.

I won $250 on my first play.

George Junior didn't mind. Whatever was going on, I had permission. I would play each of the 250 dollars, win $250 on each play, walk away with $62,500; I knew 25 squared and could compute in my head. The man sitting next to me leaned over, said, "Time for you to go home," and went back to playing his machine. I looked at him. I never had seen such a good-looking man up close. Black hair threaded with silver, Irish blue eyes with ridiculously long black lashes, a square face, skin so white that it would burn one day, go back to white the next. Seated, he was a head taller than I was, and as he pulled the lever on the machine I saw that the musculature of his arm filled out the sleeve of his polo shirt. "What're you doing here in the middle of the day?" I said. He was a fireman, he said, and again he told me to go home. I asked him why.

"If you quit when you're winning, you're all right," he said. "If you play when you're losing, then you know you're in trouble."

"That's what my mother says."

"Listen to your mother," he said, not in a dismissive way exactly, and he went back to playing. I watched him for a couple of minutes, saw that he played five credits at a time and routinely inched ahead of himself; I decided he was worth listening to. I didn't cash in the coins, instead carried the heavy sack out with me. I hadn't been in the casino long enough to accumulate a chill, and I rode back to my car on the shuttle instead of walking. I had the sense that the driver was looking at me as if I'd materialized from nowhere, but figured she couldn't possibly remember everyone who'd ridden with her from the parking lot to the casino. Although everyone riding with me was old enough to be my parent. In fact, the fireman was the only person I'd noticed who was below retirement age. Working for the fire department looked as good as pushing the change cart in the casino. Jobs were somewhere in the far back of my mind, but only as a way of life for someone else. My mother said I was entitled not to want a regular salary. My father had fallen off a building working laborer's wages, and my mother had lost her conscience decapitating rats.

Her car was in the garage when I returned home, and I took the stairs up to the kitchen two at a time, brimming with news. Before I could open the door, she opened it, stood blocking the doorway with her arms folded across her chest. I hadn't turned on the light in the basement, and it was dark on the stairs. I wouldn't go into the basement at night; having to come back up those steep stairs with that maw behind me frightened me as it would a child. "What're you doing home?" my mother said.

"Let me up," I said, and she stepped aside.

Gregor was sitting at the table, a bowl of ice cream in front of him. I started to fuss at my mother, and then I saw the arm. "I was going to surprise you," Gregor said. Attached to his left shoulder was a device, in the color of a flesh-pink crayon, that had the outer contours of a small human arm. But visible at the joints were sockets and cables, substitutes for nerve and sinew. I found it strangely repugnant, but when I look back I think it was the liberty that disturbed me. With enormous concentration, Gregor was moving his shoulder to make the elbow flex. "Watch," he whispered, as if noise might make his good luck disappear. The elbow locked into place, and with another shoulder motion he made the hook that protruded from the wrist grasp for a spoon my mother held out to him. It closed and missed; I felt I was going to have to put another quarter into the claw-game machine. "Again, honey," my mother said, and this time the hook wrapped around the spoon, which fell onto the table when my mother let go of it. "I really ate some," Gregor told me apologetically. I looked in the ice cream bowl, saw that it was almost all melted. "Hey, you really did," I said. He grinned proudly, but I saw tears of frustration in his eyes.

"So you're left-handed?" I said. I couldn't think of anything else.

Gregor started to respond, and my mother jumped in. "Twins usually mirror," she said. "And George Junior . . . "

"I'm left-eyed, see?" Gregor said. "They make you look through this piece of paper, and the eye you can see with, that's your eye."

"Here they are with all this electronic circuitry, and they tear this hole in a scrap of paper and tell the boy to look through it; I've never seen anything so primitive in my life," my mother said.

"I saw the doctor with this eye," Gregor said, shrugging, and the elbow unbent, caught the bowl on the rim, tipped out half the ice cream. Gregor let out a yelp of disappointment, and I winced.

"We're working hard, Anna," she said evenly as she wiped the table. I told her I needed to see her in the other room; I spoke with high-pitched cheer. "I could practice?" Gregor said. My mother nodded vigorously but removed the half-full bowl.

"George is going to have a fit," I said as soon as we stepped into the living room.

"He doesn't live here anymore."

"Glad you think so."

My mother plopped down on the sofa, behind first, hands raised, as if she were testing a law of physics. "Well, he's forfeited *something*," she said.

"When I win a million dollars, then you tell me George is in a weak position."

"You won a million dollars the day you married him in the state of Louisiana," she said. "I mean it, Anna, you don't need a law degree to know you'll get more money out of him gone than you ever get out of him while he's here."

"You don't need a law degree to know he's going to have a hell of a better attorney than I am," I said. I heard the verb tenses I was using, wondered whether I believed I was describing an inevitable future. If my mother picked up on it, she let it go. "Besides, I didn't marry him for money."

"You're not going to win a huge pile of money," she said, ignoring me, and for the first time I felt an undercurrent of disapproval of my blank résumé. On my twelfth birthday she'd said, "Don't ever learn to type or cook or you'll be pigeonholed for the rest of your natural life." Even at that age I knew she wasn't being literal, that microwaves and computers would be all right as long as no one expected me to perform at his whim. She wasn't literal, but she was in some ways unschooled.

"I won two hundred and fifty dollars today," I said, "and I have reason to know I'm doing the right thing." I chose not to explain; she already had enough to quibble about.

"George makes that much in an hour."

"I made that much in ten seconds."

"Anna, you know what you're doing? You're making me have to think like George."

"Good," I said. She gave me a puzzled look. "What else am I supposed to say to that?"

I heard a spoon hit the floor in the kitchen, waited for Gregor to call out. He made no sound. Both of us listened, breathing shallowly. After a while I opened my mouth to speak, but my mother gestured for silence. And then it came. *Plink*, a spoon hitting metal. Like two fat men trying to fit through a narrow doorway, we jostled and bumped each other, racing for the kitchen. And there was Gregor, hanging precariously over the edge of his chair, his face red, his new arm arcing across the floor, hitting and missing the spoon. "All *right*, Gregor," my mother exclaimed.

Then she turned to me and whispered, "Now what are you going to do?"

FOURTEEN

On two counts, we need not have worried. When five o'clock came around, Gregor asked my mother to remove the arm. "When I can do everything, then I'll show him," Gregor said.

When seven o'clock came around, George had not come. "Goddammit," my mother said.

"He gots to work," Gregor said.

"No, he doesn't," my mother said.

Gregor's face screwed up as if he were going to let out a wail, not of disappointment but of terror. I figured he reasoned that if George did not have to work, then he was surely dead. I picked up the phone with the exaggerated arm motions Art Carney used on "The Honeymooners." "I think I could phone soon," Gregor said.

"*I* just learned how to phone your father," I said.

George could not be anywhere else, but George was not in his office. I reached his voice mail, covered the receiver while a recording of George told callers how to reach his implicitly reliable secretary if they needed someone right away. I noticed that he hesitated, as if he'd memorized the message, lost his concentration. I'd have done it over. "He's gone out to dinner," I whispered to Gregor, who clearly believed me.

"George," I said, clipping my tones, "this is Anna. It's Tuesday at seven o'clock. I believe you had an appointment earlier this evening to take Gregor out for ice cream. Please give me a call as soon as you return. Thank you."

"I think I could put my arm back," Gregor said.

"Naw, he might just show up any minute," I said.

At eight o'clock I phoned again, reached his voice mail. I hung up, wondering whether hang-up calls were logged electronically. "Thomas Hardy couldn't have written anything if there'd been telephones," I said to my mother, and she laughed.

"On the contrary," she said. The nineteenth century had stuck with her.

I was computing all the times and distances that were possible for George, and I knew it meant I was obsessed by a man I didn't like very much at the time, but I couldn't make myself think of anything else. He was alone—no meal could take more than fifteen minutes. No travel time was more than fifteen minutes. I needed to find George. I knew Gregor had nothing to do with it, that he was rolling with events, willing to be amused as long as no one was dead. My mother was feeding him potato chips, and he was crunching and licking salt out of the corners of his mouth, thoroughly content. I wanted to find George to satisfy myself, and the only way I was going to satisfy myself was to inconvenience George.

I dialed Kathryn Gold's home number before I could think and make myself nervous. She answered after the third ring, with the out-of-breath earnestness of someone whose answering machine will pick up on the fourth ring. "Doctor Gold," she said, and I figured out right away that she listed that number for the public. She had a private life. Perhaps George was her private life now, but only for the moment; she'd had practice making compartments for herself.

"I'm trying to get in touch with George Duffy," I said in my most midwestern, computer-generated voice.

"May I ask who's calling?" she said, and my heart made one great thud with the realization that I'd expected her to say, *I'm sorry, but there's no one here by that name.*

"Anna," I said, protecting her for reasons I knew nothing about.

The silence of a covered receiver followed, but in seconds George came on the line. "Yes?" he said.

"She doesn't know I exist, does she, George?"

"May I ask why you're calling?"

I didn't care that Gregor could hear me, hoped that Kathryn would. "Because you've got a six-year-old child sitting here waiting to go for fucking ice cream and you don't show up and you say you're staying in your office and obviously you're not. That's why."

"I said I *might* come."

"Oh, no, George, you said you *would* come. I was standing right there . . . "

"It's your word against mine."

"I was standing right there, and if you'd said you *might* come, I'd've said, 'Oh, no, there's no such thing as *might* come to a six-year-old.'"

"I don't think I want to pursue this line of discussion at this time," George said, and I slammed the phone down in his ear.

I knew my face was dangerously red, my eyes wet, and I turned to Gregor and said, "Your daddy's definitely not dead."

"I don't like my daddy, but I love my daddy," Gregor said, and I wondered what fictional character had uttered such words. Gregor was going to be able to turn pages and change channels soon, and I considered what messages he was going to pick up on his own.

"I never wanted to hit anyone before," I said to my mother.

"You never had brothers and sisters."

"No, Mama, I've never been this furious before."

She said, "This woman's the first competition you ever had in your life," and then I wanted to slap my mother, slap her across the face, over and over until I didn't have to wait for the bruises to show.

"I don't want to hit the woman. I want to hit George. In fact, I want to hit *you*, goddammit; don't you ever stop analyzing shit?"

The expression on my mother's face was one I'd seen before, that of a mother who's dispassionate enough about the stage her child is passing through; she was pretending to be wounded. "I'm sure you're a far better person than she is," my mother said.

"She's a doctor," I said, filling the word with all the meaning that doctors wanted it to have.

"I think the lady's probably ugly," Gregor said. "And fat." Gregor was going to make some woman very happy one day. He had that ferocious look on his face that was a wonderfully poor imitation of his brother's regular expression. I wondered why I was finding so many vestiges of George Junior.

"I heard George Junior's voice today," I told him. "He said, 'I don't mind.'"

"Like in the air?" he said, as if the question were quite natural. I didn't look at my mother. I nodded. "Sometimes I talk to George, but he doesn't talk back," he said. "He always does that. But only in our room. On account of he knew you'd get mad if he made me mad."

"Hold it," my mother said. "You are not going to make this child irrational."

I'd planned to tell her about George Junior, ask her to give me her best explanation of the extrasensory world. She was a Presbyterian in name only, a tyrant of science, and I'd always been grateful that I wasn't one of those children who had to listen to some person of God whisper eagerly about mysteries and faith. "The church smells good, and the music's terrific, but so was everything Proust remembered about Odette de Crécy," she would say, then drag me off to Mass to give me something sensory, a foundation for imagining. "Many great writers were lapsed Catholics," she'd say.

"I'm sure there's a perfectly logical explanation," I said to her, not hiding my irritation at all.

"George is an unsolved mystery," Gregor said, and I was as pleased for him as he was for himself; his allusion to the television show of that name was even better than he knew.

I found myself having lost the edge of my rage at George, just that quickly. Spilling a bit of it onto my mother may have helped, and I wasn't averse to doing so again. "George Junior said, 'I don't mind,'" I told her.

"If you were telling me a dream, I'd say that was a play on words."

I gave her a look of total noncomprehension.

"I don't *mind*. As in, I don't obey," she said.

"But I heard where he put the emphasis."

"Makes no difference," she said, and I was sorry I'd told her.

I decided right then that George Junior had come to me at the lake for a reason, that he didn't mind my gambling, that in fact he was telling me that this was the way I was going to save myself. The fireman had been wrong. I shouldn't have gone home. That $250 proved it. It was midway between the solstice and the equinox, and night had fallen, but I told Gregor not to wait up for me, gave him a big wet kiss on the mouth, and left for the casino. Maybe the fireman would be there. But the odds were against it.

It was three in the morning before I lost the entire $250. I'd seen the fireman in the poker room, but he hadn't seen me. He hadn't come back to the slots, and I thought maybe he was a talisman of sorts. Next time I would try to sit next to him, see if it made a difference.

For a city that everyone elsewhere imagines to be full of gunfire and people pressing one another to fight, New Orleans was asleep at three in the morning. The interstate carried more trucks than cars, more cars with out-of-state license plates, passing through, than the big local American cars with bald tires and no mufflers. I didn't fear a breakdown. And once on the city streets, I stopped at the red lights, though my mother had told me when I got my license that after midnight I should sail through and no one would stop me. I hit the remote control for the garage door before I made the corner, rather than sweep the hedges with my headlights. I wasn't fearless, I was safe.

My mother's car was in the garage, the burglar alarm was off, and the lights were on in most of the rooms in the house, but no one was home.

At first I moved in silence, running from room to room, Gregor's room, my room, down to the basement to my mother's room. Then I began to call out, for her, for Gregor, for George. No answer. I went through the rooms again, this time searching in a different way, eyes on the floor, peering under beds, into closets, pushing back hanging clothes. No one was lying injured anywhere. Another run through the house, for clues. No blood, nothing rifled through. My mother's purse in her room, everything in it. No note in the kitchen. No answering machine messages.

I had no one to call. Not a friend, not a neighbor. Not George. Some logical explanation was evading me, and George would figure it out fast, tell me I was stupid and cloying and should leave him the hell alone. Besides, if my mother and Gregor disappeared, George's life would become perfect in some way or other, and I feared seeing his delight concealed by a somber face. I already was picturing him at a funeral.

It occurred to me then that if I were a detective the first suspicion I would have was that George had taken my mother and Gregor off somewhere and killed them. George was capable of murder. We had had a talk once about revenge. I said I would want to torment my enemy every day for the rest of his life. Or at least be responsible for a suffering he knew I'd engineered. George said, Hell, I'd just kill him. And when I asked, he said no, it wasn't important that the person see him, George, pull the trigger or brandish the knife. He would be satisfied by the fact of death.

The phone rang about the time I closed my eyes and tried to disappear. I picked up on the first ring, heard what sounded like public noises, but no one spoke at first. Then, "Mommy?"

I never had spoken on the phone to Gregor before, and for a second I believed it was George Junior calling; so little made sense. "Gregor?"

"Mommy."

"Where's he taken you?" I said.

I couldn't understand one word Gregor said in response. He was sobbing, and the pitch of his voice was so high that I was about to catch the contagion of his hysteria when a woman's voice came on the line, and Gregor faded a bit into the background, just enough for me to know he wasn't on the phone anymore but not enough for me to hear the woman. "Mama?" I guessed.

"I can't hear your mommy, sweetie," the woman said, and Gregor wound down his cries until they were nothing more than dramatic hiccups. I was giving the woman about five more seconds, and then I was going to lose control of myself.

She told me her name and she told me she was with a particular hospital, but both facts were gone as soon as she uttered them.

"Yes," I said, suddenly ready for her to take her time, delay as long as she could.

"Everything's being taken care of."

"Yes."

"Your mother's Dorothy Riggs?"

Present tense. I exhaled. "Yes."

"We have her here in the ICU."

There was no blood in the house. There was some mistake.

I heard Gregor in the background. "I want to tell her." He came on the line; I could hear his sweet, excited breathing. "I'm a hero, the man says I'm a hero," he crowed, and then I knew I could wait, that this was not what he would be saying if my mother had been harmed beyond repair. "Gammy had a headache, okay? Like she was practically crying, and I told her, 'You know, Gammy, you better call 911.' And she wouldn't do it, and I kept saying, 'I'm scared, Gammy, I'm scared,' so she called 911, and then she fell down."

A stroke. "Oh, Jesus."

"No, Mommy, listen. You know how they have this operator on police shows on TV? Well, I talked to her. I mean, I couldn't hear her or anything, but I *hollered*, and you know how they just know your address on their computer? But they want to know, are you on fire, like, or maybe there's a man in the house. I told her, Gammy got a headache and she fell down, and I said I can't go to the door, because you know how the kid always stands out on the street? The fireman broke the door down."

I shuddered. I'd gone everywhere in the house but the foyer. My mother and Gregor almost never used the front door. "Fireman?" I said. My fireman was in the poker room. It didn't seem possible that there were others, though of course a city needs hundreds.

Gregor sounded terribly self-important. "I told him, 'This isn't a fire, it's on your computer,' and he said, 'Oh, firemen come for emergencies,' and I remembered about George and he checked her heart and everything, and then he let in the ambulance guys, because they didn't have to knock down the door. I think I'm going to be on TV." He hesitated. "You know, they'd have to have me be the actor who's me, on account of nobody looks like me."

I was glad I didn't cry over Gregor anymore, because he was close to breaking my heart. I told him I'd be right there. "You know what room I'm in?" he said, and I realized I didn't know where he was at all.

FIFTEEN

A dog dead beside a highway may seem to grimace, a cat in the road may trail viscera, but each retains form; my mother had been hit by nothing more than a tiny embolus deep inside, and she had lost all that defined her for me. Hours ago she had had a thick coif of white-streaked hair and facial contours as round as a child's; now she was an old woman, hair wet and stringy on the pillow, cheeks sunken as if she had lost most of her teeth. She was breathing and eating and peeing through tubes, and I ached with homesickness as I stood over her. "You can talk to her," the nurse said as she checked the clip on the IV line. I told her I would wait, and she nodded with understanding, moved more quickly so I could be alone. Still I said nothing. My mother wasn't going to answer me, and I felt embarrassed by the idea of speaking; I could imagine her saying to me afterward, Anna, *I had the silliest out-of-body experience, and there you were, talking to me when you knew very well I couldn't hear you*. Tentatively, as if she were a dangerous animal, I reached out and patted her arm. She might accuse me of affection later, but she would have to forgive it. The skin on her arm was soft and smooth, and I remembered that fifty-three was young to die. Maybe it was across the line from tragically young to die, but it was close. The doctor in the hall had said,

"Thirty-five percent don't make it, but mortality increases with age. You're lucky she's youthful and vigorous." He looked as if he were in his forties, a man who had reason to believe fifty-three was reasonably young, so I accepted what he said.

I stayed in the room the full ten minutes I was allotted, though I had no idea what to do and, in fact, was feeling more and more frightened by the sight of her. Her chest was moving up and down raggedly, and though her eyes were closed I couldn't pretend she was asleep. Gregor was in the hall, jabbering to a volunteer about his heroics, but in an emergency I could not wake my mother up and ask her to go tend him. Suddenly I didn't want to leave the room. I studied the monitors, followed the numbers I could understand, but I wasn't sure if I wanted her heartbeat and blood pressure to rise or fall, so I quit trying to exert my will, turned away. I understood a ten-minute limit in the ICU when the patient was conscious, when polite conversation could kill her, but the restriction for someone unconscious made no sense to me. Ten minutes passed, and I wasn't going to leave voluntarily; I took comfort in watching that no cuff or electrode detached. My mother wasn't moving, but the air was. Fifteen minutes, and still no one came in to ask me to leave. I was thinking I could probably stay all day, that Gregor would find a way to make someone enjoy taking care of him. He was still wearing his prosthesis, and I shuddered to think that maybe he had been transported in the ambulance, a tiny boy with no tethers or balance, attached to an apparatus that would clip him nastily in the face if the driver took a corner too sharply.

After twenty minutes the nurse returned and said, "Ordinarily there's no reason to ask you to come out, but your little boy kind of wants you." I took a long look at my mother, willed her to survive the next forty minutes, when I could come back. If I could leave Gregor again. If strangers weren't inclined to tend him, he would be all mine, and I was both thrilled and frightened by the prospect. If I could hold out, I would wait a few days to tell George about my mother. Though George would find nothing to blame himself for. He would be indignant, claim he cared deeply about my mother, rant at my thoughtlessness. With George, I realized, I was saving up the memories of bad behaviors for a time in the far future when he might change his ways and look back, hear my litany, feel sorry.

"Gammy's not going to die," Gregor announced when I found him next to the nurses' station. He was in a small wheelchair, and I liked the hospital, its readiness to take care of us. Perhaps if I asked, someone would provide me with a bed, and I could slip in between the cool sheets and sleep, eat my meals from a tray, have nurses look at me with concerned expressions. Shifts would change every eight hours, and I would have fresh, ready caretakers each time, with no questions. "No, Gammy's not going to die," I said.

Gregor gave me a look that made me know I'd been caught condescending. "The *doctor* said she's not going to die."

"You're right, sweetie," I said.

"No-o-o-o," he said. "He said tell you that's a prognosis." He enunciated the word as if he'd been using it for a long time.

"Really?" I said, not caring that a doctor had no business giving opinions to a five-year-old. Six-year-old. God, I was tired.

"He told me, 'Your grandmother's going to walk out of here.'"

I thought of my mother, who showed external signs of nothing. "How can he say such a thing so soon?" I said.

Gregor's mouth tightened into a line of superior knowledge. "They can look at your brain."

Even though I knew about brain scans, the primitive part of me imagined my mother's head filled up with spilled blood, like that covering a wound which can't be seen until peroxide washes away the blood and dirt. I wanted her skull opened and cleaned up. "She's not badly hurt?" I said.

"I guess not," Gregor said patiently. "He told me, right now she probably can't do things on her left side. Not even her eye or her mouth. I told him it doesn't matter, on account of Gammy's right-handed. You know she's right-handed?" I nodded. Gregor was the only left-handed person in the family, as far as I knew, though I hadn't known about him long enough to try to think of others.

I looked around, wanting to speak to the doctor myself. He'd told Gregor so much more than he'd told me, and for some reason I respected him for that. Probably because he'd clearly been careful to make no comparisons; had he done so, Gregor would have parroted him. A nurse passed by, and I asked her what I could do. It was a roundabout way to get answers. "Go home and sleep," she said.

"What if . . ." I said, and I imagined my mother saying, *What if I die? Well, what on earth good will it do me, you standing over me?*

The nurse put a cool, moist hand on my arm; when she removed it I felt a thin residue of lotion, hoped it was Jergens. The smell of Jergens always reassured me. "She's stable," the nurse said. "Nothing's going to change for at least twenty-four hours."

"So I know my mother has twenty-four more hours guaranteed than I do," I said.

"Beg your pardon?"

"*We* might get killed in the car," Gregor said, and both the nurse and I looked at him in amazement. The nurse scurried off before we could confuse her more, and I giggled with Gregor. "I don't think people in hospitals laugh a whole lot," I whispered to him.

"My doctor tells jokes," he said, and I pictured his pediatrician, who was so accustomed to slipping needles into screaming babies that he hardly spoke. "He told me I look like Arnold Schwarzenegger with my arm. I know that's a joke."

"Oh, that doctor."

"Well, he's mine. George never went to him."

"Hey, mister, I guess I'm going to have to meet your doctor."

"Gammy takes me, Gammy'll take me," he said.

"Well, I want her to take you," I said. "I mean, I want you to go."

"Okay," he said, as if it had never occurred to him that I might have misgivings.

Sleep didn't seem like enough. Sleeping in my house, where the phone could reach me, where Gregor might waken, where George still had a key; it wasn't enough. Gregor had toppled over in midsentence in the car, no doubt dropping quickly into dreams of watching himself on television. He was more difficult to carry upstairs when he was asleep; unable to cling, Gregor would usually mold his body to mine, put his head on my shoulder to shift his center of gravity. But now as I tried to mount the stairs, his neck snapped back with as little control as that of a newborn, and I found myself pitching backward, almost falling down. "Wake up, Gregor," I whispered, and he came to just enough to cooperate, the new arm hanging loose and snagging once on the railing. I was wide awake by the time I put him in his bed, and I could think of nothing else to do but phone Ella.

I realized I'd never had to tell bad news with forethought. I didn't enjoy the dishonesty of it. To protect Ella, and to keep Ella from taking more power over me, I would have to be easy, casual, but I would have to impress upon her the need for her to show up at my house within the hour.

Melvin answered the phone before I could figure out what to say, anyway. Melvin was better than an answering machine. The message would get through to Ella, but it would be reworked ever so slightly by a man who knew what to emphasize. Coming from Melvin, the story of my mother's stroke would be one of a crisis long past, needing acknowledgment but not emotion. And I could relate the story with hysteria if I chose; he would filter it out. "My mama's had a stroke," I said, and the words choked me up, to my surprise.

"Miss Anna?" he said.

"Oh, sorry."

"You mama dead?"

Something in the way he said it made me smile. I told him no, not by a long shot.

He was silent for a moment, not coming up with his next question. "I just need Ella," I said finally.

"Oh, Lord, she out by the country. Her sister bring her back around dinnertime," he said. "You at the hospital?" I told him no, I was at home—there was nothing I could do at the hospital. "What you need Ella for?" he said, not in a critical way but rather as if he wanted to gauge how much off-the-books money Ella might bring in.

"I need a baby-sitter," I said, knowing he wouldn't ask where I was going, if not to the hospital.

"Ooo-wee," he said.

"What?"

"I get the impression Mr. George going to kill Ella, she ever sit for you again."

"That was four years ago," I said. I wasn't in the mood to tell him that George had moved out. Melvin had stuck with Ella for more than forty years, letting her clump around in her church shoes on Sunday mornings while he dozed, letting her take back each of her four grown children every time one slipped up, giving her good reason to believe he never had fooled around on her. "Besides," I said, "that whole fuss was over Gregor's arm, and now he's got one."

"No fooling. His daddy move out or something?"

I chortled. "Well, his daddy doesn't know about it yet."

I could hear Melvin let out a stream of air; then I realized it was smoke. Melvin smoked, and Ella let him, and they had a balance. "I don't think Ella ought to be getting in the middle of that," he said.

"Okay, George moved out. Okay?"

"I tell you I'm sorry to hear that, but Ella going to tell you she glad, yeah."

So Melvin would deliver the message. And Ella would sit. But Ella wasn't coming back until dinnertime, and if I didn't find a way to leave the house soon I was going to give in to the urge to phone George. "You have a neighbor who could sit for me this afternoon?" I said.

"I don't got a neighbor I let walk your dog. You pay off a mortgage, look like that the very day the trash move in. You got boys hanging on the corner, across the street, I mean all day long, don't tell me they out there having no prayer meeting. Mess like that, you can't give away this house. And Ella foolish about this house anyway; she know where every light socket at, say she can go blind in here, have no problem."

"If she goes blind, she won't need a light socket," I said, wishing Melvin would be willing to talk to me for the rest of the afternoon.

"That's a good one, yeah," Melvin said. "Got to tell that one to Sis."

"Sis?"

"Ella, I mean, Ella. We call her Sis." He fell silent.

I was going to have to get off the phone if I didn't think of something quickly. If I hung up with Melvin, I had no one to call. All the mothers who'd tousled Gregor's hair at the funeral and promised invitations had lost their nerve. I knew that's what had happened. Tending Gregor took a lot of touching, and there was something taboo about touching other people's children. If I called one and asked her to keep Gregor for me for a few hours, I would scare her to death. "Do you baby-sit?" I said to Melvin finally.

"Baby-sit? Shoot," he said. "Sis tell these children, you have a baby, you have three babies, you run into trouble, just come on home. This year the first year I can remember we *don't* got Pampers under the sink."

He thought for a moment. "I got to change his diaper? No, wait, they got those bags, I seen it on HBO, that Christopher Reeve special. You seen that? Got a little boy just like that, he roll all over the floor. But he good, he just roll."

"He goes to the bathroom," I said, sensing we were negotiating something. "You just lift him. His aim's as good as any six-year-old boy's." I didn't say, *And he tries; George Junior liked to pee circles on the wall.* I still hadn't decided what to do about the wallpaper in the boys' bathroom.

"Never knew a six-year-old boy could hit the side of a bus," Melvin said. "But I know a lot of sixteen-year-old boys done *tried*."

"So you'll sit?"

"You can bring him right now," Melvin said. "Sis fix enough food for ten grown men to last two weeks, and she only gone two days."

"There?" I said. Melvin had just finished telling me that half the murderers in New Orleans spent their days standing on the corner across the street.

"I'm waiting for the gas man," he said, and I sensed he wasn't telling the truth. The gas man only came when a person moved into a new house or when the neighborhood was about to explode from a leaky line. Melvin just had paid off his mortgage. And in neighborhoods like Melvin's, if an explosion was imminent, no one bothered to tell the residents.

"No, you're not," I said good-naturedly.

"For the new neighbor," he said.

"Right. Would that be the one wanted for grand theft auto or the one who killed his wife?"

"Hold on," he said. I listened for what took him away from the phone, but I heard nothing, not a downturn in the TV volume, not footsteps, not a toilet flushing. When he came back on the line, I knew he hadn't been anywhere but inside his own head. Melvin worked on the river before he retired; he wasn't accustomed to wrangling with women, particularly white women. "You know, anything get stolen out your house, you got a colored man in there, you going to point your finger at that colored man. I don't go in no white people houses."

"As long as you've known me?" I said, though in Melvin's life a half-dozen years was close to no time at all; six years could build only a few hundred dollars' equity on a home loan.

"Losing trust in a friend worser than losing trust in a stranger," he said.

I half-wakened Gregor, figuring that if he protested I wouldn't take him to Melvin. "You want to go to Melvin's house?" I whispered.

"Ella lives in his house?" he asked softly, without opening his eyes. I told him yes. "There's about a million honeybirds in her yard," he said groggily, his eyes still not open.

"Is that good?"

Now he looked at me. The expression on his face said, *And what could be bad about a hummingbird?*

SIXTEEN

Melvin and Ella's house was somehow reassuring. It was as narrow as a shotgun house could be—probably no more than fifteen feet across—but it stood high on its pilings, so close to the river that the ground had not subsided under it. To break in, a person would have to use a ladder to reach the windows, and the shotgun was not so deep that a noise in any one room would not be audible in all the others. The outside was covered in shingles that looked freshly whitewashed, giving a message that someone cared but had nothing worth stealing.

Much of the street had no curbing, just clamshell aprons, but their block had unnecessarily high curbs. Melvin was waiting on the stoop of his house, and he was standing, as if not wanting to give the impression that he ever spent more than a minute or two out there. I couldn't open the passenger-side door of my car, and Melvin said, "They put in a curb, but they forget to raise the *street*." He went around to the driver's-side door, reached across the seat, and unfastened Gregor, lifted him out as if he did so every day. I scanned the block, saw no one. It was too early in the day for idleness.

I started to follow Melvin into the house, and Gregor said, "You don't have to come in." His eyes were unfocused and wide, like those of someone suddenly awakened by a good surprise. I couldn't remember him being carried by a man before. But I did have to go in, because I had to use the telephone. Earlier, as I was about to carry Gregor down the basement stairs to the car, the phone had rung, and I'd quickly parked him on the kitchen table and stood next to the answering machine, monitoring the call, fearing that if my mother were dead the people at the hospital would not leave a message. My answering message seemed to roll too slowly, and I felt as if I were phoning from overseas and paying by the second. I took in a secretive, tremulous breath and waited, and several seconds of silence elapsed before George's voice said, "Well, how come no one's there? What's going on, Anna? If you're listening— Dorothy, if *you're* listening—pick up, please. All right, call me back when you feel like it. I'm at my office. I think I could see the boy today. After work, maybe." He hung up without another word. Right then I felt I needed to call the hospital to check on my mother, but I didn't dare use my own line. If George came up with an afterthought, and I were on the other line, the machine wouldn't pick up, and he knew that could only mean someone was home using the phone.

Clearly Melvin was close to sickened by the idea of a white woman walking into his house in the daytime when everyone in the neighborhood had watched Ella leave with a valise. I could see it in the way he didn't pick up his feet. I looked around, hoping to say something good that he'd want to tell Ella. For a shotgun house with windows on both sides of each room, it was dark in the front room; I realized the shutters were closed. The wood floor was bare, and if there was air conditioning in the house it wasn't seeping into that room. It was hot as an attic in there, with an attic smell of hot, clean wood.

Ella had only four pieces of furniture in her living room, but the faux Chippendale sofa was covered in plastic and the coffee table and two end tables both buckled slightly with too much

Pledge on veneer. Only the mantel gave the impression that this was not a storeroom in a secondhand furniture store. Ella had managed to line up close to fifty photographs, all in frames, on a surface no deeper than a hand span, no wider than an arm span. The mantel in my mother's old house had been no bigger, and she had succeeded in making it look full each Christmas with the half dozen cards she received, including one from the car insurance agency and one that had come attached to her Kris Kringle gift at work. I saw no dust on Ella's pictures. From even a short distance, the brown faces in the photographs made a fine pattern of dots, like musical notes. And nestled in, somewhere around the third bar, were two half notes among the quarters. George Junior and Gregor, last year's school pictures, each in a heavily scrolled silver-plated frame.

"Gregor, look!" I said, pointing at his picture. Melvin carried him over, indulging me, and Gregor studied the full lineup of photographs. None were large, but they clearly spanned many years, some sepia-toned with hand-tinted lips and cheeks, some with the fried hairdos of the fifties, others with blue backdrops bleeding into blue mortarboards and gowns. The newer photographs showed no one over the age of eighteen, while the older ones were more likely to be formal portraits of fortyish grandmothers, or wedding pictures of couples who looked terribly old to me but in fact were probably no more than eighteen. In the obituaries in the *Times-Picayune*, the postage stamp–sized pictures that went with the write-ups came from both categories: I would see a grainy picture of a middle-aged woman with fancy curls and a veiled hat and would read that she died last Tuesday at the age of ninety-six. "You might have some dead people up here," Gregor hinted to Melvin.

"How else you going to remember somebody?" Melvin said.

"Oh," Gregor said, and I tried to imagine what he'd been thinking. I had photos of both boys, one from each year of life, in my wallet. George had none of either. As Gregor could see each time I spent money, I had made no changes in what I carried. And surely George hadn't, either.

We had to pass through two bedrooms to get to the kitchen where the phone was. The beds were made as neatly as I'd have made them only if I expected judgmental company. "Ella sure keeps a pretty house," I said.

"The kids move out, got to be worth something," Melvin said, chuckling, and Gregor bobbed around happily against his chest.

Melvin didn't have a phone book. "They leave it on the porch, you don't see when they come, it be gone by morning," he said. "What they going to do with a phone book, can't spell they own name, I don't know, but last phone book we got in 1992."

"You could call directory assistance," Gregor said. Large words were no problem for Gregor; it was the small, familiar ones that evaded him. I told him it cost money. Melvin and Ella were not the sort whose phone bill varied from one month to the next.

"Go ahead," Melvin said. "My great-niece run up a bill calling a psychic 800 number, we don't even blink over a couple dimes."

The ICU nurse said my mother was doing fine, that there was no change, but that was absolutely to be expected. "What if I'm out of reach for a while?" I said, not trying to hide how desperate I was for honest permission. She said not to worry, just to phone for my own benefit whenever I felt like it. I could hear a bit of Mississippi in her voice, slow goodness that wouldn't seem to work in an intensive care unit. I looked at my watch, figured she had five more hours on her shift, considered going to the hospital instead, letting her take care of me. But the pull of the casino was too strong, the need for immersion in the mental silence created by ambient noise. For Gregor's sake, I should learn to take care of myself.

"I don't mind, either," Gregor said when I walked out the door.

Melvin looked at me for an interpretation. "Maybe he needs a nap," I told Melvin, and I kissed Gregor once for a long time. I was halfway to the interstate before I figured out what Gregor was talking about.

The fireman was still in the poker room. He had on the same shirt as the night before, and I saw four trays of white chips in front of him, and I realized that in some ways a great deal of time had passed and in reality no time had passed at all. I, too, had not changed clothes, or slept, and I didn't see myself doing either in the near future.

The Hold 'Em game he was in was the only one running, and I seated myself at an empty table across from where he sat. He'd already folded his hand, and he caught sight of me quickly, motioned me over with the same thrust of the chin Gregor used to refuse a spoon; the difference was in the eyes. I moved tentatively, as if someone might lose concentration or accuse me of cheating, and then he waved me over with a broad gesture of his hand, causing the woman opposite him to turn around and look at me. There were two women at the table, and I sized them up, decided they were too blowsy and card-happy for the fireman to see as women. "You ever go home?" he whispered to me when I edged up behind him. I didn't get too close; I was sure I smelled of anger and fear that hadn't been washed off in days. "Yes," I whispered back, "for what it's worth."

He pushed his chair back, almost bumping noses with me as he stood up. "You won the slots last time you sat by me," he said. I nodded. "Trust me," he said, "I am not good luck."

No one at the table was paying attention to us. The dealer was dealing a new hand, bypassing his place, and I marveled at a game where a person could slip out and make no difference. "Coffee?" he said, and I felt that same anecdotal pleasure I'd had in school when a boy spoke to me: Remember it all for telling because it feels like nothing at the moment.

We didn't walk anywhere or pay any money; the coffeepot was on the buffet table along the wall of the poker room, and we sat at the empty table. "Don't you ever work?" I said to him. *The best defense is a good offense*, my mother always said.

"We rotate, one day on, two days off, every fifth rotation I get off."

I definitely might consider working for the fire department. Or at least consider complaining that they were given too much free time. But there was something about firemen that made me want to let them get away with whatever they could. They seemed so impossibly gentle, though the only other place I'd been this close to one was in the checkout line at the supermarket. I loved looking in their shopping carts. They would come in a pair, wheel out a cart with a half-dozen Rock Cornish game hens, Stove Top stuffing, a gallon of milk, three bunches of broccoli, and six Hubig's apple pies. And they would high-five both my boys, finding ways around George Junior's protestations that his brother couldn't do it.

"I'm surprised this place isn't wall-to-wall firemen," I said. "Why?"

I shrugged, caught out.

He grinned. "Most of us have more predictable ways of moonlighting."

I knew there was a moving company run by firemen, because my mother had wanted to use them when she put her things into our house. But she hadn't, because George had said, "You want a bunch of guys who go through doors with pickaxes carrying your crystal?" and at the time she was trying not to resist George. For all I knew, all the good-looking men painting houses and selling real estate were firemen. From now on I wasn't going to worry when I saw such men, wasn't going to wonder what they did when the money wasn't good.

I noticed a mean red burn mark on his arm, tried to picture him in fire-fighting clothes—the helmet, the fireproof slicker—and found the idea terribly sexy. "How'd that happen?" I said. He looked at the arm as if he were always damaged some way. "Cigarette next to me at the poker table." He laughed. "I'm a chief; most of my risks are right in this room." A chief. That was as impressive as a dermatologist, I thought, and I was disgusted with myself for a second until I realized that was George's way of looking at things.

I ached to ask him the question, sensed the answer would be the one I wanted, feared it would not be. I wouldn't have to tell anyone if he didn't say what I wanted, but I would know, and that would be just as bad. "Do you have priorities?" I said. "At a fire, I mean."

I'd made the question too vague to follow, easing myself into it. "Well, I prefer that everybody go home alive," he said.

"The people in the fire. What about the people in the fire?"

He was losing the mood to be funny. Moving slowly with me toward what I wanted to know. "Is this a lifeboat question?" he said patiently, and I was sorry I'd started. Probably every time he sat down at a poker table with strangers he eventually watched conversation drift that way when he said what he did for a living.

"I guess." Though it wasn't. George had no trouble with the idea of a Sophie's choice, the placement of value on a life, but George had not been the one in the pool that day.

"I don't go up to a house and say, 'Let's see, IQ of eighty-seven, let him die; too many black ancestors, let her die.' You save the one who's got the least chance of saving himself."

"That's good," I said. "That's very good." My eyes filled up with tears, but they were tears of exhaustion, the kind that would make crying oneself to sleep feel excellent.

The fireman's name was George. I didn't ask him his last name, because I couldn't bear to know. There were four George Duffys in the phone book, and I didn't know what I would do if he were one of them. George the fireman agreed to give me ten minutes, thinking he'd prove something to me. He cashed in his chips, sensing his streak was over for the day, and I said, "Either you believe in luck or you don't," and he said, "I believe in it, and I know when I don't have it." But he sat down next to me at a slot machine, not the one I'd played the last time, and I began to win steadily. No big payouts, but five, ten, twenty; I was ahead by more than $250 in ten minutes. I turned to him. "So?" I said.

"So I've got to go home or I'm in trouble."

"Oh," I said, not wanting to know what that meant. He was probably not even to the parking lot before I was out the $250 and ten more.

I went through all the rest of the coins in my sack, trading in nickels and quarters for silver dollars. I wanted to play quickly, either to win big or to prove to George the fireman that he was wrong. But I couldn't tell whether I was winning well or losing well; my credits moved up and down like a sine curve. Or so it seemed, and then I was out of money.

In the car I realized I was truly out of money. I had nothing with which to pay Melvin. I'd planned to pay him ten dollars an hour to make up for whatever I'd run up on his phone bill. I always paid Ella with a check. He would take a check. George couldn't complain if I had to pay for child care while my mother was in the hospital. Fifty dollars was reasonable. Though the going rate for healthy children was half that much. George could complain. I dared him to complain. I hoped he'd complain.

George was in the kitchen when I came in with Gregor. Gregor had not stopped talking since I picked him up. Melvin had seduced him into napping by promises of a tour of his yard and his own approbation. And Gregor was as energized as if he had been sucking sugar all day, going on about the honeybirds. And frogs. And a garter snake. "We saw this crow. You know what a crow is?" He didn't pause. "Anyway, Melvin says, 'One crow is bad news, two crows is happiness,' so we waited for that crow's wife, on account of we didn't want bad news."

"What the hell is going on?" George said as soon as we emerged into the kitchen from the basement stairs.

Gregor fell silent, and I was grateful for the wisdom he was born with. George Junior had had the flip side of that same wisdom, the ability to size up a situation and know what would get me in trouble. "I wasn't here," I said.

"*Nobody* was here," George said.

"Were you here, Daddy?" Gregor said in a fact-gathering sort of way, and I hugged him tighter. He was riding on my right hip, and his new arm was concealed behind my back. Neither Melvin nor I could figure out how to release the suction, and all I could do for now was make sure Gregor stayed comfortable.

George ignored him. "I call here, and no one answers, and you've got to admit that's damn strange. I mean, that woman hasn't left the house since she moved in." I opened my mouth to speak, to protect him from saying something he might regret, something I definitely would never forgive, but he rolled over me. "Let me finish, Anna. I figure you've pulled some stunt, moved out or something, so I come over here, and nobody's home, but your clothes are all here, so I don't know what the hell to think, and then the phone rings, and it's some fucking hospital." I breathed out with relief. Even George would not announce my mother's death this way.

"And?"

"And where in God's name were you?" he said.

"What'd the hospital say?"

"What else? Your mother's awake and asking for you. I refrained from saying, 'So what else is new?' You want to tell me what's going on?"

"I was a hero, the fireman said I was a hero," Gregor said, and then he buried his face on my shoulder, embarrassed.

George looked at him as if no one, including Gregor, had the right to have the delusions of childhood. Certainly George had never been credulous, had never had wide-eyed faith that could make him tremble. The Church had seen to that. He had no photographs of himself from the time before I knew him, and when I was pregnant, thinking I would have one child, I pictured a miniature version of the adult George and assumed the child would feel fine about himself in the world because George felt fine about himself in the world. The corollary of that, of course, was that the child would have to put nothing through the pastel filters of innocence. I was relieved when neither boy took on George's contours; I figured both could stay ingenuous for a long time if George didn't speak to them. "A fine thing," my mother said sometimes; "you *shield* those boys from their father as if he were Charles Manson."

"Do you see any reason to have this discussion in front of Gregor?" I said.

"Your mother's not here to watch him."

This was the time when, if I were Gregor, I would proudly announce that I was a lot more independent than I had been the last time George saw me. But Gregor didn't speak, and I could feel him straining to keep the arm out of view. He'd never used those shoulder muscles in that way, and I imagined an isometric burn that would set him back tomorrow. I shifted a bit to my right, but Gregor didn't release the tension in his body. We were trapped in that corner of the kitchen unless George left the room, and George wasn't interested in leaving the room. I stroked Gregor's head reassuringly and said, "Show Daddy."

Gregor shook his head no, kept his face buried on my shoulder.

"What'd he do?" George said, as if Gregor were a child who did something wrong every single day.

"Something good," I said in that high voice adults use when talking about a child who's listening.

"I'm not ready," Gregor whispered wetly into my ear. I'd forgotten he was planning to surprise his father.

I let out a jovial chuckle that didn't fool me, but it seemed to fool Gregor, who looked up into my face expectantly. "Oh, this boy is *very* ready," I said.

George was leaning back slightly on his heels, his arms folded across his chest. We were wasting his time. Either he had billable hours that he'd walked out on in his rush to find me doing something wrong, or he'd told someone to expect him ten minutes from now. Gregor craned his neck, trying to catch his father's eye, but George wouldn't look up from the floor. "Daddy, I got a arm," Gregor said shyly, and he slowly lifted the piece over my head as I turned to model for George.

As if he were doing me a favor I should never forget, George looked at the prosthesis with an expression that showed nothing, not anger, not disgust, not even normal curiosity. "Congratulations, son," he said dully.

"I can eat ice cream with it," Gregor said. "And I think I could of called 911 if Gammy couldn't, but Gammy could. I'm practicing." He held up the claw. "You can get a hand that's pink and has nails, not real nails, because you don't *need* nails. Because nails keep your fingers from getting hurt, and you don't feel it if it's fake. But I got to practice, see?" He opened and closed the grip, and I could feel the shoulder muscles moving.

George was so pale I thought he might vomit or fall over. He was now transfixed by Gregor's demonstration, but he was under a spell much stronger than a natural love of horror; he seemed actually to be punishing himself by watching. "Daddy?" Gregor said. "It doesn't hurt, Daddy."

"I have to go," George said softly.

I wanted him to leave, and I was ready to tell him so. He was in the room with me, and my mother wasn't in the room with me, and that was not the regular order of things. I expected I would send him away and tell her she could come out now, and we'd find something for Gregor to do and I'd repeat George's every word, mimic his every gesture, and we'd get happily indignant. "I have to go to the hospital," I said, remembering. "Are you taking Gregor for ice cream?" I felt Gregor take in a deep breath.

"I *tried* to set something up with you this morning," George said. "I've got to be somewhere in twenty minutes. Sorry."

SEVENTEEN

When I was school age, I read about birth order the way other girls read about emerging sexuality and astrology. I was looking for clues or, better still, definitions of the possibilities on which I could build my dreams. First children, fourth children, only children: history was full of them, the ones driven since birth to be equal to the people around them, and all the people around them were grown or near-grown. When I was four, I was thoroughly humiliated by my secret knowledge that I couldn't read. And so it was to go from then on, my mystification that everyone else knew more than I did, but if I watched carefully I might catch up. My mother always looked so happy having things to tell me, and I assumed it was because she was better than I was. I had tried never to leave either Gregor or George Junior alone with an adult. They were a package, shielding each other from false notions that they were being outpaced by their elders. Now Gregor was falling into the unprotected company of adults, and I marveled at how much he thought he had to tell them. At the hospital, I parked him by the nurses' station and he stopped everyone who passed with more explanations of musculature than he'd given me, never mind that half the people he spoke to had thought about nothing but the human body for most of their working lives.

My mother was awake when I tiptoed into the room. She was still in the ICU because the blood vessels in her brain had surprised her once and they might do so again. She hadn't filled out since I saw her in the morning, and I wanted to squeeze the IV bag, pump and pump until she was round and useful to herself again. "Come here," she said, sounding drunk and careless, and I was afraid she wanted me to kiss her. I approached slowly, gingerly, as if a footfall might loosen a blood clot. I remembered us driving down the street holding my third-grade classroom's bowl of fish: My mother's car kept hitting tiny bumps, spilling water on my hands and my skirt, and I was beginning to imagine ten fat fish in a cupful of water at the bottom of the bowl. "I wouldn't do this to you," I had wailed.

I stood beside her bed, and she said something unintelligible. I said, "What?" She was too groggy to be peeved, and as I tried to follow the movements of her mouth as she repeated herself I could almost see the midline of her face, marking the border between control and noncontrol. "Please tell me you weren't out there again," she said, each word coated in saliva.

"I wasn't out there," I said. I'd never lied to her before, but only because I'd never considered protecting myself; besides, the truth hadn't seemed dangerous to her before. Until now, insult and disappointment might have broken through her skin, but she'd absorbed both so well that sometimes I was frustrated. She just wasn't the type to knead her temples or pat her belly in the region of her lower colon and try to imply that I was killing her slowly.

"You see what happens," she said, the two sibilants messing her up, but she couldn't wipe her mouth. I searched for a tissue and did it for her. I was repelled, and I didn't know if it was because I never liked to touch her or because her helplessness infuriated and relieved me at the same time. She hadn't come to George Junior's funeral until the last moment; she'd set up a covenant with me, and she kept breaking it.

I apologized, my eye on the wall of monitors. Her blood pressure rose, her heartbeat slowed, and I wondered if she had any secrets I could pull out of her, the way police did with lie detectors. "I love you," I said, and her heartbeat speeded up, from seventy-three to eighty-nine in a matter of seconds. She saw what I was doing, gave me the crooked half of a smile. "Not fair," she said. "I'm supposed to see through you."

"Gregor's outside," I said after a while.

"Oh, shit," she said, and I raised both eyebrows. Some barrier in her brain had been breached. My mother had no aversion to bad language in and of itself; unless a word's inflammatory it's just a bunch of phonemes, she always said. She preferred to avoid four-letter words because she thought they indicated vagueness, the same way the passive voice did.

"Oh, shit, Mama?" I said.

"What day is it?" she said.

I had to think. The ICU had no windows; I wasn't even quite certain what time it was. And if I'd seen a clock, I would have taken a moment to figure out if it was A.M. or P.M. I told her it was late Wednesday afternoon.

"What day was yesterday?" she said, then considered. "Wait, that's not what I want to know."

"Gregor, you want to know about Gregor."

"There's nothing wrong with me, you know," she whispered. "I just lost track of time. I mean it. Gregor, what day did I take Gregor to the doctor?" I told her yesterday. "The first day, he's not supposed to keep it on. He have it on?" I nodded, then explained that I didn't know how to remove it. I was afraid to tug, imagining tiny blood vessels popping from the suction. "You're in a hospital, Anna," she said and burst into tears.

"Hey, he's doing fine," I said. "He's out there giving all the nurses physiology lessons. And the doctors, too. He waylays all of them."

She couldn't stop crying, but she smiled, slurred out, "I'm all emotional."

"Maybe it's menopause," I said, and she laughed and sobbed, and the monitors went haywire, but no one came in. The numbers raced and scrolled, but they must have been signs of life. My mother began to hiccup and sniffle, and I preferred to watch the numbers as they dropped, settling down and hiccuping along with her.

"Anna, I was paying the difference," she said. I didn't know what she was talking about. "The house money, I was using the house money." I told her I didn't understand. "The *prosthesis*," she said, and looked surprised that she'd put the syllables out in the right order, never mind that her tongue slid halfway out of her mouth in the process and the word was reduced to a slippery growl.

"For Gregor?" I said, and she raised her right eyebrow to remind me that I didn't have to be simpleminded with her. "I mean, why're you paying for it?" She lowered the eyebrow, raised it again. "Oh," I said. "Well, he knows about it now." She tried to raise herself up at that, flopped miserably to the left, but she didn't start crying again. "He'll pay for it?" she said. She thought a moment. "Never mind. I haven't lost *all* my faculties."

An enormous feeling of well-being washed over me, the kind I had experienced in my lifetime perhaps once every few years, when I was almost feverish with comfort. She had not been in the next room when George learned about Gregor's arm, had not been waiting to make me laugh at him, but she was here now, and the story was fresh, and it was hard to quit our two-person clique when it was so much fun.

"He didn't even notice Gregor had it until I showed him," I sang out.

Her face was filling out, coming back, even with no animation on one side. "You *showed* him?"

I clasped my hands together in pleasure. "I was backed into a corner. He'd've seen it unless he walked out of the room, which wasn't likely. Besides, I wanted him to see it. Best defense is a good offense, Mama."

"What'd he say?" she said, and I realized I couldn't remember. I thought perhaps he had said nothing. "I got the overall impression that he wasn't thrilled," I said. "But you know, somehow it doesn't seem to me that he was upset over the *fact* of it. He wasn't angry. He was something, but it wasn't angry."

"Probably jealous," she said, reducing the five syllables to about three, but I could understand her.

"Jealous?"

"Jea-lous," she said, more clearly this time. "Your father didn't last long, but I do remember that. A father gets like that, last thing he wants is a happy child."

"No," I said, "I don't think that was it. He may not want Gregor happy, but I don't think that was it." It was coming back to me, the morbid fascination in George's eyes: He looked as if I'd opened Gregor's chest and begun massaging his heart while Gregor chattered away proudly, telling of auricles and ventricles. "It's like extreme measures, you know? Like I went too far."

"Nice topic," my mother said.

"Meaning?"

"Meaning I'm in the ICU. I *want* extreme measures." I cocked my head. "No, I'm serious," she said. "Never put a 'do not resuscitate' sign over my bed."

I stifled a smile. It sounded like one of her jokes. "Never?"

I saw fear on the right side of her face; it gave her an ambivalent expression. "Oh, God, you know how you think you're too young for a will? I don't have a will. I don't have anything written down."

"So tell me."

"So resuscitate me," she said, letting the sibilants flow. "There's no such thing as no hope. When I'm finished living, I'll stop on my own, thank you very much. Doctors shut off the machines so they can harvest your organs. Don't donate my organs, you hear me?"

I asked her why, not to be argumentative, but to get some reasons for my own decision about myself. So far I had failed to get a donor card just because I thought it would be bad luck. I hoped I could come up with a more principled reason, or else I'd feel a need to do the civic thing, to do some good for which people would remember me. Even in anonymity.

"I told you. If you've got your heart pumping, they'll keep it going until they take whatever else they need. Then they'll take your heart. Remember that baboon in California?"

I smiled in spite of myself. Some topics were funny because that's all they could be.

"Goddammit, Anna." *Goddammit* wasn't a four-letter word. "I mean it. They say he screeched in terror when they took him away. I do not want to be lying in this bed, *watching* them get ready to cut me open."

"You remind me of Kathleen." Kathleen was the only girl my mother ever found good enough to be my friend. She was the one in my seventh-grade English class who wrote story after story of waking up in a coffin underground. She thoroughly terrorized all of us until one of the boys wrote a parody of her stories, and I think most of us quit thinking about death about that time.

"Kathleen was, well, unconventional," she said.

"Kathleen's an attorney in George's firm." I said. "Real estate law." I realized she'd been on the track her entire life.

"Sit down," my mother said. I sat in a nearby chair, but it was too low for me to see her. I perched on the side of her bed instead, careful to jar nothing. "None of this occurred to me," she said. She was getting ready to cry.

"It was a mild stroke," I said. "As strokes go. The doctor says you're lucky, you got a major warning sign."

"Fifty-three was long dead a hundred years ago."

"Half the women my age were dead in childbirth a hundred years ago," I said.

She reached for my hand with her good hand, and I let her take it, surprised that the softness of it didn't make me uneasy. "You're trying to jolly me up," she said. "And maybe later that'd be a good idea." Okay. "But not right now." Okay. "I want something in writing. Go get Kathleen." I cocked my head to the side, and she said, "You can laugh at that." I shrugged.

"I don't want to donate my organs. I do want extreme measures. I don't want George to get any of my money, though he earns about that much in a month. I do want Gregor to keep going to the doctor. He tell you this is just a start?" I nodded. "You can't sign on my account, can you?" I told her no. "I want power of attorney. You go get power of attorney, all right?" Yes, yes. "What time is it?" I didn't know; I assumed it was late afternoon, remember? "Get a lawyer."

"Mama, George is the only lawyer I know. Except for all the lawyers I know through George, and obviously they're all friends of George."

She gave me that too-patient look that always made me know I was a fool. "Get George if you have to. I'm not *divorcing* him."

"You're just spelling out the terms of his greatest wish fulfillment," I said, and she had to smile.

"Listen," she said after a while. "They've got social services here. I'm not the first person to die here." I opened my mouth to speak, and she read my mind. "I'm not the first person to think about mortality here."

I said I would get right on it. I was afraid she had an ATM card.

EIGHTEEN

I had been right about the hospital. Everyone was accustomed to diagnosing, patching, prescribing, never mind that each act later was supposed to be miraculously recorded in a computer, printed out when we were less vulnerable. Without revealing our names and social security numbers, Gregor and I could move around the hospital asking for free advice; all we had to do was strike people as vaguely familiar. I learned how to release Gregor's arm, all the while listening regretfully to him whimper, "Gammy'll do it." And I learned that social services still echoed of Hull House; I could be referred to an attorney, but only if I couldn't afford one. "But it's for my mother," I told the woman who glared at me upon learning my husband was a lawyer. She had master's degree in social work written all over her—the tics and twenty extra pounds, the shade of pink lipstick I hadn't seen on anyone since I mashed an old tubeful onto my face when I was three. I had an unnatural dislike of social workers, and I knew it: Several had tried their hand at me when Gregor was born, and it had been the exasperating softness of their voices that had made me want to scream.

"Your mother lives with you, correct?" the woman said.

"Yes," I said as if I were answering a questionnaire.

"I would think your husband would want to help her." She looked toward Gregor in a meaningful way, as if she knew all about three generations in a household and who owed what to whom.

"You would think wrong," I said, with the you-know-mothers-in-law hint in my voice, but she didn't smile, which didn't help me like her.

"Gammy lives with us, but now Daddy doesn't live with us," Gregor said, as if he were the only grown-up in the room.

The social worker perked up; family pathology was as good as poverty any day. "You should've said this was an adversarial situation," she said.

"It's *not* an adversarial situation," I said. "All my mother wants is to get her affairs in order."

"Then you could ask your husband."

"Look, can't you refer me to a legal clinic or something?" I said. In a minute she was going to feel all the contempt I'd been saving up for six years.

When she told me again that I wouldn't qualify, I stood up before she could, rolled Gregor out the door so fast his head whiplashed back in the wheelchair. I knew he was thrilled by the uncustomary speed but had the good sense not to shout with pleasure. "I didn't like her," I whispered in his ear as we took a hall corner almost fast enough to tip. "She was mean," he whispered back, delighted.

I phoned George's office from the pay phone in the corridor. When he came right on the line and the tone of his voice was reasonable, I thought for a second that maybe he and I had a spiritual connection, that he could *sense* I was calling with nothing that would annoy him. I heard my own voice forming friendly words, as if he'd said something to mollify me. "There's boilerplate for someone who wants to live no matter what, right?" I said almost flirtatiously.

"I'm not going to slip in language to kill her, if that's what you're implying," he said, and I quit thinking about a spiritual connection.

"I was just kidding," I said.

George sighed deeply, as if he were the most patient man in the world and everyone but me knew it. "I don't really have time to play around, Anna."

I had a good half-dozen retorts; some were plays on his words, others uncensored attacks on his sour take on the world. But if I said something snappish to George my mother was going to have to spend the night in intensive care avoiding sleep in case she died intestate without knowing it. I needed George to draft papers for her before his secretary went home. "Can we do this quickly, then?" I said. "I know what she wants." I looked at the hall clock. "I could be down there in half an hour."

"This is not a storefront, you know."

I wanted to say, *It could be for all I know*, but instead I said, "I'll go home and change." Right then I would have been embarrassed to walk in somewhere that had no emergencies. I'd passed a number of women in the hospital who'd obviously left home unexpectedly; probably I'd passed men, too, but men in summer all tended to look that way if they weren't in coat and tie. At the casino it had been different. Cold killed every smell but cigarette smoke, and only the rumpled were truly serious.

"You have the kid with you."

"Aw, George," I said.

"I mean it, Anna."

"Look, half the partners in your firm came to the funeral. Gregor's sitting right up there, looking exactly like George; they're looking at George, and they see Gregor, they know who he belongs to."

"Whom."

He had me. He always had me. I could rage, I could hang up, but he would quietly put down the phone, shrug, leave his office and go to his doctor woman who didn't need him, and I would have to go back to my mother and say *sorry*. "Whom he belongs to. To whom he belongs," I said. The crescent of hot pain sparks in my belly came on, relaying a threat that I would vomit if I didn't get cool air. "Tell me what I need to do," I said as casually as I could. If George knew I needed to get off the phone, he would filibuster until I got sick there in the hallway. In that way he had a spiritual connection to me.

He enunciated slowly and clearly. "Let me write all this down." He had to get paper and pencil. If I were a client, he would have paper and pencil. I heard pages rustling. "Okay." O-k-a-y. I was getting lightheaded, and I needed to sit, but there was nothing to sit on in the hall. I tried sitting on the floor, but the receiver was on a short steel cable that didn't reach far enough. I leaned against the wall, pressed my cheek against the cool plaster. My peripheral vision closed in, but I held on to the phone. George's voice was clear and loud, but I couldn't pay attention, and the dark frame around the telephone in my line of sight became larger until all I could see was the small blue instruction panel, and I fell to the floor.

I came to slowly because I didn't want to be there, didn't want to find out that my panties showed or that my breath stank or that a passerby was telling George something was dreadfully wrong with me, come right away. When I decided to open my eyes because I had to be fair to Gregor, I figured I'd been lucky. The only other person in the corridor was a girl who looked no older than seventeen. She squatted beside me in a pose that let me know she'd be gone as soon as she was sure I wasn't dead. "I told the guy on the phone you, like, passed out," she said behind her hand. "He is seriously pissed off."

I looked up, saw the receiver was still hanging from the phone, saw Gregor was watching me with mute fascination, as if it was just a matter of time before everyone he knew disappeared, and he might as well get used to the idea. I told the girl thanks, I was fine, and she uncoiled with no wasted motion, walked off at a brisk pace, turning back only to look at the phone with wide eyes. "George?" I said, kneeling to reach.

"If you think histrionics is seductive, you're wrong," he said.

"I passed out, for Chrissakes. You can't *make* yourself pass out." I realized I was arguing the wrong point.

"Know something, Anna? The funny thing is, I was trying like hell to get your attention, and now when it's too late you're trying to get mine."

"I can't do this over the phone," I said. Suddenly I was irritated with my mother.

"I'll come over there," he said. Then, before I could become angrier at my mother, he said, "Look, what she wants isn't out of the ordinary. She wants it all to go to Gregor." His tone implied that he knew she was trying to sidestep him, but he was letting it go to prove something. Yes, I said, all to Gregor. "I presume she has less than a million dollars?" he said. Very funny. "No, I've got to ask. Over a million, there're tax consequences." Not over a million. "Well, you're over twenty-three and *you're* not disabled, so there's no forced heirship. I can get it on one page."

"What she wants is the resuscitate stuff," I said.

"I think if you don't spell out 'no extreme measures,' then they automatically keep you going. You'd have to *sue* to pull the plug on her."

"Surely you'd represent me," I said, and he laughed before he caught himself.

I was actually looking forward to seeing George, waiting in the visitors' lounge with hopes he would come in suddenly so attractive that I'd set aside all anger. Maybe if he spelled out all my mother's terms correctly, with full understanding, I would find that incredibly sexy, the way I sometimes had crushes on doctors who gave me effective medicine. I assumed that once I met Gregor's orthopedist I would fall hopelessly in love with him, even if the love lasted only a few days, seeping into my dreams where the feelings for the doctor could be transmogrified into something more acceptable. Each time the door opened into the lounge, I had a heart-stopping surge of adrenaline, the kind that only comes when the expected doesn't happen. I was sharing a Coke with Gregor, shimmering with nerves from drinking my share too quickly. I always tried to take my half first so that Gregor could release all the warm spit he wanted into the can and never know I preferred not to drink after him.

George arrived within the hour. And he had a sheaf of papers with him. "Couldn't have done this ten years ago," he said, handing me pages that looked typeset. The document was only two pages long, but he'd made four copies, one for my mother, one for me, one for his office, and one for the hospital. He'd thought of everything, and he looked good being a lawyer. His white shirt was starched and pressed as only a laundry could do it, and he'd had a gentle haircut, a quarter-inch off instead of the bimonthly hack-back that showed the fuzzy island in the middle of his pate.

I reached out and touched his hand, under the guise of thanks; I wanted him to take my hand in return, stroke my palm absentmindedly with his fingers as he had done before he ever kissed me the first time. But George pulled his hand away as if I were another man. "Where is she?" he said, all business.

"I thought we might talk," I said.

George pulled a pocket watch out of his waistband. I'd never seen it before, never known he had a watch pocket. "Can't," he said.

"You said on the phone you'd come over here so we could talk."

"No, I didn't, Anna," he said impatiently. "You're always twisting around everything I say."

"I said, 'I don't want to talk on the phone,' and you said, 'I'll be right over.'"

"See?" See what. "You interject what you want to hear into everything."

I told him to forget it. Overall I thought I was probably more intelligent than George, and my mother certainly had planted that notion and nursed it along. But George had dedicated the working, knowing part of his mind to tripping up other people. Early on I'd enjoyed his ability to knead and slam the truth around until it took new form; that was what made him rich. But that talent eventually became indistinguishable from power, and all I knew about George after a while was that he was a lot more powerful than I was. Talking to him was like being Joseph K. in *The Trial,* screwing oneself deeper and deeper into a presumed guilt.

I didn't want to send him into the ICU alone, or even with just a nurse as witness. If George walked in without me, all the blood in my mother's body would flood her brain as if she were upside down; it would rush out of the vessels that carried it and fill her head like a balloon until it popped. She wouldn't have a nice, neat stroke, she would have an explosion. Luckily, George wasn't interested in entering alone, and he used his professional voice to push his way in. Lawyers and doctors were like scissors-paper-stone: Each could trump the other if the circumstances were right.

I went in first, and George held back, almost shyly if I didn't know better, and I saw she was asleep. I gestured with flattened palm for George to stay back, and he stood in the doorway out of her line of sight. If he was affected by how helpless my mother looked, he didn't show it. "Mama?" I said, and her right eye shot open.

"I was just resting," she said, and I realized I was going to have to relearn understanding her speech each time I saw her. I told her George was here. She processed that piece of information, not searching for meaning, it seemed to me, but rather rummaging around in her mind for the right words for the occasion. "George the cheating husband or George the lawyer?" she said finally, and I was glad her words were slurred.

"Jesus, Mama," I whispered.

"I'm sure she has nothing lovely to say," George said, looking straight at her. "Dorothy, I'm here pro bono."

"Did you read it over?" she said to me.

"God, I hate this," I said.

George pulled out his pocket watch again, and with paunch and posture he looked so much like the White Rabbit that I resented him for his absurdity. "I get the hint," I said. "I read it, Mama."

"Get my glasses," she said.

"Your glasses're at home," I told her. I hadn't brought toothbrush or comb or deodorant. I could pretend that I thought bodies didn't need toiletries when they didn't move and took in only sugar water, but the truth was that I hadn't thought about her wanting anything from home. Certainly not glasses.

She ignored me. "George, there's a nurse out there, glasses bouncing off her chest, ask her please may I borrow them."

George stood stock still. George never had fetched in all the time I'd known him. Scissors-paper-stone; my mother must have thought that she fit into the equation somewhere, beating out law and medicine with the urgency of her needs.

"I read it, for Chrissakes," I said.

"All right," she said. "If you think about it, *I* won't be the one having to deal with this mess if I'm unconscious." She paused, turned her one-eyed gaze toward George. "Or dead," she said.

"Dorothy, believe it or not, I don't want you to drop dead," George said softly, and I was sure my mother could see through him as well as I could.

She let out a little sniff of annoyance, and I wondered if it came from both nostrils. "If you don't want to stress people to death, try behaving yourself."

George didn't move, but I knew he was thinking that she hadn't signed the papers, and he hadn't notarized them, and she'd better think about treating him right. "Believe it or not, what I do with my life has nothing to do with you," he said evenly.

"Fine, fine," she said, and I knew she'd figured him out. "Get me a pen, Anna."

No sooner had George squeezed his notary's stamp onto the final copy of the papers than my mother said, "Know what I'm going to do when I get out of the hospital? I'm going to call your mother."

Neither one looked even slightly stunned, though disbelief may very well have been the reason. "You deserve each other," I said with the sincerity that comes only when a person is close to hysterics.

NINETEEN

Going to the casino felt right, responsible, as if I were going off to work knowing my household chores were done. Gregor was at home with Ella, who planned to have him writing calligraphically by day's end. My mother was being moved into a private room and was too cranky to want more than a fifteen-minute visit. And I'd figured out that George had not become dangerous over the threat of being turned in to his mother because he'd confidently underestimated my mother's tracking abilities. I went to the Whitney Bank, became a signatory on my mother's accounts, and took a hundred dollars as a loan, an investment. She had more than sixty thousand dollars in a savings account earning 2.5 percent interest. With such a phlegmatic attitude, she'd never notice a hundred here and there, as long as I controlled myself and paid back when I could.

As soon as I was on the parking shuttle bus and had watched the side doors meet tight at the gaskets, I felt like a fugitive who'd caught the last flight, a commuter who'd caught the last train; it was that sort of flop into the seat. I would think about slots, I would think about the fireman, I would play the game in which I pretended I was seven and I knew nothing of what had happened since. A future would come to me; showing up for it was what I was supposed to do. I leaned back and closed my eyes so I wouldn't see the parks and piers. I didn't want to hear George Junior.

I traded the hundred dollars for coins. It was my mother's money, which she wasn't sure she had, so I could play differently with it. The coins didn't fill half the carry cup, and I felt marginal. Maybe I should have taken two hundred. Or an odd amount that looked as if it paid for something. I had an ATM card for her account. I didn't need to quibble.

Late morning, only one poker game was running, and the sign said it was Omaha. George the fireman wasn't at the table, but last time he'd played Texas Hold 'Em, and for all I knew he had a preference. I approached the floor man at the desk, asked if a game of Texas Hold 'Em was making up. I wanted to sound as if I knew what I was talking about, and I clearly fooled him, but to myself I sounded like an uptown woman walking into a barroom on Louisiana Avenue and trying to pass for black. "I'll put your name on the list," he said, and I said no, thank you, I was looking for a friend who played. "Oh, yeah," he said. "You're looking for Duffy."

I had that same adrenal lurch I'd had the day before when I was waiting for George in the visitors' lounge, the one that came with an unsurprising surprise. "Pardon?" I said, though I needed no explanation.

"You the one hung out with the fireman," he said.

"George?"

"That might be his name. Here we call him Duffy. Something about firemen, they all got those kid names. Jerry, Eddie, Scotty. But they got limits, can't go calling a guy Georgie, I don't guess."

I gave him the sort of laugh a man who lives by his wits deserves, but I wondered why we never had called George Junior Georgie. Maybe it would have made a difference. I made myself stop thinking about that; all I needed was to hear his voice and I'd have run out of the casino.

George Duffy. I wondered how often he'd gotten our phone calls. The only other George Duffy we got calls for was a piano tuner. Women with voices hungry to sing along with sheet music would call and ask what the rates were, and we'd say right off, "Oh, you want the George Duffy who tunes pianos," but we never went to the trouble to find out his number. "There're four George Duffys in the book," George had told the boys. "One day there'll be five."

"You can be G. Duffy in the phone book," Gregor had said. "Maybe George and I'll both be G. Duffy in the phone book."

I knew what George Junior was about to say, and I interrupted quickly. "Maybe you'll be in the New York phone book," I told Gregor. I was thinking about George Junior again. The fireman. I would think about the fireman. I couldn't play without him.

"You have a list going?" I said to the man.

"You want to know if Duffy's here?"

I nodded, but then I realized I should explain. "I need him for luck," I said.

The man guffawed generously, and I could smell the sourness in his mouth that came after too much sugar. "Not this week you don't. I think he was down about two hundred bucks last night."

"Know how some people carry a disease and don't ever get it?" I said. The man obviously didn't look too kindly upon analogies, but I wanted to hear this one come out for its own sake. "He's a carrier."

"You know, not too many good-looking women come in this place," he whispered. He was over sixty and didn't sound flirtatious, and I couldn't follow him. "Duffy noticed you, that's for sure."

"Oh," I said, understanding him now. I was surprised to feel a sexual lick go through me, the way it did when estranged lovers finally kissed open-mouthed on television.

"You could call him. Not too many George Duffys in the fire department."

I enjoyed having a private joke with myself. I reminded him that all I wanted was luck. "He doesn't have to talk to me—or *anything*," I said.

"Mmm, hmm," he said, and I felt a lot younger than he was.

There was a telephone book tucked into the pay phone shelf in the ladies' room. I'd been so ready to drop quarters and dimes in case the phone company charged for directory assistance that I'd changed ten dollars' worth of my unused silver dollars. This gambling was a business with operational expenses. Now I would need no more than three quarters and three dimes, thirty-five cents for each George Duffy to whom I was not married. A new bet. Odds were I'd find him on the first or second call. I figured I'd say, *Is this the George Duffy who's a lawyer?* And the person would say, *No, this is the George Duffy who tunes pianos*, or *This is the George Duffy who's a fire chief*, or I'd find out what that other George Duffy was. Rich man, poor man, beggar man, thief, doctor, lawyer, fire chief. A lot of redundancy there. I dialed the one on Napoleon Avenue first. It was the address closest to my house, and I might as well go for a big win before the small losses.

"Chief's office," a man said when he picked up on the fifth ring. By the time he picked up, I'd realized I might get an answering machine, and didn't know what I'd do about it.

"What?" I said. I heard a lot of noise in the background, static and a nostril-pinched female radio voice.

"Can't hear you. Wait." A lull. "Sorry. Who's it you're trying to reach?"

"You say chief's office?" I was getting ready to hang up. I hadn't thought out all the slender branches of the flowchart. The noise on the other end picked up again. "This's the chief's line. You want the chief?"

"Sure," I said. I wondered if the fire department had computers that flashed the number where a call originated. It would say, *Pay phone, ladies' restroom, Isle of Magic Casino, second floor.* That would be his problem, not mine. But I didn't want to get him in trouble. Maybe this was his secret life. He was a chief, he had a wife, he had a lot to lose. Then I remembered I'd found this number in the phone book under his name.

"Yeh," he said when he came on the line. I heard rebuke in his voice.

"This the George Duffy who's a fire chief?" I said. I never before had phoned a man who wasn't going to give me an appointment and get paid for it, check out the air conditioning, power wash the stucco. That's how I'd made George want to marry me, my mother said, later admitting that perhaps being coy wasn't necessarily a good idea.

"Yeh," he said.

"The one who plays cards?" I said. I chose the words carefully, no game or venue of choice mentioned.

"Who's this?"

"Anna from the casino." He didn't answer right away. I figured a Fantasia of casino women was dancing through his mind, and he was trying to put my voice on hippo women who played cards and ostrich women who served drinks. "I'm the one who can't play the slots when you're not here," I said, helping him out, hoping he was thinking only of women less appealing than I was.

"Hey, Anna." Nice.

"How come you're in the phone book?" I said.

"So you could find me." He sounded playful, almost cynically so, and I was relieved. "I *do* work," he said.

"Could you take a break?" I figured he could make it to the casino from Napoleon Avenue in twenty minutes, help me win for twenty, make it back in twenty.

"This isn't a three-martini-lunch kind of job," he said. Right then an alarm went off somewhere near him; it was loud, but low enough in the register not to hurt my ear. I thought he would have to hang up, slide down a pole, but he told me to hold a second. The alarm stopped, and he said, "I couldn't have timed that better if I'd tried." I asked him why he was still on the phone. "I don't roll on car fires," he said. "I'm the chief, remember?"

"So you could take a break." I said it like I didn't mean it.

"I'll be there tomorrow."

Tomorrow wasn't a notion I could deal with. I was sleep-starved. Eight hours last night had whetted my hunger for more sleep, but I couldn't stay in the bed. I had to see my mother and leave Gregor in good hands so the phone wouldn't ring and frighten me. For me all "tomorrow" meant was evasion, and I couldn't promise what form it would take.

"My mother's in the hospital," I said. "She's stable *today.*"

He laughed with the complicity of one who realigns his priorities until their order doesn't look too bad. "Maybe I could bless your money or something, like you've gone to Castel Gandolfo or something," he said.

"You're a Catholic, George Duffy." The name came out like a pet name.

"How the hell'd you know that?"

"Because my husband's name is George Duffy." For some reason I added, "My husband I'm separated from." George would have caught that preposition hanging out there.

He cleared his throat. "The lawyer or the piano tuner?" he said. "Wait, let me guess. The lawyer."

"How do you know it's not the piano tuner? Or the one who lives on . . ." I flipped back into the phone book quickly. "The one who lives on Constance?"

"Because piano tuners don't have wives like you. And the one that lives on Constance Street is me. At home."

"Oka-a-a-y," I said. Firemen had strange lives, like nuns. Even as an adult, I wanted to know what nuns' undergarments looked like. I found the way they lived together, nuns and firemen, locked inside stone buildings, thoroughly erotic. I could drive past the fire station on Napoleon Avenue at six-thirty in the morning and see a half dozen of the men in their navy-blue T-shirts milling around at shift change, and I would want to kiss them. I checked the address of George Duffy on Napoleon Avenue in the phone book. It was around where I figured the station was. Maybe I'd seen George Duffy in his navy-blue T-shirt. But he was a chief; if he didn't roll on car fires, he didn't go outside in the summer heat just to gossip.

"I could come there," I said. "You know, for luck."

"You wouldn't be the first woman to sneak in this place," he said. "Though you'd be the first to sneak in for *that*."

"I could get you in trouble?" I said.

"You sound kind of hopeful."

I didn't have an answer for that. I could be there in twenty minutes, touch him for luck, be back in twenty minutes. "Where do I get in?" I said.

He asked me where I was, and I said, "Where else would I know you weren't at the casino?" and I sensed I was flirting but wasn't quite sure.

"Car fires never take long. But this hour of the day, it's eighteen minutes if you catch the shuttle right out the door, twenty-two if you don't. My house is two minutes past here.

So I'm an expert." Yes. "I'll be at the back door of the station. Not where the trucks go in, not on the side street."

"Back door," I said. "I know what a back door is. I could probably work for the fire department." Now I knew I was flirting, because I was bouncing up and down on the balls of my feet and hoping this conversation would go on this way for a long time.

"I'll be down in eighteen minutes," he said. "In case you have good luck."

I hit traffic on the interstate, I got stuck behind a bus on Carrollton Avenue, I cut through the university section to try the back way and came up against a Sewerage and Water Board barricade that detoured me onto a one-way street going the wrong direction. I hated New Orleans. I had no concept of how much time had passed, but I wasn't making average time.

Instinctively, I parked a block from the station, though at first I didn't know why. Then I realized this was probably the station that served St. John's School. New Orleans was such a small town; I could park next to the fire station and before I would know it all the teachers at St. John's would walk out of a pre-opening meeting and recognize my car and build months' worth of gossip on all the wrong conclusions. That's what happens in New Orleans when a woman is freakish. Or lonely. Maybe it was time to know some of the teachers personally.

It was terribly hot out; according to the radio the heat index was a hundred-ten degrees. The car had not cooled off in the time it took to come all the way into the city, or maybe I wasn't able to keep from perspiring. There was no shade near the back door of the fire station, and I told myself I'd walk off if George Duffy didn't respond by the count of ten. He opened the door before I knocked, and I noticed a peephole in the door. "Big brave boys," I said cheerfully, pointing at it.

"Some stuff's standard," he said. "They don't just build fire stations where all the well-behaved people live."

I was still standing in the direct sunlight, and the scalp where I parted my hair was burning. I was holding my carry cup of coins. I hadn't figured out how I was going to siphon off his effect on me, but the money seemed like a possible place to start.

"I think even the pilgrims at Castel Gandolfo get some shade," I said.

He looked down in the cup. "I'd say something sacrilegious, but you're probably too superstitious," he said. "Come on in. Evidently it takes longer to put out a car fire than to drive all the way in from the casino." I didn't understand. "Nobody's back yet."

"I *can* get you in trouble."

I stepped inside, found myself in a stairwell that wasn't air conditioned. I smelled grease, cooking grease, machine oil, and a hint, if I moved right, of Mennen Speed Stick. My father had used Mennen Speed Stick, and after he died my mother wore it until her anger at him broke through. George Duffy gestured me up the steps with a wave of his hand. Concrete steps. I supposed no one cared how safely firemen went up, and surely this wasn't the way they came down.

We reached no exit until we'd gone up a story and a half, then I found myself, winded from the climb, in a room more spare than even religious devotion would require. A single bed covered only by unpressed sheets, a desk with a radio and telephone, a computer terminal, nothing on the walls. "Well, you're definitely not gay," I said in three unfit breaths.

He looked around the room as if he'd never noticed it before. "We rotate," he said.

"And?"

"And if I put up my photos of Judy Garland the guys on the other two platoons'd be quite pissed."

I was shimmering with interest. This was better than a tour of a convent. With nuns, at least my imagination was fueled by movies with Audrey Hepburn, Meg Tilly, and Whoopi Goldberg. All I knew of fire stations were children's books and field trips to look at the engines. Three different men slept in that bed. "You change your sheets?" I said.

"You're a funny lady, Anna Duffy," he said. "I assume it's Anna Duffy." I nodded. "You really come here for luck, Anna Duffy?" He didn't move closer to me, but rather stepped back, sat down on the bed.

I shrugged. "I only win when you're in the chair next to me," I said. "I'm sure there's a scientific explanation for that."

"Why do you play?" he said, patting a spot a respectable distance from himself on the bed.

"It's personal," I said. I thought I had figured out that I played because I didn't want to feel anything about George Junior, and I assumed I must have been doing a good job because I hadn't gone mute or starved myself to death. So maybe this was about responsibility. I wouldn't have minded him knowing all about that, but I didn't want to waste his time telling it to him.

"Sorry," he said. George Duffy the lawyer would have said something different, some polite form of *fuck you*.

"No, I wouldn't mind telling you, I just don't want to have to *tell* you."

"So," he said, slapping his knees. He wasn't looking straight at me anymore. Suddenly I was embarrassed, the way I pictured people got in psychiatrists' offices when they spilled out a shame and then noticed a painting on the wall that the doctor's wife probably had picked out.

"I don't know," I said. Now that I was there, I couldn't imagine what I'd expected to happen. I put the carry cup on the floor where my skirt hid it from his view. I was going to replay this moment over and over again when I was trying to sleep. And worry it down to an ugly, humiliating nub. This was why I played the slots. I couldn't stand to think.

"I guess you know anybody raised Catholic doesn't like to wave his hands over things," he said, smiling. I hadn't thought about it, but I figured he was about to make this easy for me. I'd never known anyone with an inclination to do so. My mother and George liked nothing better than to see me squirm. "I mean, by my First Communion I knew they weren't kidding. That it wasn't just *symbolism*." I looked at him funny because I didn't know firemen were interested in abstractions. "Wine is wine, for Chrissakes," he said.

I liked his take on Catholicism. "So what do you do for luck?" I said after a while.

"I play well."

"I hear you were down a couple of hundred dollars the other day."

"I had bad luck?" He cocked his head to the side. "No, look, you're playing a random game. I'm not, at least not completely. If skill weren't part of it, I wouldn't be doing it."

"Thanks a lot," I said.

"But you've got your personal reasons." He spoke gently, not mockingly, and I wondered if there were other men like this. George had led me to believe that he was the norm. In fact, better than the norm.

"You don't really think I can do anything for you, do you?" he said.

"You have to." I spoke with the urgency of a child who honestly believes in his need.

He considered for a moment. "The way I see it, you've got a couple of choices. You can go home and hold onto your money until I'm out there. And I *will* sit next to you, as long as you don't tell anyone." My eyes widened. "I mean, that I'm playing into it. Those guys in the poker room are merciless." Okay. I knew some dollar slots far out of view of the poker room.

"Or."

"Or."

"Or you can go out there today and find out you don't need me at all."

"Or."

"Or?"

"I can go out there and find out I do need you after all."

"You're a gambling lady, Anna Duffy," he said, pleased with his joke, laughing and pitching his head back so I could see that all his teeth were either perfect or capped.

I was thinking again, listing in my mind all the rituals I'd imagined I might ask him to do. Saying words over my cup, putting his hands on my hands, giving me something that smelled of him. I couldn't figure out how I'd let myself come so close to being a fool, but I was grateful he hadn't let me.

"Tomorrow," I said, and when he put his hand on the small of my back to lead me to the door I had to strain to face forward, not to turn around and hold him like he'd been my lover for years.

TWENTY

I broke even. No clocks were visible in the casino, surely for good reason, and my only way of gauging the passage of time was by hunger. When the second cycle came, and I knew I had to get home to relieve Ella, I had ninety-seven dollars. I could draw no conclusions from ninety-seven dollars. Count the money spent on the phone call; I was still down $2.65. Count the four dollars I had to pay for a sandwich because it was too early to comp, and I was up $1.35. I was at least holding on, failing no one, and all the figures would make me interesting, give George Duffy the fireman something to think about. I had the feeling he spent his working day in that cell like a prisoner, hoping for a real conflagration.

No one was in my house when I returned. Not Gregor, not Ella; I didn't need to look under the beds. Reflexively I picked up the phone and called my mother's room at the hospital. It rang a half dozen times, but I'd asked for her by name, and the operator hadn't said, "Oh, sorry, she's dead," so I wasn't frightened for her. Only for Gregor. She answered on the eighth ring, sounding groggy and irritable. I asked her if everything was all right. "Do you know how hard it is to answer the phone?" she said miserably. The side table was on her left, now that I thought about it.

"I'll be right over," I said. I liked the notion of someone else's problem I could solve.

"No, no, this's the first time it's happened." She was matter-of-fact, not implying anything.

I phoned Melvin next, and Ella answered. I should have called there first, but I was trying not to think, and evidently I was being successful. "You're home?" I said without identifying myself.

"Miss Anna?"

"Yes."

"I could say the same about you," she said.

The clock in the kitchen indicated that it was after seven, but we were midway between the solstice and the equinox, and the light outside had deceived me. I told her I'd lost track of time. "So where is he?"

She didn't answer right away, and I was starting to be nervous, getting ready to negotiate down in my mind from Gregor's sure death. "You didn't leave no number," she said.

"He's over there," I said, relieved. Melvin's truck had no effective means of strapping in Gregor; she had no right to take him home, but then I had forfeited some of my rights and they had to accrue somewhere.

"He got me to dial his daddy," she said.

"Aw, jeez, Ella, you could've taken him home with you."

"You know Melvin got no good seat belt, not even for me."

I asked her where they had gone, though I knew George would not tell her and she would not ask. Ella was still sure George despised her, and she was probably right. I saw Gregor's arm lying naked and unprotected on the kitchen counter, as if he'd been swept out of the room so quickly that parts had trailed behind.

"I don't talk to that man, and he sure don't talk to me. Feel like *I* got a divorce from him."

I apologized, meaning it, waited a bit before I asked if she could come in tomorrow. "You call me first," she said. "I can come, but you call me first."

Within a half hour, I hated my house. I paced through, noticed where the paint was coming off the wall plaster, leaving little brown islands. Wads of greasy dirt had accumulated wherever the baseboards met. A patch of dust clouds clung to the wallpaper next to the stove vent. For a visitor, who would avoid the peripheries, the house was all right. But all the bad patches were going to spread, if not in actuality then in my mind, and I thought it would be a good idea to move out, let the next occupant clean the parts Ella ignored before the furniture moved in.

I needed to have Gregor. Not to find him, to have him. I wanted to carry him around, feel him close to me, kiss him, delude him about what he could do, listen to his wisdom. I got into the car, determined that I wouldn't return to the house without him. Though I only had two possible places to look. If he wasn't at either, I would ask questions of whoever was there, follow the leads, tamp down panic.

Kathryn Gold's house was not on my way downtown. It was farther downtown than my house, but it wasn't on my back route to George's office. New Orleans's street grid is a matrix moiréed by the curve of the river. No streets are labeled east or west, and South Carrollton Avenue intersects quite neatly with South Claiborne Avenue. In terms of time and mileage, it made more sense to go to the office first, then pass her house on the way back. But I didn't want to do that, preferring to eliminate the worse possibility, even though as I turned onto State Street my heart raced so fast I didn't think I'd be able to speak a word without breathing hard and giving myself away.

George's car was parked out front, the only car parked on the street in the entire block. This was the dinner hour on

State Street, where I assumed all the families worked hard at being intact to prove how right their wealth was. I wondered what the neighbors thought when Kathryn Gold moved in alone, or when Kathryn Gold's husband moved out.

I slammed the car door hard to convince myself of something, and it worked, because I walked up the brick path to her house with long strides and good posture. If any neighbors were sitting in their dining rooms with a view of the street, they could see my anger, break the silence, say, *Oh, my, that Dr. Gold has definitely overstepped her limits*.

The doorbell was set in a security panel, in case anyone had any doubts, and as I pressed it I could hear deep chimes. I heard a woman call out that she would get it, and I was amused that she still had ideas about George being helpful until I realized she probably had a housekeeper who didn't leave until after nightfall.

I liked Kathryn Gold until she spoke. She was not much taller than five feet, with a stocky no-nonsense body and black every-whichway curls. Girls like her in my experience always looked up from under their lashes, not sexily, but rather as if waiting to be hit. "Yes," she said, as if I were selling something better marketed in a less fine neighborhood.

"I'm Anna Duffy," I said, looking straight at her and trying for the life of me to remember what I was wearing. I couldn't picture myself in the casino, or getting dressed; only when I recalled that it was today I'd hidden the coins behind my skirt did I get an image of myself. I'd liked the way I looked at the fire station.

"Oh, come in," she said with the kind of embarrassment that meant, indeed, that she'd seen in my face that my father was a construction worker.

George came up behind her. I could tell he wanted to lash out, but he hadn't shown Kathryn that side of himself. I failed to conceal a smile. He tried to catch Kathryn's eye, remind her how he'd told her I was insane, but she didn't look at him. "No one could find you," he said too gently.

"*I'm* home most of the time," I said.

George looked toward Kathryn again, as if hoping she would leave the room so he could quit behaving. But Kathryn had some questions she wanted answered, and she folded her arms across her fine no-babies chest, waited. She was getting another chance with me. "If you call spending all your waking hours as a compulsive gambler being at home," he said.

"I don't think this is the time or place for this," I said.

"Oh, I'm having a wonderful time," Kathryn said.

"You want the boy?" George said.

"His name's Gregor," I said. I turned to Kathryn. "Did he tell you the boy has a name?"

She smiled. "Actually, I asked Gregor."

The house was a rectangular solid on the outside, but I could see from the foyer the floor plan had the intricacies necessary for arranging rooms in a space with no protrusions. I couldn't figure out where Gregor might be. I asked where he was. "Upstairs with the maid," George said. "Kathryn's paying her time and a half."

"I'd've paid Ella for extra hours," I said. I didn't say, *And Ella doesn't ask for time and a half*, because that would make Kathryn look foolish, and she already was finding out about one mistake.

"Are you divorced?" Kathryn said to George.

"I don't think this is the time or place for this," he said, and I winced.

"What's the girl's name?" he said to Kathryn, ignoring me. She had no clue as to what he was talking about. He pointed up the stairs.

"Tyresia," Kathryn said.

"Tyresia, bring him down, would you, please?" George called up the steps. We stood in silence, probably for no more than a minute, but surely each of us was ticking off seconds. I thought about saying, *Um*, to scare George into thinking I was going to tell Kathryn the truth, but I didn't do it. We heard footsteps, and George exhaled audibly, and I saw two skinny black legs start to shuffle-kick down the curved staircase. Tyresia was holding Gregor, but he wasn't molding his body to hers the way he did when he trusted someone, and Tyresia was clearly not strong enough to make it down the steps with that sort of resistance. I ran up and met her, and she handed Gregor over with relief. "Thanks," she said. Gregor leaned his head on my shoulder, whispered as we descended, "She's nice, but this is a scary house."

"I apologize for all this," I said to Kathryn on the way out the door. If George had told her I was crazy, she wouldn't believe him. She probably wouldn't even believe I lost track of time.

He followed me to my car. Loading Gregor into his car seat was a back-screwing job, and George stood to the side and watched me, not with interest in the process, but with irritation that I was taking so long. Night had fallen just that quickly, and the switch was in the wrong position to turn on the overhead light when the car door was open. I couldn't find the buckle for the seat belt, which was twisted once, making it too taut to secure easily. I lifted my head, as fumbling in the dark was better when I didn't look, and saw George's image contorted in the streetlight. His face seemed to have been stretched over a huge, dim lightbulb rather than a solid-jawed skull; his nostrils flared sanctimoniously. I'd have said that I could use help, but I didn't want him so close, heaving around and scrambling everything up and probably pinching Gregor thoughtlessly. The seat belt clicked just as I began to feel the first itch in the armpits that signaled I was going to break out in a great sweat. I left the car door open; even at night it would be unbearably hot in a closed car. I assumed George wanted to talk to me. He reached over to shut Gregor's door, and I said, "Oh, okay," and proceeded to walk around to the driver's side. "I have something I want to say to you," he said.

"Then don't close Gregor up in the car."

"Private," he said.

I took a few paces away from the car. In New Orleans, you developed an instinct about how far you could be from a child and still keep him safe. In a public park in daylight, it was about twenty feet. On a quiet street at night, it was half that distance. "You'll just have to whisper," I said.

George pulled himself up and flattened himself out the way a cobra frightens its prey. "Thanks a fucking lot for what you tried to do in there," he said.

"I came to get Gregor." I, too, kept my voice down.

"You came to mess up my relationship," he said.

"Did you hear what you just said?"

He became taller, not knowing someone shaped that way looked preposterous trying to threaten. "You know what the trouble with you is, Anna? The trouble with you is you think you're so goddamned smart."

"No."

"Don't tell me you don't. Your mother got this idea, if you tell a kid something, she starts believing it, and here you are, never having done a damn thing with your life, and you think you can make fun of me."

I ignored the insult, realizing at some later date I'd prove he wasn't as sharp as he thought he was. "I can't believe what you said. You've got to admit it's funny." He gave me a look that I knew meant he couldn't remember what he'd said. "You said

I'm here messing up your relationship. Who do you think I am, your college roommate?"

"No, I'm the star boarder in your house. I pay rent, and I get two hot meals a day."

"*My* house?" I hoped all his violations of Louisiana civil code would take spectral form and dance around his head.

"You can have the house," he said with what might very well have been genuine sadness for all I knew.

"I don't want the house," I said. "I want what we had before George Junior died."

"We had jackshit before George Junior died."

"No, we didn't," I said.

"Please stay away from Kathryn," he said.

"And you stay away from Gregor."

All the way home in the car, Gregor uttered only one phrase. "Mommy, do you love me?"

Yes. Three blocks in silence. "Mommy, do you love me?" Yes. "Mommy, do you love me?" I said yes, all the way home.

TWENTY-ONE

I let Gregor sleep with me that night. I wasn't afraid of crushing or smothering him, because Gregor could roll over; he simply couldn't use limbs like curb feelers or whiskers to sense if I came too near. It had struck me as odd that of the two boys, George Junior alone was a bed wetter. Gregor had to wait or call out, and he always waited. George Junior could have done either, or gone to the bathroom on his own, but I figured maybe he had been sad in ways I didn't know about. I lay on my side of the bed, and in the lamplight I'd promised him for the night, I watched Gregor sleep. He preferred his back—a sign of security in animals, my mother always said. George Junior preferred to sleep on his belly, and I once mentioned to my mother that maybe I'd stayed on my back while I was pregnant, and that they liked the positions I'd kept them in before they were born, George Junior on top, Gregor crushed under him, failing to develop. "This sounds like your wonderful notions about Ansel Adams," she said.

"What about Ansel Adams?"

"When you were younger you used to ask about how pigment was patterned in a litter of kittens."

"I was seventeen when we got Ansel Adams," I reminded her, and she raised that eyebrow.

No sooner had I fallen asleep than Gregor began to scream. His screams weren't powerful enough to stop my heart the way an alarm in the night could. They were more like dream cries, emanating from somewhere so deep inside him that they were muffled. I wasn't certain what to do; all I'd ever heard was that waking a sleepwalker was a bad idea. I hadn't lived with very many people, and I knew nothing of others' nightmares. I reached out and held him, figuring his body would register safety and slowly calm his brain. But he stayed rigid, every poor little unused muscle in his body rock tight, and the screams didn't stop. I whispered his name, the quietest intrusion I could think of, and he took in a great breath, waited as if listening for his name again. "Gregor?" He opened both eyes halfway, blinked, let out a whimper. "You had a nightmare," I said, brushing his hair off his fore-head.

"Mommy, do you love me?" he said.

"I love you more than anything on earth," I said, and realized I meant it.

"I listened, you know."

"Listened to what?" One day I would be able to read his mind as well as my mother read mine, and I would use the connection as a way of letting him go.

"He was talking to that lady. Me and Tyresia listened. She doesn't like her, either." I said nothing, waited with a delighted sort of horror. "Know how sometimes you can tell things? I could tell she didn't know he was a daddy before. He ought to've told her at least about George. He really loves George. But he never *did* tell her about George."

"He's sad about George. I don't talk about George, either, sometimes." I didn't like myself for sounding as if I were tak-ing the high road when I really wanted Gregor to say, *No that's not it.*

"No, that's not it."

"No?"

Gregor whispered, as if George Senior were in the room. "He doesn't want to be a father."

"Aw, baby, that can't be true." This time I wanted him to believe me.

"Know what he said? He said, 'Sometimes I think about drownding that one, too.' He said that to the lady. I'm not making it up."

I struggled not to exhale, knowing my breath would come out ragged. "No, I know you tell the truth."

"I asked Tyresia, 'Does she have a pool?' And Tyresia said no, so I wasn't scared before you came, but you know what?"

"What?"

"I could get drownded in the bathtub. I think even grown-ups can, I've seen it on TV. And they could get *up*."

I sat up in the bed, propped Gregor up. "Listen to me, buddy. Sometimes people say things they don't really mean. Your daddy is not going to drown you."

He thought that one through for a while, trying to decide whether he should accept his mother's unbelieving tone or his father's sure one. "He couldn't be a lawyer if he killed a person, right?"

"He doesn't want to kill you," I said, resisting an urge to kiss him all over, on his face, his tummy, his neck, the way I could do when he was a baby and wouldn't protest. "He was just trying to impress that lady."

"I hope she thinks it's a bad idea, killing people."

"She's a doctor," I said, then tried to muffle a laugh. Gregor gave me a bemused, quizzical look. "Doctors take this oath, see? They *swear*. They're not going to hurt anybody— more than anything they promise that. So they go out and save lives, and you know what this doctor does?" He shook his head no, his eyes wide the way he must have imagined an attentive adult's would be. "This doctor goes out and picks at your pimples!"

"What's a pimple?" he said. "Like a pimple dog?"

I was still struggling not to laugh. "A pimple dog?"

"A pimple dog. I don't want a pimple dog. They get loose in people's yards and they eat kids to death."

"Oh, my God, a pit bull dog," I said, and I rolled on top of Gregor, giggling and tickling him and generally ruining all chances that either of us would fall back asleep anytime soon.

At three in the morning, when Gregor was sitting up in my bed watching *A Night to Remember* with a fierce, tearful intelligence, I finally got angry. I told him I was going to the kitchen, but if he heard me he paid no attention. He was fighting sleep by then, and though he knew at the outset how the movie would end, he had to see for himself who survived.

I dialed Kathryn Gold's number. "This is Anna Duffy. May I speak to George, please?" No sense in being rude; she already had enough to be regretful about.

"It's the middle of the night. People are sleeping," she said.

"Well, clearly *I'm* not."

George was on the line in a matter of seconds, not at all interested in pretending he was sleeping in a guest room. "This had better be good," he said, and his voice wasn't muffled. He had learned that Kathryn Gold could witness an enormous amount of ugliness and allow herself to be told it was justified.

"I am sitting here with a child who screamed in his sleep until he woke himself up."

"It's the middle of the night," he said.

"Of course it's the fucking middle of the night." I kept my voice low so that Kathryn wouldn't hear me letting go.

"Anna, I've bent over backwards to be patient with you . . . "

"Do you want to know why he woke up screaming in the middle of the night? I'll tell you why. You take him to this strange woman's house, you hand him off to a baby-sitter—"

"I remind you—"

"You hand him off to a baby-sitter, and then you proceed to tell this strange woman that you'd just as soon see him drown, too."

"Who told you that?" he said.

"Who do you *think* told me that?" I paused, because it occurred to me that he honestly didn't know. "*Gregor* told me that, for Chrissakes."

I could hear ambient sound disappear as George put his hand over the receiver. But he was too loud to cover everything, and I was sure I heard something about "that crazy maid of yours."

I called his name into the phone, loud as if he had stepped away and forgotten to come back. "What," he said.

"Is that all you have to say?" I said sadly.

"Look, the girl that works here, she's new, she probably lives in one room with six people, she's probably never heard of privacy, and taking care of kids is not exactly in her job description, so you can't really blame her."

"George, she isn't the one who said she wanted Gregor dead."

He didn't even hesitate. "Hey, I have every right to be having a private conversation. It's not *my* fault the boy was over here."

I told him to put Kathryn on the line. I wasn't going to tell her he was married, I was going to tell her that if she were smart she'd have George out of her house before daybreak.

"You must think I'm out of my goddamn mind," he said and hung up.

Gregor was asleep sitting up when I returned to the bedroom. A commercial for Frankie and Johnny's furniture store was playing, and Gregor's eyelashes were wet. I knew I didn't need to move him gingerly; he was too far down into a sleep of pure exhaustion.

The call wakened me. "This is Dr. Louviere's office. Mrs. Riggs?" the nurse said, and for a moment I was confused, thinking this was some sort of emergency involving my mother, but not understanding why someone would phone her to tell her about herself. I mumbled that I was her daughter, heard my voice come up out of dreams. "Oh, Mrs. Duffy?" she said.

"Yes."

"We're calling to remind your mother about Gregor's appointment." I told her my mother was in the hospital, and she was silent for a moment. "Do you want to reschedule?" she said finally.

I had no choice but to come awake, think. Gregor was stirring next to me, grumpy; I had no idea what time it was, but assumed it was after nine. "Will it mess him up if someone new comes?" I said, and Gregor's eyes came open. "Who?" he said, and I told the nurse to hold. "It's your Dr. Louviere. You have an appointment." I half wished he'd insist on going with his grandmother; as long as I was not directly involved, George could not one day reveal in court that I was responsible for whatever he seemed to know was terribly wrong about prosthetics.

"Ella could take me," he said. I didn't cross his mind at all.

"Don't reschedule," I told the nurse.

When I seated him at the island in the kitchen, I noticed the prosthesis lying on the counter. I tucked the Rice Krispies box under my arm, picked up the implement with both hands, walked toward Gregor. "You don't have to be scared of it," he said.

"I don't want to break it." I couldn't say, *I don't want your daddy to see me with it*. I wondered why George was scared by it.

"Dr. Louviere says it's a boy arm, so it's very strong."

I asked him if he wanted to practice, all the while holding it out in front of me the way Kunta Kinte's father had held him. Gregor giggled. "You're still scared of it," he said.

"You're a sweetheart, you know that?" I said, and he let me feed him his Rice Krispies, with milk and no sugar. George Junior had liked his with three heaping teaspoons of sugar. George Junior never had had a cavity, and Gregor had had six. "I brush his teeth twice a day," I'd told the dentist, not saying that George Junior on his own never cleaned much more than the upper incisors. "It's not your fault," he said to Gregor. "And it's not your fault, either," he said to me.

When I phoned Ella as promised, she said, "I could be there eleven, that all right? Melvin getting new seat belts, figure he's going to need them."

"I'll pay for them," I said.

"No need," she said. "I been telling that man he going to get a ticket if he lucky, a concussion if he not. He doing it because the baby fuss at him."

"Gregor?"

"Gregor tell him, 'You can live with no arm and leg, but no head *hard*, yeah. Melvin crazy about that child."

This one time, Ella and Melvin could find Dr. Louviere. I would learn about Gregor's arm soon, once I knew what George knew. I would be *deus ex machina* for now; that was a good one, but I felt no urge to share it with my mother. I told Gregor, "Next time."

"Don't worry," he said, "it's *my* arm."

TWENTY-TWO

I felt no need to rush to the casino, because George Duffy was the sort to stay awhile. It was almost noon by the time I left my mother. Now that she wasn't completely helpless, she was bored and irritated and trying heroically to hide it. I caught her during physical therapy, and she was being a good soldier for the therapist, clenching her teeth and letting the woman push her limbs much farther than my mother wanted them to go. "Talk to me," she said, breathing hard as her knee bent almost to her waist.

"I met George's girlfriend," I said, then felt I should be polite, let the therapist in on the conversation. "My estranged husband," I explained, and the woman stopped in the middle of an ankle wiggle to process the information.

"Go on," my mother huffed to one of us, and the rotation of her ankle resumed in earnest.

"She's sort of short and sturdy and dark, and she's a doctor, but I already told you that, right?"

"I don't care what she looks like," my mother said. Her speech was coming back, I noticed.

"I went inside her house."

"Don't care what her house looks like, either," she said and let out a yelp of pain.

"She wants to know what happened," the therapist said.

"Gregor overheard him say he hoped Gregor'd drown."

"Stop," my mother said to the therapist, and made me repeat what I'd just said.

"He passes the child over to the housekeeper, who evidently enjoys putting in a stick and stirring it, and Gregor eavesdrops on his daddy seducing some woman. He's going to grow up thinking the way to a single woman's heart is by telling her you'd just love to kill off your last child."

"Gregor's going to grow up thinking something far worse," my mother said.

"Poor baby," the therapist said. I realized she didn't know the half of it. And I felt no need to explain; the story was bad enough.

When I was walking out of her hospital room, my mother's words to me had been, "You use directory assistance, you use the Internet, you call one of those services they advertise on TV, but I want his mother's phone number." On the way to the casino, I realized I probably could sidestep all those processes. I hadn't seen George pack his address book. And he was the type to put his mother in an address book. I might leave fingerprints on it, unfold a handkerchief or two in the drawer where he kept it, dare him to confront me.

Two games of poker were running when I reached the poker room; the sign over both read "Omaha," and I almost decided not to bother looking for George Duffy. But he was impossible to miss in that day's crowd. No one young, no one female, no one, really, with a full head of hair. But George Duffy just had pitched back in his chair, laughing at something one of the old men had said. I liked men among men; I'd never seen my husband talk to another man without sounding as if a microphone were thrust in his face and he was covering up something.

My mother once had said to me, "Do you think George ever played team sports?" and I'd said, "Too bourgeois," and she'd said, "Lacrosse?" and I'd said, "Too agile."

George Duffy stood up when he saw me, and I felt like tossing my hair to the side like a popular girl. The men sitting on either side of him looked at me and smiled with no innuendo. "Ready?" he said. I saw he had three trays of chips, and no one at the table was doing as well. "You're ahead," I said.

"And I will be when I get back," he said.

As we walked toward the slots, I told him I'd forgotten my money at home. I'd realized it when I drove up to the hospital and tried to decide between a parking meter and the garage. All my wallet held was a quarter and two nickels, and when I thought about borrowing from my stake I learned I didn't have it. I found a meter with thirty-seven minutes left on it, held onto the quarter and nickels in case I needed to make a phone call, planned to use the ATM at the casino. I couldn't backtrack.

George Duffy stood back when I put my mother's card into the machine. "You don't have to do that," I said.

"You shouldn't trust me," he said. "I mean, you should trust *me*, but really, you shouldn't trust anybody."

"I don't trust anybody, I just trust you," I said, and I took out three hundred dollars.

He wasn't close enough to see the PIN, but he couldn't help seeing the machine deal out all the twenties. "Maybe you shouldn't trust *yourself*," he said.

I felt lucky, and I played the five-dollar slots, and with George Duffy at my side I lost three hundred dollars in about twenty minutes. He sat back in the chair next to mine, let out a great sigh of relief. "Thank goodness," he said.

"What?"

"That was a big responsibility, all that power I had over you."

"Hey," I said, "I'm down three hundred. The day's not over." I rose to go back to the ATM. He grabbed me by the wrist to hold me back. So this was what firemen were all about. The grip was firm, but it told me he'd let go if I wanted. I imagined that firemen made love gently, that they could carry a woman as if she were burned all over. "Three hundred more and I'll quit," I said.

"It's your money," he said.

"No, it's my mother's money." I realized what kind of person I sounded like. "She's not going to die. I'll pay her back."

"I won't tell your mother on you, if you won't tell my mother on me," he said, and I smiled because it was funny, not because I would have to go home that night and rifle through George's dresser drawer so my mother could tell his mother how he'd gone wrong. My mother-in-law seemed like the type to rejoice that George was sloughing off trash, but my mother clearly thought the woman would see only the unseemly behavior. No one in Mrs. Duffy's circle knew George was married to the daughter of a construction worker and a rat decapitator; that she could keep to herself. Probably none had been told her grandson was a freak. But she'd have a harder time containing herself over news that her own son fooled around. Broadcasting one's indignation looked good.

I took out six hundred this time; a debt of an even thousand was easier to remember. George Duffy watched with what looked like consternation. "Stop expecting me to lose," I said.

When I was down three hundred more, he spoke for the first time. "If you play when you're losing, you have a problem," he said.

"A hundred more," I said, and with will I made that hundred last half an hour. George Duffy was patient, sitting beside me as if he didn't have several trays of chips waiting for him. When

I played the last of that hundred, I spoke before he could. "I'm not losing. I'm up and down, and you know it."

"How about a break?" he said, as if he'd sat there for a while deciding that was what he needed to say.

"A hundred more," I said. It was gone in ten minutes, and to show him I could stop, I offered to treat him to lunch. "Not from your stake," he said. "Never from your stake."

"I'm investing," I said, feeling flighty and ambiguous. He said he had a comp and would pay for me. "See, I already made something," I said, and he gave me a qualified smile, the sort I'd give if I couldn't resist a child's naughtiness.

He cashed out his chips, ordered a muffuletta with French fries. I chose a green salad, and he told me I didn't need to skimp on cost, that he might be an employee of the City of New Orleans but he wasn't destitute. "I'm thinking longevity," I said, looking at the ham, salami, and provolone soaked in olive salad on his sandwich. He shrugged. "All firemen do is plan meals and eat them and start planning the next one, and maybe sometimes we go to fires."

"Like you're always having your last meal?"

He looked as if that had never occurred to him before. "Nah," he said. "We just like to cook." He shook enough salt on his fries to season a cauldron of soup.

"You're insane," I said, and I stuffed an uncut piece of lettuce into my mouth to show I wasn't prissy.

"Tell me the last time you saw a fireman in the obituaries."

"How'd you know I read the obituaries?" I said. I'd been reading them only recently, in the weeks since George Junior had died. Most children listed died in infancy or succumbed to tumors they probably were born with. A stray bullet took one every now and then. In almost every case, parents were helpless.

"Lucky guess," he said.

"You have children?"

I could tell he followed my non sequitur, because he looked me in the eye in a way I could not explain. "No," he said, "I'm still a child myself. Why?"

"Just asking."

"Okay," he said. "You'd say if you wanted to."

We ate in silence, and I tried not to watch him because he had no way to eat a sandwich like that without looking disgusting, it seemed to me. "I want to tell you something," he said finally, and I could tell he wasn't speaking with his mouth full, so I looked up at him. He had a modest streak of oil in the crease above his chin, and I liked him for it.

"Okay," I said.

"Whatever you think you did, to make you want to destroy yourself, it can't be that terrible."

"Good God," I said.

He shrugged. "I spend a lot of time at the card table."

"Meaning?"

"You're blowing money like you want to get caught or something."

That I didn't believe. "You don't know my circumstances," I said.

"No," he said softly, "I don't."

"I'm here to win. Pure and simple. Either slowly or quickly. But I need to win. I have to have a lot of money. All right? I mean, I'm not in it for the pleasure of it."

"You think alcoholics like the taste?" he said.

I felt like getting up, walking away, but he didn't deserve it. "I don't like this," I said, surprising myself. I wondered why I'd never uttered that phrase before.

"I'm not saying you've got a problem. Yet."

"Ah, catch her before she gets too compulsive," I said, and because my voice was sardonic I tipped my head to the side, let him know I wasn't a mean compulsive.

"Think about it."

"Look, you want to know my situation?"

"No," he said, and for a moment I wondered whether he was married or instead was one of those men who would look away if a woman showed too much flesh or too much honesty.

"I'll be impersonal as hell about it," I said, and he laughed. "I've got a lot of responsibilities and no resources," I said. "How's that for general?"

"Why do you think they blink that progressive jackpot figure in three colors of neon?" he said.

"Okay," I said. "But you've got to admit it's a dream that isn't too farfetched. I mean, it's *local*."

"You throw the sweepstakes mailings in the trash?"

"Every time," I said proudly.

"Tell you what. You take that hundred home, buy a share of Merck, I'll feel better."

I'd heard of people who watched CNBC all day long; I'd seen TVs set on it during market trading hours in restaurants. I'd tried it a time or two, watching the Dow Jones rise and fall second after second, tracking a single stock. But George had walked in on me. "If you get all your information from television, you'll be broke inside a week," he'd said with contempt. I didn't tell him that I was mesmerized by the game of making little bets with myself: If I hold my breath until Coca-Cola comes up again, I win; if Pepsi closes down one point today, I win.

"A person can get pretty badly hooked on the stock market," I said, though I knew he could argue that the stock market wasn't random, that it was hard right then to lose everything.

"One share."

"There's no anonymity in investing," I said. With the slots, I faced a machine, my back to other people, and I could make all the mistakes I wanted.

"Give me the hundred, I'll do it for you," he said, and when that sounded like a good idea, I knew it was because I would see him again. I smiled. "You think I'll abscond with your money," he said.

"That never occurred to me."

"I know," he said. "Firemen may siphon off premium cable channels, and we may run bookie joints in the stations, but generally we're sitting ducks."

"That's not why it never occurred to me," I said.

"I know," he said, but he didn't look me in the eye.

TWENTY-THREE

Ella and Gregor came home after I did. It was more than two hours past his appointment time, but because I knew nothing of the process I didn't fret. Ella bounced through the house carrying Gregor at a good clip. "You got to let me have this child," she said.

"I told Mommy I was a winning boy," Gregor said.

Ella smothered him in kisses, which he wouldn't have wiped off if he could have. "We been standing up in the E-Z Serve over a hour," she said.

"Show her," Gregor said.

"Wait, wait," Ella said, and I had a feeling I knew what was coming. "I tell him, 'You want a Coke?' He say, no, he want a scratch-off."

"How much did you win?" I said, knowing Ella wasn't dancing around over petty cash.

Now Gregor was bouncing up and down. "Wait, wait," Ella said. "You know that was my dollar, right?" she said to me.

"Whatever deal you two sharpies worked out is okay with me."

"Three hundred apiece!" she shrieked. "I just stand there, this boy tell me, 'Get five of them,' and sure enough, the fifth one, you get a twenty-dollar payout. Then he say, 'Ella, get ten of those, somewhere in that bunch you get a hundred dollars.' Six hundred dollars, Miss Anna. This child know what he saying."

"Gregor?"

He shrugged, but only his right shoulder. He was wearing the prosthetic arm, but it was nestled so neatly in the happy folds of Ella's chest that I hadn't noticed it. "I think I have very good luck," he said.

I wanted my hundred dollars back from George Duffy. It was a stake so much larger than Ella's; we'd do well. I could stand there and look at Gregor and love him, see him as my partner. Moses and Addie Pray, running our *Paper Moon* scam, our honest scam that could make us giggle over our secret. We could go from convenience store to grocery store to newsstand so no one would notice us, make six hundred dollars a day, tell George we didn't need to see him again.

"No, Mommy," Gregor said, seeing my glassy eyes.

"No, what?"

"I think you want to play it all the time."

"You've got to admit, it's a lot of fun."

"Nothing's fun if you do it over and over," he said.

Ella planted another big wet kiss on his cheek. "You too much," she said.

Gregor's face registered mock disdain. "That won't get you anywhere, Ella," he said, and she let out all the giddy laughter that came of having more cash than she expected.

As I watched Gregor practice using his arm that evening, taking half an hour to put about a hundred calories in his mouth, I saw he didn't believe that repetition was necessarily bad. But I'd had time to picture myself, standing up in crowded public places, quizzing him on our plays as if he were a ventriloquist's dummy, and I saw no pleasure in the idea. It wasn't mindless or numbing; it meant the stress of others' scrutiny. And it meant unpredictability. With a slot machine I could think of nothing at all, or watch the patterns on the grid in front of me, trying to please myself visually. *Buy five of those, now try ten of those, there's nothing good here, let's go somewhere else*: Attention was necessary. And if Gregor lost or made an error, I would have to see his disappointment. "We could of been rich," Gregor whispered. "I'm sorry."

I waved a hand around the kitchen of George's three-hundred-thousand-dollar house. "This isn't what I call *poor*," I said.

"Daddy says this is his house."

"True," I said. "Very true."

I could have told him his daddy was a lawyer who thought I didn't know the law, and then I'd have had to explain concepts that bored me. But I let it go because I was thinking too much about getting money from somewhere besides George. My half of the house, my half of his piece of the partnership: I owned these because I'd taken on the job of rounding out George's life plan. Even though I hadn't done well at it. All he had to show for knowing me was a child he preferred to see dead. I wasn't sure what was supposed to come of a marriage anyway, surely not definition, possibly not entertainment except in manageable doses. I'd figured early on that George simply liked the comfortable contours of the word "wife"; it had a protective sound to it. He had to have one, just as he once had had to have Order of the Coif, and now had a tennis club membership.

My mother phoned shortly after I put Gregor in bed. "Hey, you're doing well," I said to her.

"It took me half an hour to do this maneuver," she said.

"Sorry."

"I'm joking," she said. "If you're not difficult, nurses don't mind doing favors."

"I could be there if you want," I said, although I was tired; I was certain she would refuse. Since she wasn't going to die, I found her absence simplified my life in every way except the purely practical. And assuming little fragments of her responsibilities in return for no longer being the repository of all her hopes seemed like a fine deal, if I thought about it.

"I'd have to amuse you all day," she said. I asked her what she was calling for. If she was using up her chits with the nurse, she wasn't calling to alleviate my boredom. "You get the phone number for George's mother yet?" she said.

I told her no, I'd forgotten about it. That was true, though I wondered what excuse I would use the next time she asked. This could amount to nothing more than my mother-in-law being given a fine chance to insult me.

"I'm going to keep after you on this one," she said, and I felt the old tightness in my stomach that came of having my mother's hand pressing against the small of my back, urging me to speak to someone older and taller. "If you don't get it for me, you know I'm going to look for it as soon as I get out of here. And you're not the type to hide it from me, either. Not successfully, anyway."

"Jesus, Mama," I said, "does it ever occur to you that this is not normal?"

"Someday you'll have children of your own." She'd been saying that all my life, and she hadn't stopped for even a day when the boys were born.

I told her I was serious. She was quiet for a moment, and I thought she might be getting weepy because she was so emotionally friable.

"Mama?"

Her voice was dry and terribly cheerful. "I don't have a lot to do in here except think, you know. That mess on television is horrid. And this little girl comes in with a cart of magazines,

I take one so I don't hurt her feelings, but I'm not about to make myself hysterical trying to turn a page. I'm afraid you're the entertainment." I sighed, and she asked me what time it was. It was quarter to nine.

"You're going to have a visitor," she said. "Are you presentable?"

"Are you insane?"

It had to be George. I was looking forward to going to bed as soon as I hung up the phone. Being in the bed alone, reading, turning off the light when I was good and ready: I never had done that before. Either I'd had my mother poking around our little house, waiting for me to go to sleep so she could read and turn off the light when she was good and ready, or I'd had George. If George didn't want sex, he wanted the lights out as soon as he'd slipped in between the sheets. I didn't want George to come over and rile me up so that when I finally went to bed my eyes would skim past the words on the pages while I thought of what I should have said.

"I called Kathleen Andrews."

"Who's that?" It was a nice name for a nurse; all I could picture in my mother's life were nurses.

"Kathleen. We talked about her the other day. Who's had the stroke here?"

I couldn't remember talking about a Kathleen. I associated the name Kathleen with the girl in school who wrote coffin stories; whenever I saw an actress named Kathleen who didn't have that Black Irish coloring of the girl I knew from school, I felt something was amiss. We *had* talked about Kathleen the other day. "Kathleen Christopher?" I said.

"It's Andrews now, and I'm here to tell you she's as moody as ever."

"Thanks a lot." Now I would go to bed thinking about being buried alive.

"Anna, she's a lawyer. Yes, yes, I know, a real estate lawyer. But *every* lawyer knows domestic law. They love nothing better than protecting themselves."

I tried to imagine what was going to show up on my doorstep momentarily. An attorney who made housecalls was silly enough, standing on the porch wielding a briefcase like a doctor's black bag. I put a homburg on her head. Kathleen had been bone-thin in school; her arms could bend backward at the elbow. Her mother had given her perms, and she had walked around with her head down, the erratic curls often failing to cover her face. No breasts, a homburg and no breasts, poor Kathleen.

Kathleen wore no homburg; otherwise she was the Kathleen I imagined. She stood framed in my doorway, head down, as if she still expected a crowd to mock her. Suddenly I was terribly shy, as if I were responsible for protecting her. "Thanks for coming," I said.

"No problem," she said and walked into my house. I realized now that she kept her head lowered so she could charge into rooms. Her briefcase was hardsided, and when it bumped my thigh I knew a bruise was coming.

"I have no idea why you're here," I said when she was seated on the edge of the sofa, briefcase on lap, knees together, sheathed in panty hose that had one small, forgivable run.

"I owe your mother," she said with what sounded like affection. "She may be meddlesome, but sometimes she's worth it." I gave her a look that said I had no concept of what she was talking about. "She raised unholy hell when we were twelve; she said *then* she wasn't going to tell you. Though I guess I wouldn't have minded. You never talked to anyone, either."

It was coming back to me, but only in nonsensical fragments. My mother the rat executioner had heard the tale of Kathleen's aborted horror-writing career—from me—when twelve-year-old Kathleen was probably still sitting in her own bedroom, pale with defeat, too humiliated to tell her own parents. My mother had responded by urging me to invite this terribly misunderstood girl over, and I had refused flat out. Evidently she hadn't stopped there.

Kathleen gave me an undecipherable smile. "Your mother hollered at the teacher—what was his name?"

"Kenyon."

She rolled her eyes up in her head. "She hollered at Mr. Kenyon until he kept Phillip after school and made him apologize for making fun of me. She said, and these are probably her exact words, 'You get one sensitive kid in this school, and all you do is shut her up.'"

"So my mother says you're a lawyer," I said, a little peeved. I didn't like the idea that my mother had gone to school to save another girl, even if perhaps she was saving her so she could be packaged as a friend for me. I was sensitive, and my mother never had noticed.

Kathleen shrugged. "Well, I'm not exactly sensitive anymore." She smiled, and I had to smile back.

"You're in George's firm. You're in real estate. I told my mother we should leave you alone."

"You should've known better," she said. I heard that affection again, but it seemed as if it might be washing over onto me a bit.

"Yeah," I said, and I wondered what it would have been like if I'd asked Kathleen over after school, taken her to my room, laughed with her under the approving supervision of my mother. I offered her something to drink, hoped she'd want a Coke. Wine or coffee would intrude on my fantasy.

"Thanks, but I promise I won't stay long." Kathleen might break kneecaps with her briefcase, but she still had a deep lode of seventh grade in her. She didn't speak for a moment, as if she'd come with a good phrase and now didn't like the way it might come out. "Hell," she said finally, "I might as well be blunt."

"Okay."

"I can't think of anything I'd rather do than screw George Duffy into the ground."

"Oh, shit," I said. "She's given you the impression that my marriage is over."

"I've got the impression your marriage is over."

The jolt of adrenaline that went through me was so powerful I thought it would make me stop hearing. And in fact, Kathleen's voice seemed to become muffled, the same way grief can be covered over by shock.

"If he's fucking around, I don't want to hear it."

"Your mother said you knew he was fucking around."

"I know he's fucking one person."

Kathleen flopped back on the sofa, clearly relieved that we had the same information. "That's not enough?"

I knew nothing of her life, and almost as little of how much she knew about mine. I could forgive George for falling in love after George Junior died, but the idea of explaining that exhausted me. "It's not so bad," I said. "I mean, it doesn't embarrass me so much if it's just one, you know?" I heard what I said, and it didn't sound believable. A satyr with no feeling was a fool, and so was a woman whose husband replaced her with one other. "I don't know what I mean," I said.

"You better get over the idea that all this reflects on you," Kathleen said.

I shrugged. "I don't know why image matters. It's not as if anyone's looking at me."

"God, I hate your husband," Kathleen said.

"Please have a Coke," I said, and she laughed as if she knew I wanted to go back almost fifteen years, lie across beds and be passionate about boys the way we assumed other girls had done.

She stood in my kitchen as familiar as could be and said, "He almost cost me the partner track. He tell you about that?"

"Of course not." For all I knew, George went down to his office every day and sold drugs.

"I'll never know why he was out to get me, but he gave me an unsatisfactory on every criterion. With reasons, all trumped up, like I didn't bill enough hours or I couldn't draft documents or anything he could think of. He's not particularly crazy about women, you know."

I shrugged. It never had occurred to me that George had opinions on anything except my failings. "Later someone told me that the partners told him he was setting me up for a sexual discrimination suit and he'd better cut the crap. He still gave me a bad evaluation."

I was astonished by my own reaction: I pictured George in a crisp white shirt and a red tie delivering strong arguments in front of those partners who were powerful men, and I found the image attractive. But attractive in a way I could handle: Either I'd lure him back at all costs, or I'd damage him in a way he would notice.

"I don't want to divorce him until I have my own money," I said.

"That's why your mother called *me*."

I liked the way Kathleen talked in riddles. She threw a cryptic phrase at me, let me quickly travel its synapses, find nothing, and say, *I give*. "I assume she didn't call you to give me money," I said. "And I know she didn't call you to get me a job where you work."

"She said, and I quote, 'Please talk Anna into going after George's money.'"

"God, that's sickening," I said. Kathleen gave me a quizzical look around the side of her upended Coke can. "My mother's whole life plan revolves around my being a freeloader. No wonder George treated you like shit. He probably thinks all women are like me. And, come to think of it, like my *mother*."

"Right," she said. Another enigma. "I'm definitely the person who's going to come over here for that. You've got to stop thinking about George supporting you and start thinking about your taking community money. Your mother says it'll punish him; I'm willing to suggest you use it to save yourself."

"Our kid died," I said quietly. George had said that when I'd killed George Junior—and eventually that was the way he put it—I'd killed him, George. A better version of him. Not because my genes were an improvement, he always hastened to add, but because George Junior would have had him for a father. I would ask what his father was like, hoping to learn something, and he would refuse to answer. My boy would have as little knowledge of his origins as a child in a tight-sealed adoption. "George sort of got punished already."

"And you didn't?"

I shrugged. George Duffy the fireman had told me, with his answer to my lifeboat question at the casino, that what had happened in the pool that day had been a *disaster,* and I'd done what anyone would have done—save the one who was helpless. But George Duffy the lawyer had said that I'd drowned the one I didn't like, and his word reached me in a place where a good man's could not. George Junior's death was no retribution for me, because George said I wanted it.

"Look," Kathleen said, and she slammed down the half-empty Coke can with exactly enough force for no liquid to spew out the top. I could see in that second why she was able to pretend she was a fierce lawyer and not a woman who should have grown up to wear black and write haunting stories. "You may be the first woman George has bullied into thinking she's worthless, but you're hardly the last. I guarantee if you drag him into court, you'll have a dozen female attorneys working for you pro bono."

"You know, just once," I said after a while, "just once I'd like to have an idea that didn't come straight from my mother." I fought back tears the way a humiliated child might. Kathleen was, after all, permanently twelve years old in my mind.

"She figured you'd say that."

I groaned. "Kathleen, I wanted to get money on my own."

"You don't have a degree?" I told her no. "Your mother said to remind you there aren't a lot of fun jobs out there." Oh, God, my mother surely had told her how she'd earned a living. Imagine word about that getting around the seventh grade. "So go to school. On George's money. He owes you. It's called restitution."

"School?"

"School. You can read every book in the library, but if no one's graded you on it, all you're good for is entertaining your mother with your imagination." She winced with disloyalty, but the wince wasn't real; she was clearly proud that she knew so well what went on between my mother and me. "And trust me," she said. "George is terrified by knowledge he can't master. As long as it's formal."

George always said, "Trust me," but I didn't tell Kathleen that. "What if he wants to come back? He might come back, you know." My mother might come back, too, I realized.

"He might," she said with no conviction. "You know who the woman is?"

"I know she's a doctor," I said, more proud of her than I was of my mother. "Not exactly the kind of woman George can look down on." Kathleen folded her arms across her chest and raised her eyebrows. "Oh," I said, "sorry."

"For your information, Kathryn Gold used to weigh about three hundred pounds."

I felt like hugging Kathleen, like making her my best friend since seventh grade. "Aw, jeez, no wonder I felt like liking her," I said.

TWENTY-FOUR

Merck vacillated that week. Up one and five-eighths, and I considered calling George Duffy the fireman and buying more. Down a quarter, and I thought about going out to the casino and finding him, telling him he'd led me astray. By the time I'd negotiated my mother home, it had closed out the week up one and a quarter, and I'd translated that into $1.25, hardly the route to solvency. I took it as a sign. George Duffy the fireman wasn't going to save me; George Duffy the lawyer was going to buy me a good liberty. I phoned Tulane. "I'll major in psychology, minor in statistics," I told the admissions officer.

"Sounds good," she said gently, as if people my age hung up quickly.

"I plan to be a famous poker player," I said, and she laughed with relief. Maybe I would make friends at college.

The physical therapist had told my mother she could go home if she could continue with her exercises. She told her that in front of me, and I wanted to say, *Keep her until she's fixed; I can't bring myself to touch her*, but the woman was young, with a terrible generosity of spirit, and I could see her years from then, remembering me badly, using me as an example of one who thwarts recovery, perhaps writing an article about me.

"We could get someone in," I said instead to my mother.

"We were hoping you'd say that," my mother said with a conspiratorial wink to the therapist, thinking she was still bilking George, and I realized that I was ready for her to go out and find new daughters.

"I want the Virginia phone number," she said as soon as I had her headquartered on the living-room sofa.

"You're pushing too hard, Mama." I'd never mentioned Kathleen's visit, and to her credit she hadn't asked, but we both knew this was her second major interference.

"Sit," she said, patting the sofa cushion on her right. She was perched on the center cushion, leaving nowhere comfortably distant to sit beside her. I sat, crosslegged, facing her, the small of my back pressing against the arm of the sofa. "I know you'd feel better if I moved out," she said, meaning it, and some of the revulsion subsided. "In the meantime, I've *got* to meddle." She cocked her head to the side in case I'd forgotten she was, after all, a funny lady. I unfolded.

"What would you say to her?"

"I don't know. It'd depend on how she acts."

I'd known George eight years, and every few months I'd cycle into rage about his mother, daydream about telling her off. Usually I'd imagine myself hopping a plane at full fare when I had my nerve, hiring a driver to soothe myself, pulling up to her house, ringing the bell. I pictured her house as a Thomas Jefferson sort of building: All I knew of Virginia were the pictures I'd seen of the university, bricks and Monticello-nickel lines. I'd be dressed in linen, uncreased by travel, and her housekeeper would be impressed, let me in. She would come down the steps, in linen, too, and I would say, *I'm Anna Riggs Duffy, and you're no better than I am*. Then I'd turn on my heel, walk out, and she'd run after me, grab my linen-sheathed arm, cry because she'd misjudged me. At George Junior's funeral, I wasn't at the apogee of the rage cycle. And if I had been

I wouldn't have known it. Three feet away from me: She'd have heard me if I'd called out, *I'm Anna Riggs Duffy, and you're no better than I am.* Everyone would have heard me; the story would have traveled across the city, unembroidered.

"Have a plan, Mama."

"I've got an opening line," she said. "And I've got one point I'll *definitely* get across."

"Yes?"

"I'll say, 'This is Dorothy Riggs in New Orleans. Do you know who I am?'"

"And she'll say yes. Or she'll say no."

"I don't want to think that far in advance," my mother said, and she wasn't kidding.

"But you've got your point to make."

"Trust me, it won't be hard to get to. All I have to say is, *Oh, by the way*. . . Now, get me the number. Please."

George was so compartmentalized that I went where I expected his address book to be, and there it was, nestled in his top dresser drawer along with his nail kit, handkerchiefs, and the wristwatch he wore before he decided to be sophisticated. Under D, she was listed as MLD, as if he couldn't figure out what else to write.

I listened in on the extension phone, a portable I kept in the bedroom. For some reason I trusted my mother. The voice that answered wasn't what I expected: not a gentle horse-country drawl but a smoke-scratched Outer Banks twang. My mother delivered her line smoothly, and I relaxed into a low level of good excitement, as I might after the opening bars of a piano recital. "Is something wrong with George?" his mother said, sad alarm in her voice. My mother couldn't have counted on that.

"No, no," my mother said, and affection leaked out of her. "I just thought we needed to talk."

"Does George know you're calling?"

"Actually, George has moved out." Ah, the point. I scurried into the living room with the portable phone, caught her attention, punched the air. My mother waved me away with her good hand, as if I were going to ruin her performance.

"I was afraid of that," Mrs. Duffy said. "I'm so sorry."

She didn't sound as if she meant she'd figured George would eventually come to his senses and leave me. But my mother didn't seem to have picked up on that. "What do you mean by *that?*" she said.

"I just figured he'd walk out after the other one died."

The other one. No one had ever referred to George Junior as *the other one.* George Junior was the child; Gregor was the leftover protoplasm.

"The other one?" I said, knowing it was going to be all right if I spoke. "This is Anna, I was listening in, and I apologize."

"Hello, Anna," she said, and I liked the way my name came out in her accent.

"Nobody ever called George Junior the other one," I said. By this time I was in the living room, facing my mother again, daring her to interrupt.

She was silent for a while. "George wouldn't want me talking to you," she said finally.

I saw my mother open her mouth to speak, and I shook my head vigorously, no. "George doesn't have a lot of privileges left," I said. "He's involved with someone else." My mother looked furious, and her body lurched forward with a wish that she could get up and grab the phone from me.

"Please don't let that bother you," Mrs. Duffy said.

My mother, who was tipping precariously to the left, screeched, "Are you out of your mind?"

I told Mrs. Duffy to hold on a moment. I covered the receiver, held the phone behind me at arm's length, came within whispering distance of my mother. "Let me finish this," I said. I reached for her phone, but she put the receiver deep in her lap. "You've got to trust me on this one," I said. My mother shrugged, tipping another five degrees, and I righted her, hung up her phone.

"I've never met you," I said to Mrs. Duffy. "That wasn't your idea?"

"Good Lord, no, what kind of person do you think I am?"

"*Try* to imagine," I said, and after she'd thought about it a second she gave out a tentative chuckle.

"George sends me money, I guess you didn't know that, either."

"Why?" I said, imagining her in the foyer of her house, talking on the phone that sat on the eighteenth-century table in the curve of the staircase.

"Why? In some ways I suppose he's a very good man."

My mind cut two hundred years off the age of her phone table, then moved it into the hallway outside the bathroom of a one-story house.

"Okay, look, I'll tell you what I thought, and you can correct me." She was going to be amused by this, not offended, or I wouldn't have gone forward. "I thought George was some Virginia gentleman, FFV, bloodlines that mean a lot in Virginia, a family tradition of law school, in other words far too good for me, a fairly ordinary girl from Louisiana." I didn't say how far below ordinary I fell, just in case I was wrong about her.

She let out a whoop that no Virginia aristocrat would allow to escape. "You're probably the first and last person George fooled with *that* act. Forgive me." My mother could only hear my side of the conversation, and her scowl deepened each time I leaned closer into the phone with disbelief.

"Let me get this straight," Mrs. Duffy said. "George marries you, and no one from his family shows up at the wedding, and you think it's *our* idea? And then you never meet us, and you think it's *our* idea? Oh, Lord, this isn't funny," she said.

Sure.

"Honey, I'm not going to beat around the bush." Beat around the bush, an expression George scoffed at the first and last time I used it in his presence. "I got the same problem as the little boy. And so does George's sister."

I cried so hard I had to hang up the phone, and then I cried so long that my mother became alternately frustrated and frightened. It was a strange sort of crying, because ordinarily I only could cry looking at something, a memory trigger, another person whose pain was too close to my own. This time I cried with my eyes shut and no thoughts, no images, and I'm not sure I would have stopped if Gregor hadn't called out for me from his room. Still sobbing, I went and retrieved him, propped him on the sofa on my mother's left, as if the will to keep from falling on him and hurting him would strengthen her somehow.

I stood in front of them, and now I was crying because I was going to change everything with what I said, and I found the moment almost more than I could bear. I addressed my remarks to Gregor. "You remember how we saw your other grandmother at the funeral?" He nodded. "And how we thought she was acting like she was better than us?"

Gregor looked up at my mother, who'd probably told him that and told him not to mention it. "So?" my mother said.

"That lady didn't have a real foot," I said.

"I know that," Gregor said.

"What?" I said.

"*What?*" my mother said.

"Then it must be genetic," I said to my mother. And then to Gregor, "You knew that?"

He nodded. "She showed me. You couldn't tell or anything, if you were in a crowd, you know? I mean, people don't look at people's feet. She said she trusted me. Maybe she's a very rich lady, but she trusted me."

My mother had the sort of goofy smile that might mean having only half the information and might mean having only half the facial muscles. I leaned over clumsily, kissing them both, leaving their cheeks wet from my face, half hoping I'd slip and land on top of them and force an out-of-control embrace. "Mama, don't you get it?"

"I'm not sure," she said, and now I knew the goofy smile was within her control. "All along I thought it was something else."

"Gregor, you want to go watch TV?" I said.

"Are you crazy?" he said with the confidence of the newly enfranchised.

I wasn't in the mood to make George look less than bad, but I controlled myself, speaking like Mr. Rogers, who could wrap up evil in cotton wool and be sure children would be wise if they ever saw it. "Okay, buddy," I said. "I gather you got these different arms and legs from your daddy, and it made him a little nervous."

"I'll say," my mother said, and then I spent the rest of the evening giving Gregor the driest facts imaginable about human reproduction, leaving out the love part because it wasn't relevant, all the while trying to decide what I would say to George.

At breakfast my mother said, "I don't want to talk about it," but evidently what she meant was *I don't want to have a dialogue about it,* because she held forth for a good twenty minutes. I tried to stay deep in the moment, because if I'd stepped back, looked at her propped at the table, struggling to rely on her right hand, and Gregor, propped at the table struggling to use his left, and my mother all the while failing to censor herself, I'd have begun to scream with frustration.

"I dare anyone to give me that rotten-childhood excuse," she was saying. "A boy has a mother who takes off half her leg at night, and a sister who uses her toes like fingers because she has no hands, that boy does not have to grow up mean. A boy like that should have spent his childhood helping out, a boy like that should grow up empathetic as hell."

Her reasoning was fallacious, of course, but I never got farther than inhaling to speak before she found a new line of attack. She was talking very fast, as if Gregor were a stenographer who couldn't possibly keep up and therefore would take in none of her words. "He *knows* it's genetic, maybe he thinks it only happens to women, but with all his fancy studies does he bother to find out how to avoid it? No." He's Catholic, I whispered, but she rolled right over me. "You know how you avoid it absolutely? You don't get married. George Duffy had no business getting married, at least the way *he* did it."

"You said you thought it was something else," I said. "And I have a feeling it had nothing to do with George Junior taking up too much space."

My mother tried for a defensive posture, but without balance she looked more like someone who'd suffered a keen blow to the head and wasn't letting on that it hurt. "Your father took LSD before you were born," she said. "I thought it might explain a number of things, but clearly it *didn't*."

I had nothing to say; an entire life of too much caution had to be rethought.

"If Daddy never got married, George and me never would of got born," Gregor piped up.

I rose, pulled my mother's coffee cup out from in front of her. "This is enough," I said. She'd been taking the cooled coffee in with a straw, and the straw flipped out of the cup, spattering a few drops on her right hand, which she could remove only by shaking that hand.

When some landed on Gregor, she remembered him. "I'm sorry," she said. "I'm glad George Duffy got married."

"I think you can have babies and not be married," Gregor said, looking to me for approval.

"Technically, yes," I said, and he beamed.

I took my shower while the physical therapist worked with both of them. I had considered staying in the room, to watch and learn, find escape in the repetitions, but my mother and Gregor were not machines. They liked to talk. I missed the slots for mindlessness. The nickel slots would have been a good compromise, but I no longer had an excuse.

I did dialogues with George in my head in the shower; I wasn't ready for my mother. I never got past the first exchange with George, because whatever I imagined saying to him elicited a cruel defense. *I understand now why you did what you did. Well, it took you long enough.* The opposite tack. *There's no excuse for how you've treated your mother. Look, Anna, your mother may be no rose geranium, but at least she didn't raise you in a circus sideshow.*

I had no perspective, that was the problem. It would have been easy to adopt my mother's stance, as I always did, on God, the governor, the health benefits of brown rice. She was, even now, frighteningly correct all the time. But I wasn't going to have her in the room, and I needed belief in my wisdom. George knew I had been raised to have none of my own. So he viewed me as an opposing attorney who took eight years to finish law school and didn't pass the bar until the fourth try. He could say anything, tell the story of the princess and the pea and claim it was Cinderella and know I'd have to acquiesce.

I phoned the fire station. George Duffy had a peculiar way of answering, chopping the first syllable off "hello" to make a caller think he was being bothered. "He-e-ey," he said when I identified myself, happily giving me a couple of extra syllables. "How come you don't call me at home?"

"You get a lot of calls from strange women at home?"

"Nah," he said. "It's kind of hard meeting women at fires, you know? Usually they're not dressed too presentably, and they've got other things on their minds."

"You're not married." I wasn't the type to say sweetly, *What about your wife?*

"Not in a while. You'd think, a woman gets rid of a man a guaranteed twenty-four hours out of seventy-two, she'd be the envy of the block. But no, she preferred seventy-two out of seventy-two."

I couldn't imagine George the lawyer mocking himself. "You told me you had to get home, you were going to get in trouble. With what, your cat?"

"My mother takes care of the cat."

Oh. A mama's boy couldn't be a lot better than one who locked his mother in a closet and tossed a check through the door every month. Probably there was virtually no difference. Maybe men were supposed to hate their mothers. George Junior definitely had been planning to go to another continent and tell everyone his family was dead. Gregor I didn't know about.

He must have known what I was thinking, since a fire chief who lived with his mother was surely no stranger to flak. "She's got glaucoma. Sits two feet from the TV all day, making herself more and more blind—I figure I'll bunk there, change her lightbulbs, you know. I'm probably the only fireman lives in the Irish Channel anymore, but this is hardly permanent. She's almost eighty."

"Lucky boy, my mother's only fifty-three," I said.

"Merck's up half a point."

"That's not why I called," I said, then realized I'd called for him to tell me I was wise enough to face George. I'd assumed he was married. "But never mind."

"Aw, you're not getting away that easily," he said. George would have told me *okay*, *good-bye*.

We agreed on coffee, tomorrow, Café Luna. None of that bothered him. He liked the Russian tea cakes at Café Luna, he said; in summer he always had the iced Kahlua coffee. Was the crowd too effete? "How can you be *too* effete?" he said, and I laughed. I figured that between now and then I'd come to an understanding of what I wanted from him. Even if I had to look at my dreams.

George-the-husband-the-lawyer was screaming when I answered the phone five minutes later. "You had no right," he said.

"You've spoken to your mother."

"Damn right. And before you go passing judgment on me as a son, I just want you to know I've phoned her every weekday morning since I left home. And that includes when I was in law school. And had no money."

I hadn't thought she'd call him after last night. She wasn't on his side.

"Do you know how hysterical you've made my mother?" he said.

For the first time I didn't believe him. He lived in compartments, so even without imagination he could tell lies about one when he was in another, but I'd crossed over. His mother had been amused last night—with irony, with horror—and people like that didn't slide all the way down into plaintive fussing. "I find that hard to believe," I said.

"What do you call it when she hears my voice and immediately lashes out at me for being a lousy father when she hasn't got a clue as to how I'm handling this whole mess?"

"I don't call it hysterical. I call it justifiably disgusted." I wished my mother were in the room to hear that one. But George hearing it was enough.

"What'd you call her for? Or rather, what did your mother call her for?"

"To tell her you'd moved out. I figured she was this upper-crust matron who'd fuss at you for being so unprincipled."

"Bullshit."

"You want to tell me what else I'd call her for?"

"Your mother'd call her for."

"In your mind, we're one and the same, so don't go off on that tangent," I said. I wasn't trying to be careful with my words. For the first time, I knew absolutely that I was never going to like George, and that I had a reason not to ever like George. Up until then I'd been convinced that I had a skewed view of the world; all I had to do was get wiser and then I'd finally appreciate George the way he told me I was supposed to.

"Look, Anna," he said, still thinking he had power, "if I wanted you to know anything about me, I'd've *told* you."

"That's obvious."

"You have to understand: I wasn't hiding you from her, I was hiding her from you."

"Am I supposed to be flattered?"

"Do you want to talk or not?"

"You know, I sort of figured that maybe tomorrow I was going to call you up and tell you that now that I knew you had a screwed-up childhood I felt bad for you and wanted to understand you."

"I hate that social-worker crap."

"So how would you like me to feel?" I said.

"You ought to feel damn grateful. You want to be a clone of your mother, high-school diploma, sitting down there on Tulane Avenue with the most distasteful job this side of the Chicago stockyards? No, you don't lift a finger, and you live half a block off St. Charles Avenue in a house that could hold four of her house. And no matter what you've done, I've stayed married to you. Yeah, *grateful* about sums it up."

"I'm grateful for Gregor," I said.

"Well, good, because he's more your fault than mine." I said nothing. "Kathryn researched it for me. I mean *thoroughly.* Like a doctor, not like a lawyer. And you know what? Whatever this is, it isn't hereditary. If he had heart problems, *maybe* there'd be a genetic link. But he doesn't. It's an accident, Anna, a fucking accident. Three times in one family, but an accident."

I hung up the phone slowly so he wouldn't hear the click.

On the way to Café Luna I remembered a conversation I'd had with George Duffy the fireman, and then I knew what I wanted from him. I'd told him about Gregor's ability to choose winning scratch-off tickets, and we'd talked about lottery tickets, which made no sense to me. Buying a lottery ticket was like watching a situation comedy on television: If you didn't get in on it at the very beginning, it was too embarrassing to ask later what it was all about. George Duffy said he chose random picks each week. When he explained the system to me, I said it seemed to make more sense to have favorite numbers and play them each time, narrowing the odds, building the meaning if not the tension. "If I skipped a week, and my favorite numbers came up, I'd have to kill myself," he'd said. From George Duffy the fireman, I wanted reflected sense.

"Try Duffy," was the first thing he said to me when we were seated. Despite the heat outside, I had hot chocolate and a heated blueberry muffin and pretended in the air conditioning that it was winter. I asked him what he meant. "You don't have a name for me, do you?"

"I think of you as George Duffy the fireman."

"That's a lot to call out across a room," he said.

"Duffy," I said. "I always hoped someone would call my sons Duffy."

He was silent a while. "So tell me."

"That's quite an opener," I said, and I couldn't look him in the eye because I knew I'd keep on looking.

"So tell me," he said again. "You've got a mother of some proportions, and you've got sons. And from the way you play the slots, I'd say you've got places you'd rather not be."

"What do you need to know to be a fire chief?" I said.

"You need to know technical stuff. You *don't* need to know human behavior."

"Okay, okay."

"Look, I go to Baton Rouge, major in psych, come back here because you know no one ever really leaves, figure out the only job for a psych major is in city civil service. You sit in city civil service, and after a while you see the only happy people are the firemen. And that's the sum total of my insight." He took a big mouthful of tea cake, nuts and figs catching obscenely on his lower lip. "Well, one more insight. You sure have a clever way of not talking about yourself."

"That's because it's all I really want to do," I said.

"So talk."

"Right," I said.

"You're married," he said.

"I guess that's one of those places I'd rather not be."

"So tell me," he said, and I told him everything. I found if I tried I could tell him all my important facts so quickly he couldn't be bored. George, George Junior, my mother, Gregor, George's mother, a sentence apiece and the mosaic was there, even if, from a distance, it did not make a picture. I didn't mention myself, because he knew all there was to know about me, which was nothing.

"This is all too bad, but I'm not surprised," he said.

"Meaning?"

"Meaning, why'd you pick me?"

"I didn't pick you." He wasn't the type to take mincing steps toward a woman, moving a few inches each day across a lawn, protecting himself and wasting his time. But that had been George's one valuable quality, his ability to avoid frightening me until it was too late. I wanted Duffy to be ambiguous, and slow. "You happen to be the person who sat next to me on a very good day." As soon as the words were out, I realized how euphemistic they sounded.

"Something subconscious kicked in, Anna. I sat next to you and you knew I didn't really live anywhere and you knew I'd learned my lesson about intruding."

"I don't think so," I said. "To tell you the truth, I came here because I *wanted* an intrusion. I mean, you make sense of everything."

"You want me to tell you what to do."

I didn't like the way that sounded. It was true, but not the way he put his intonations onto it. "What would you think of me if I weren't married?"

He thought for a moment. "Depends on *when*. Five years ago, right now, or five years from now?"

"Right now," I said, because the me of the present was the actual me; I figured my nature was never going to change, in fact hadn't changed since the day my father died.

"I'd think, 'Hey, when's this girl going to take me home to meet her mother.'"

I felt my face reddening. "I bet you say that to all the girls," I said, as if I talked this way with men all the time.

He smiled, and I pictured him at fires looking at women who were wrapped in blankets and disheveled and sad. He probably gave such women chances, despite what he said. That was what made firemen so thoroughly erotic in my mind, their willingness to do a two-finger compression on an infant's chest, to carry an eighty-year-old woman as if she were a bride, to breathe into another man's mouth.

"I'd rather know you five years from now," he said.

"Why?" I said, still picturing him with old women.

"You're going to be a hell of a person when you feel better."

We were standing on the porch of Café Luna, and I was trying to figure out how to see him again, when the car hit the dog. I'd noticed the dog on the other side of Magazine Street, and I'd had the same low-current anxiety I always had when I saw a stray on a well-traveled street. Until then I'd successfully wished them to stay in place until it was safe to move across traffic, but this dog saw something on my side of Magazine, perhaps me, and couldn't be willed to wait. It darted into the downtown flow of cars, and they stopped; drivers coming uptown, also traveling on a green light, seemed like me, believing the dog would come to its senses, dart back to the other side of the street. But the dog kept on coming, and though the silver Nissan braked, there was an audible impact. I screamed no, began running toward the street, Duffy trailing me. Now all cars were stopped, and the dog rolled three hundred and sixty degrees, righted itself, and scampered the rest of the way across the street, tail between its legs, stopping short only when it came within a few feet of us, now that it trusted no one. "Go grab something off someone's plate," Duffy said, and he extended his hand slowly toward the dog, as if any sudden movement would send it dashing back into Magazine Street, where cars quickly had resumed normal speed. I ran up the steps of Café Luna, called, "Food, food," to the three tables of people who were eating outdoors in the middle of an August day. A boy of college age proffered an entire Prussian, and the girl with him said, "That's bad for their health." He gave her a look that said she probably wasn't going to see him again after today, handed off the pastry. I returned slowly to Duffy, afraid of sudden moves, but the dog was learning quickly now what was dangerous, and it took one tentative step toward him, then another. I stood a few feet behind Duffy, broke off a good quarter of the Prussian, waved it in hopes that the scent might travel through the wet, bus fume–filled air. The dog took another step toward Duffy, and it was close enough to be touched. I stepped forward with the Prussian, and as Duffy patted the dog on the head it promptly rolled over, feet in the air, showing us submission and no blood.

"I think he's all right," Duffy said, and I shoved the food in the dog's upside-down face; when he took it into his mouth it rested on his palate, and he hacked at it with his back teeth, making sure none of it would fall to the ground. I gave him another piece, smaller, wanting to ration it out now.

I never had seen a dog that looked quite like that. He was what my mother called a Louisiana cayoodle: a short-haired, medium-sized dog with stand-up ears and a pointed muzzle. But what distinguished him was his coloring, black and white, much like a Holstein cow. He was lean, but not underfed, and he wore no collar. "You have time?" Duffy said. "I'm taking him in."

Taking him in, to me that meant Japonica Street, the SPCA, a place I had visited once searching for the young Ansel Adams when he'd run off, a place I would never go again, no matter what. I figured if I ever had a pet, I would have it tattooed, microchipped, and tagged; if it ran off I would wait for a phone call. "The SPCA?" I said, ready to intervene and never see the man again.

"Naw, I'll pay. My mother's vet's on Freret Street," he said, and I hugged him without thinking.

Duffy drove a generic car—white, boxy, American-made sometime in the past ten years. The interior gave away nothing, no stains on the cloth seats, no nicks in the vinyl, no dried oak leaves peeking out from under the floor mats. He covered the backseat with a large towel he kept in a trunk so neatly arranged with a lug wrench, motor oil, bungee cords, and a lantern that I couldn't believe he had ever turned a corner sharply. "Up, man," he said to the dog, and when he patted the backseat the dog hopped in, using every joint and muscle the way he was supposed to. We rode in silence, and I half hoped someone would see me. I sat up straight, my face close to the window; people tend to disappear to passersby if they move too deeply into the interior of a car.

Dr. Eugene took only ten minutes to assure us that nothing inside the dog had exploded on impact—not his heart, his spleen, his bladder. He had no broken bones, he didn't even have any sensitive muscles. He did, however, have scrapes on the pads of his feet, and more fleas than a well-kept dog should have, even in summer, even in Louisiana. Dr. Eugene let the dog lick him in the face, then turned away with a jolly grimace. "Garlic, somebody thinks garlic repels fleas," he said, his tone implying that this dog needed a much better owner than he currently had.

"Maybe it repels small Japanese cars," Duffy said.

It was a slow day at the vet's, late summer when all the Tulane students were up north with their pets and all the locals were out of town, counting on housesitters and no emergencies. Dr. Eugene said, "How about a bath and dip while you go figure out what you want to do with Lucky here," he said to Duffy. Duffy ruffled the top of the dog's unmarred head and said, "That's the least I can do, besides refrain from calling him Lucky."

We took seats in the waiting room, which smelled impressively of absolutely nothing. "I'll take him for Gregor," I said before Duffy could think of an alternative.

No one who worked honestly for the City of New Orleans, not even the mayor, could afford a house like mine, and I didn't want Duffy to see it. I reminded him he had to drop me and the dog off at my car at Café Luna. He had paid the vet's bill; he had offered to stop off at Walgreen's to buy a collar and leash, then take me and the dog to my house. "I've exploited you too much already," I said, though I should have known he was not one to be fooled by niceties.

"Trust me," he said, "I've been inside too many places in this city to judge anyone by her house."

I'd forgotten that firemen caught people as they were. Duffy had told me of the woman whose three-story was hit by lightning the day she'd had her carpets shampooed. She'd sent the firemen around to the back door, and as they'd shuffled around the house, it had burned to the ground. Duffy had not been impressed.

He was excited the way only people without children could be. He wanted to see Gregor's face, to be the one Gregor associated with the totally fine experience of getting a dog. So we stopped at Walgreen's after all, but I ran in while he kept the motor running, aiming the air-conditioning vents toward the backseat while I was gone. When I gave him my address and asked him if he knew where that was, he said, "I could even tell you the cross streets. And probably the location of the nearest hydrant."

Again, he stayed in the car with the motor running. I left him ripping the price tags off the collar and leash, trying to put the collar on a dog that had clearly never owned one. Duffy was probably dreaming of a grand entrance, with the dog high-stepping like a show horse; I pictured him dragging the poor animal up the steps. But Duffy had a way of being right, and I thought I would like to have him around sometimes, making decisions for me, slicing away at my worries over what would go terribly wrong.

My mother and Gregor were sitting on the living-room sofa watching television. "Notice anything?" my mother said. She didn't exactly say it with a hint of a good surprise. I looked around, looked them both up and down, saw nothing different. "We're sitting on the sofa watching television," she said.

"I've got a surprise for you," I said to Gregor.

"We're sitting on the sofa, Mommy," Gregor said. "Don't you notice anything?"

"I give."

"It's all we can do," my mother said.

"Oh, shit," I said. They might have been sitting like that for more than an hour. "Why'd that therapist leave you?" I said, then realized I sounded like George. "I take that back."

"We'd've figured something out," my mother said. "It's good practice—especially for me." I didn't feel so good about the dog anymore. Surely some mistake lay covered by my intentions, and as soon as Duffy came in with the dog my mother would good-naturedly point out my lapse. Allergies? Responsibility? Psychotic animal? I was terribly tired of anticipating, of fearing I would destroy someone with my thoughtless decisions, and I decided not to care, to rely instead on good sense—if not my own, then someone else's.

"Don't move," I said, and I ran out of the room, flung open the front door, motioned Duffy to come in. With leash in hand, unattached to the dog, he lifted the animal out of the car, kicked the door shut with his foot, and carried the animal up the front stairs and into the foyer as if it were a wrapped gift of glass.

I watched my mother's face, saw the neutrality that comes of ambivalence, quickly shifted to Gregor. His mouth was closed, his eyes wide open, as if an exclamation of joy would only bring a mocking *Sorry, it's not for you.*

"He's yours," Duffy said, and he put the dog on the floor to see what he would do. The dog took one look at my mother, one look at Gregor, and rolled over with his feet in the air. I ached for Duffy, but he said, "Hey, Gregor, he thinks you're his master," and Gregor bounced up and down with delight.

I stroked the dog's belly, and he righted himself, edged over to sniff Gregor, trailing a vague scent of pesticide. Then he pressed the dome of his head against Gregor's chest, rubbed it back and forth. "He's petting hisself," Gregor said.

Duffy let out a sigh of relief, and I mentally scratched "psychotic animal" off my list. "I know you," he said to Gregor. "You go to St. John's." I hadn't told him that.

Gregor nodded vigorously. "I know you, too." Then Gregor turned to me, the obvious outsider. "He came to visit our kindergarten room. He said, "Stop, drop, and roll," and George Junior said, 'What about my brother?' which was maybe nice and maybe mean. Tell her what you said," he said to Duffy.

"I said, 'He can drop and roll, so *you* stop.' Right?"

Gregor looked up at my mother, who up to that point still hadn't figured out how she felt about Duffy and the dog. She broke into a lopsided grin, and Gregor giggled with pleasure. "I'm going to call him George the Third," Gregor announced.

My mother slapped her forehead with the heel of her right hand; I knew her well enough to know her mind had traveled to the British history books, where few were madder or sorrier than George III.

"Hey, Gregor, my name's George, so how about George the Fourth instead?" Duffy said. He turned to my mother and winked. "*He* opposed the Catholic Emancipation Act—couldn't have been all bad."

My mother for once was speechless. She had the expectation of rescue in her expression. I caught her eye over Duffy's shoulder, vigorously shook my head no. Before I paid my tuition, I would get her thousand dollars back to her.